The E.M.P. CHRONICLES

Book One:
458 Miles and 24 Days

OZ MCTATEY

A Modern-Day Series Based on Survival, Perseverance, Adaptability, and the Importance of Family when the Power Grid Goes Down

Practical Survival Techniques and Strategies for a Highly Probable Event

1

This is a work of fiction. Names, characters, businesses, places, events, locales, and incidents are either the products of the author's imagination or used in a fictitious manner. No identification with actual persons (living or deceased), places, buildings, and products is intended or should be inferred. As you read this book it is intended for entertainment purposes only. Statements should not be used as, or in place of, medical or survival advice.

To contact the author email at oz@eyeonprepping.com

Design and composition by Teresa Muniz
Cover design and illustrations by J. L. Alfaro

Print ISBN-10: 109-227238-0
Print ISBN-13: 978-1-09-227238-4

Second Edition

TABLE OF CONTENTS

PROLOGUE

WE LIVED IN NEW YORK when 9/11 happened. We saw the fear. We saw the pain. We saw the deaths. Through our friends, we experienced the anguish of not knowing if family members were dead or alive. Though I was not directly affected by 9/11, it changed my world. This book is written and based on my true concerns and fears should I directly experience a Stuff Hits the Fan (SHTF) event. As a prepper with eighteen years of experience, I share, through fiction, how my family and I would react and the actions we would take. Through the characters, I provide real skills that should be learned and practiced.

So, what exactly is an SHTF event? It's an event that significantly or permanently affects your life in an emotional, physical, financial, or other matter. As I write this book there were a significant number of rather large-magnitude manmade and natural SHTF events occurring. For example, The California "Camp Fire" decimated 9,800 homes and 149,000 acres. The most upsetting fact is that there were over 76 dead and 1,300 unaccounted for residents. Or consider North Korea. As nice as the United States tried to play with North Korea, they still announced the acquisition of a new "high-tech" tactical weapon. Is the weapon an upgraded Electromagnetic Pulse (EMP) long-range missile or are they now experimenting with chemical warfare? Regardless of the new "high-tech" tactical weapon, the fact of the matter is that North Korea is unpredictable in addition to having nuclear capabilities. President Donald Trump met with Kim Jong-un several times, yet the rogue nation and the United States have not agreed on a nuclear arms treaty.

Yet another concern is the United States government's prediction of the flu in future years. Yes, the flu. Some predictions show that future flu outbreaks could be worse than previous decades and could potentially lead to a pandemic. The worldwide spread of a new flu virus could be as simple as one sick person getting on an airplane. It's not ironic — probably more coincidental — that as I write this book there are numerous articles on the 1918 Spanish flu drawing comparisons to future flu outbreaks. From history, we learn that the Spanish flu of 1918 infected an estimated 500 million people worldwide (about one-third of the planet's population at the time) and killed an estimated 20 million to 50 million victims, including some 675,000 Americans. The Centers for Disease Control and Prevention noted:

"The pandemic was so severe that from 1917 to 1918, life expectancy in the United States fell by about 12 years, to 36.6 years for men and 42.2 years for women." (Prevention, 2018)

At the time of this writing, we're in a global trade disagreement with China. President Donald Trump threatened to impose 35 percent to 45 percent tariffs on Chinese imports to force China into renegotiating its trade balance with the U.S. Experts agree that if a trade war were to occur, it would have a devastating effect on the United States as compared to China.

Also, tensions between Russia and the United States have been escalated when compared to previous years. The souring U.S.–Russia relationship has the potential to ignite a new deadly conflict. Specifically, the United States and Russia have plans to withdraw from the Intermediate-Range Nuclear Forces Treaty. On March 8, 2019, President Trump said:

"[The U.S.] cannot be the only country in the world unilaterally bound by this treaty, or any other. We will move forward with developing our own military response options and will work with NATO and our other allies and partners to deny Russia any military advantage from its unlawful conduct."

Prior to this, Russia created and tested new hypersonic missile technology that makes it much easier to evade U.S. defenses.

Lastly, in March 2019, Venezuela was hit by a cyberattack, allegedly, from the United States. The cyberattack brought the power grid down in twenty-two out of the twenty-three Venezuelan states. News agencies report that murder, rape, hunger, sanitation challenges, and no communication paralyzed the nation.

Now, to the true reason for this book. You see, as I write this book, I'm the one who lives 458 miles and 24 days, by foot, away from my family. The reality is that it would probably take me over a month to get home if you consider 24 days does not include eating, sleeping, and resting. The decision for me to move away from my family was a complicated decision but one that my wife and I agreed to. We both agreed that the job opportunity at hand was a perfect fit for my skill set. The downside is that I would have to move to southern Georgia from Kentucky and we both knew I would be home, my true home, Kentucky, once a month at best. Sure, I could have settled for a job but that is just what I would have done, settled. I had "settled" for far too many jobs in our life together and she was happy and supportive that I found a great opportunity albeit in another state.

After a couple of months away from my family, I found myself in a psychological conundrum. The new job was great for our retirement but what if I never saw my family again because of an SHTF event? A ton of questions came to my mind. "What if an Electromagnetic Pulse or cyber-attack hits and I have to walk home?" "What if there's a viral outbreak and I'm unable to get home because of illness?" Given Kentucky sits on the New Madrid fault line, I also wondered, "What if a magnitude 8.0+ earthquake occurs, and transportation routes are blocked?" The only thing I thought to myself was that I sacrificed the love of seeing and being with my family daily for money; the root of all evil.

From a real-world experience and in the short time I've been in Atlanta and away from my family, I have experienced Hurricane Michael, tornadoes, and flooding all of which are serious events. None of them have prevented me from traveling, finding food or water, maintaining shelter, or compromising my livelihood. They were, however, all events that I took seriously and learned from.

For example, immediately upon learning of Hurricane Michael, and given I was away from Kentucky, I purchased a Coleman® lantern, a dozen 16-ounce propane cans, extra wicks, several packages of freeze-dried food, and 12 gallons of purified water. The lantern would provide light, heat, and the ability to cook while I ensured I had three days of extra food and water on hand.

I knew to do this before the rest of Atlanta panicked. Sure enough, two days before the arrival of Hurricane Michael, the entire population of Atlanta seemed to have panicked. Walmart® and the local grocery stores literally ran out of the staples (water, eggs, milk, flour, flashlights, batteries, heaters, and candles, to name a few). It was not the hurricane I was afraid of. It was the people who panicked. In my world, the "people" will always be the ones I protect against.

As I struggled with what to do in a life-altering SHTF, I began planning multiple options of how, regardless of the SHTF event, I would return to my family to protect and support them should something happen. This book is a journey and planning tool for how you can prepare for an SHTF event with the hopes you never experience such a thing. However, after living in New York and experiencing the effects of 9/11, I owe it to my family and to myself to do everything within my control to prepare for an SHTF event while I pray it never happens.

In closing, this book is based upon my experiences and how I plan to get home during an SHTF. I use a highly possible scenario to describe my actions and what I perceive would be the actions of others. Where possible I use facts based on real data and information and provide the source. I communicated with experts and conducted extensive research on the topics in this book and pair personal experiences with the information I present. All sources can be found in the "Reference" section at the end of the book.

I consider myself a professional and well-versed in numerous subjects, including prepping, but do your own research and create your own experiences. May God bless you and your family and the United States of America.

1. REFLECTION

WE LIVED IN NEW YORK when 9/11 happened. We saw the fear. We saw the pain. We saw the deaths. Through our friends, we experienced the anguish of not knowing if family members were dead or alive. Though I was not directly affected by 9/11, it changed my world. This book is written and based on my true concerns and fears should I directly experience a Stuff Hits the Fan (SHTF) event. As a prepper with eighteen years of experience, I share, through fiction, how my family and I would react and the actions we would take. Through the characters, I provide real skills that should be learned and practiced.

So, what exactly is an SHTF event? It's an event that significantly or permanently affects your life in an emotional, physical, financial, or other matter. As I write this book there were a significant number of rather large-magnitude manmade and natural SHTF events occurring. For example, The California "Camp Fire" decimated 9,800 homes and 149,000 acres. The most upsetting fact is that there were over 76 dead and 1,300 unaccounted for residents. Or consider North Korea. As nice as the United States tried to play with North Korea, they still announced the acquisition of a new "high-tech" tactical weapon. Is the weapon an upgraded Electromagnetic Pulse (EMP) long-range missile or are they now experimenting with chemical warfare? Regardless of the new "high-tech" tactical weapon, the fact of the matter is that North Korea is unpredictable in addition to having nuclear capabilities. President Donald Trump met with Kim Jong-un several times, yet the rogue nation and the United States have not agreed on a nuclear arms treaty.

Yet another concern is the United States government's prediction of the flu in future years. Yes, the flu. Some predictions show that future flu outbreaks could be worse than previous decades and could potentially lead to a pandemic. The worldwide spread of a new flu virus could be as simple as one sick person getting on an airplane. It's not ironic — probably more coincidental — that as I write this book there are numerous articles on the 1918 Spanish flu drawing comparisons to future flu outbreaks. From history, we learn that the Spanish flu of 1918 infected an estimated 500 million people worldwide (about one-third of the planet's population at the time) and killed an estimated 20 million to 50 million victims, including some 675,000 Americans. The Centers for Disease Control and Prevention noted:

"The pandemic was so severe that from 1917 to 1918, life expectancy in the United States fell by about 12 years, to 36.6 years for men and 42.2 years for women." (Prevention, 2018)

At the time of this writing, we're in a global trade disagreement with China. President Donald Trump threatened to impose 35 percent to 45 percent tariffs on Chinese imports to force China into renegotiating its trade balance with the U.S. Experts agree that if a trade war were to occur, it would have a devastating effect on the United States as compared to China.

Also, tensions between Russia and the United States have been escalated when compared to previous years. The souring U.S.–Russia relationship has the potential to ignite a new deadly conflict. Specifically, the United States and Russia have plans to withdraw from the Intermediate-Range Nuclear Forces Treaty. On March 8, 2019, President Trump said:

> *"[The U.S.] cannot be the only country in the world unilaterally bound by this treaty, or any other. We will move forward with developing our own military response options and will work with NATO and our other allies and partners to deny Russia any military advantage from its unlawful conduct."*

Prior to this, Russia created and tested new hypersonic missile technology that makes it much easier to evade U.S. defenses.

Lastly, in March 2019, Venezuela was hit by a cyberattack, allegedly, from the United States. The cyberattack brought the power grid down in twenty-two out of the twenty-three Venezuelan states. News agencies report that murder, rape, hunger, sanitation challenges, and no communication paralyzed the nation.

Now, to the true reason for this book. You see, as I write this book, I'm the one who lives 458 miles and 24 days, by foot, away from my family. The reality is that it would probably take me over a month to get home if you consider 24 days does not include eating, sleeping, and resting. The decision for me to move away from my family was a complicated decision but one that my wife and I agreed to. We both agreed that the job opportunity at hand was a perfect fit for my skill set. The downside is that I would have to move to southern Georgia from Kentucky and we both knew I would be home, my true home, Kentucky, once a month at best. Sure, I could have settled for a job but that is just what I would have done, settled. I had "settled" for far too many jobs in our life together and she was happy and supportive that I found a great opportunity albeit in another state.

After a couple of months away from my family, I found myself in a psychological conundrum. The new job was great for our retirement but what if I never saw my family again because of an SHTF event? A ton of questions came to my mind. "What if an Electromagnetic Pulse or cyber-attack hits and I have to walk home?" "What if there's a viral outbreak and I'm unable to get home because of illness?" Given Kentucky sits on the New Madrid fault line, I also wondered, "What if a magnitude 8.0+ earthquake occurs, and transportation routes are blocked?" The only thing I thought to myself was that I sacrificed the love of seeing and being with my family daily for money; the root of all evil.

From a real-world experience and in the short time I've been in Atlanta and away from my family, I have experienced Hurricane Michael, tornadoes, and flooding all of which are serious events. None of them have prevented me from traveling, finding food or water, maintaining shelter, or compromising my livelihood. They were, however, all events that I took seriously and learned from.

For example, immediately upon learning of Hurricane Michael, and given I was away from Kentucky, I purchased a Coleman® lantern, a dozen 16-ounce propane cans, extra wicks, several packages of freeze-dried food, and 12 gallons of purified water. The lantern would provide light, heat, and the ability to cook while I ensured I had three days of extra food and water on hand.

I knew to do this before the rest of Atlanta panicked. Sure enough, two days before the arrival of Hurricane Michael, the entire population of Atlanta seemed to have panicked. Walmart® and the local grocery stores literally ran out of the staples (water, eggs, milk, flour, flashlights, batteries, heaters, and candles, to name a few). It was not the hurricane I was afraid of. It was the people who panicked. In my world, the "people" will always be the ones I protect against.

As I struggled with what to do in a life-altering SHTF, I began planning multiple options of how, regardless of the SHTF event, I would return to my family to protect and support them should something happen. This book is a journey and planning tool for how you can prepare for an SHTF event with the hopes you never experience such a thing. However, after living in New York and experiencing the effects of 9/11, I owe it to my family and to myself to do everything within my control to prepare for an SHTF event while I pray it never happens.

In closing, this book is based upon my experiences and how I plan to get home during an SHTF. I use a highly possible scenario to describe my actions and what I perceive would be the actions of others. Where possible I use facts based on real data and information and provide the source. I communicated with experts and conducted extensive research on the topics in this book and pair personal experiences with the information I present. All sources can be found in the "Reference" section at the end of the book.

I consider myself a professional and well-versed in numerous subjects, including prepping, but do your own research and create your own experiences. May God bless you and your family and the United States of America.

2. PREPARING – THE BEGINNING

TWO MONTHS AFTER 9/11, Oz and his family began their journey to being prepared. At the time he didn't even know what a prepper was, but he swore to himself that he would never let his family be caught off guard or as unprepared as they were on that day. Granted he wasn't a psychic and couldn't predict when the next disaster was going to occur, but he could be prepared to shelter-in-place and watch the rest of the world panic while he and his family remained safe.

The family would no longer shop only on paydays or live paycheck to paycheck. No longer would the family not have firearms. No longer would the family not have an emergency fund. No longer would the family sit in darkness and wait for a SHTF event. They would be proactive. They would have food and water on hand. They would have the means to protect themselves. They would have emergency cash both in the safe and in the bank. They would not be victims of the events of the world anymore.

Within two years of their prepping journey, Oz would become a well-known and established lecturer, author, and expert on prepping. This was most definitely not a path he chose but rather a path that was chosen for him. After 9/11, and as a military veteran, he felt the need to help the rest of America prepare.

Oz knew finding like-minded families would prove difficult but was extremely important. As a prepper, there's an unwritten code of secrecy. First, you never divulge you're a prepper and second you never divulge what your preparations consist of. So, the dilemma for Oz became how to create groups of like-minded people while maintaining secrecy. If the Stuff Hits the Fan, Oz knew it would require many trustworthy people with different skillsets to survive.

In a most unique circumstance, Oz was fortunate enough to have met Brian and Elizabeth Tregor. Brian became Oz's best friend and was married to Elizabeth. Brian and Elizabeth were physicians who had extensive experience in emergency medicine. They were like-minded families and over time opened up to Oz that they had been preparing food, medical supplies, guns, ammo, and general supplies for an emergency. Both families had the common belief that it was only a matter of time before the next manmade or natural SHTF event happened. Together, they would not be as unprepared as they were during 9/11 and, more importantly, the families grew to trust one another.

Oz, Brian, Elizabeth, and Nicki saw 9/11 for what it was. It was a terrorist attack that changed the lives of individuals, families, and the United States forever. Directly, it led to the death of 2,977 people and injured more than 6,000. Indirectly, it led to many more deaths including our brave military men and women serving overseas in the fight against terrorism. Just as important was the fact that the event was undetected by the U.S. government.

Five years later in 2007, the families felt it was necessary to take the next step in their preparations: find a Bug Out Location equidistant between the two households. They would need to accumulate large stores of food and medical supplies. They would need secure access to water and purification systems. They would continue to take professional training including tactical gun courses and first aid. They would practice and develop new skills ranging from how to start a primitive fire to bush crafting, but it didn't change the fact that each family lived in a dense, highly populated area. This meant that when the Stuff Hits The Fan hundreds of thousands of people would eventually run out of food and begin migrating wherever they had to and doing whatever they had to do to find food. They knew their families would eventually be visited by the hordes of desperate people who hadn't prepared as they had. It was time to purchase a Bug Out Location.

Oz was on the internet researching potential Bug Out Locations (BOL) when he heard, "Oz, snap out of it. Have you seen the news today?" Brian said excitedly.

"No. You know I don't watch the news. Fake reports, terrorism, people starving, politicians attacking each other, and ever restricting gun laws. Tell me again why you watch the news," Oz said without lifting his head from the computer screen.

"News is a compass as to how bad things really are. A gauge if you will. I agree that the majority of news is fake and not truly vetted, but it does give us some direction on potential SHTF events. Look, Georgia is in a drought, we're still fighting terrorism in Iraq and Afghanistan, not to mention that I just read an article on both Iran and North Korea's electromagnetic pulse capabilities. Both technologies could bring the United States to its knees. EMP equals no electricity for a minimum of six months but more like twelve. Most of the U.S. would starve within three weeks. This type of information gives a direction or focus of what could be next," Brian said.

"I know," Oz stated. "It's why we increase our preparations and constantly develop our skills," Oz said haphazardly but continued. "I'm surprised there's nothing on mutant viruses in the news today. By the way, Brian, stay focused on our property search. Between our two families, I'm sure we can find something economical. The Bug Out Location needs to be somewhat of an equal distance between our two houses and have backroads we can travel if the main highway is impassable. Not only will this be our 'safe haven' it could be our livelihood. You and I are smart enough to know that we'll need to get out of the city in a disaster. We'll also need to establish relationships with like-minded people to survive. We'll need different skills. We need to begin to think about recruiting others we trust. We already have medical, construction, engineering, gardening, firearms, water storage and purification, food preservation, and aviation experiences. Still, there are a ton of other skills we're going to need such as bush crafting, hunting, plant identification, tracking, trapping, orienteering, and cold weather living to name a few. Don't forget that we'll also need to set up security details, and that alone will take at least ten people if we want to do it right."

Oz was deep in thought while looking at a property that had ten acres, no water, no electricity, and no sewer. However, it was within twenty miles of a large city that had a population of over 300,000.

He silently said, "I'll pass. Too close to what will become the panicked flock."

"Brian," Oz said abruptly. "What would you look for in a Bug Out Location?"

Brian took a minute to respond and then said, "First, and ideally, I would want to be at least sixty minutes away from the nearest city that has around 500,000 people. You know that within days city dwellers will begin to venture to the forest and countryside. They'll think they can simply hunt and live off the land. We're going to encounter those types of people, but if we're at least sixty minutes out it gives us a week or two to prepare. Second, our property should be near a water source. A stream, spring, river, or well. As you always tell me, Oz, you can only live three days without water. Third, fertile soil. You've made me understand that prepping is only a short-term solution. Even the best of us who are prepared can only store so many beans and rice. Ultimately, we'll have to grow our own food and raise animals. We'll have to live off the land and live a subsistence lifestyle. What am I missing, Oz?" Brian ended.

"Pretty good list, but there are a few more things to think about. We'll need some form of electricity, whether it's solar, wind, geothermal, or hydroelectric. We'll have to look at average rainfall, the number of clear days compared to cloudy, average number windy days including direction and speeds, water table levels, and determine if the property has a sizeable aquifer. We then need to consider what percentage of the property is wooded or cleared. We want a balance, so we can hunt and attract wildlife; but at the same time, we need cleared land for gardening, animals, food plots, housing, and security. We also need to consider the cost. Ideally, we want land we can pay cash for or work out a loan with the property owner. This means it won't be the perfect property, but with hard work and dedication we can make it perfect; and the most important part, we'll own it. We need to also consider how many neighbors we have and how we can become part of the community. Since we're buying a bug out location, it means we won't be there often; one to two times a month at most. We need neighbors who trust us and will watch the property when we're not there and if, I mean when, The Stuff Hits the Fan, we need the neighbors to welcome us in. Odds are high that they will be teaching us new skills, bartering with us, helping us defend our home, or simply giving us advice that could save our lives. Cell phone service would also be a bonus. That will allow us to install and monitor security cameras from any distance and, of course, have internet access. Once we have the land, that's when the work really begins from determining where we build our houses and out of what type of materials, to where we put our Listening Post Observation Posts."

Brian interrupted, "What's a Listening Post Observation Post?"

"We can talk about that at the appropriate time. Right now, we need to do our research and find the perfect bug out location," Oz explained.

Within four months, the two families had purchased a piece of property three hours from each of their respective homes. The Bug Out Location was in northwest Kentucky. The property, which they named Zulu Papa, or simply ZP, was named after the author of the first book Oz read that introduced him to prepping — *Zion Prepper*. ZP was located forty-five minutes away from the nearest city which had a population of 75,000. The property was smaller than they wanted, only ten acres, but had the necessary requirements.

The property was surrounded by state forest yet had three acres of clear, level ground. Being surrounded by state forest gave them access to another 600 acres of land which would never have new houses, industry, or businesses. In addition, there was a stream, two natural springs, natural barriers like valleys and tree lines, only five neighbors who were born and raised in the area, plenty of natural vegetation including blueberries, raspberries, asparagus, mulberries, lamb's quarters, and chestnuts, and finally cell phone service.

The two families eventually had a metal building constructed that could easily accommodate twenty-five people while maintaining privacy for families. Within the building, Oz and Brian built a four-foot high cement block wall surrounding the entire interior perimeter, but low enough so as to not cover the windows. The cement wall was reinforced with rebar and the cinder blocks were filled with concrete. This added additional security against entry as well as protection from gunfire. Unless you had been in the building you would have no idea of the additional security features. All of this was done at a modest cost, too.

In addition to city power, they installed solar panels with deep cycle batteries that could provide up to three weeks of power if conserved. Within the building, the families stored over 600 gallons of water in two intermediate bulk container (IBC) totes in addition to having a well on the property. The IBC totes were food grade plastic totes that at one time held corn syrup. Oz had purchased them for $25 each. Once cleaned and sanitized, they were perfect for water storage. On the north side of the building, Oz created a water catch system by linking six more IBC totes together.

The purpose of the system was to catch and store over 2,000 gallons of rainwater.

In order to have a sustainable food source, the families built numerous raised bed gardens but held off on any livestock since none of them would be living there permanently. The raised bed gardens were not filled with soil, but rather mulch. Over the last ten years, Oz learned to garden with mulch. Mulch is "natures" soil as he often told Nicki. Just as important, the two families invested in their community. Oz, Nicki, Brian, and Elizabeth often visited their neighbors for advice or simply to say "hello." Over the following years, the families created strong bonds with the community.

Over the coming years and when not working on the Bug Out Location, the families individually continued to develop their skills. Oz and Brian knew that there were many skills to learn to become self-sufficient, and if ever there was an SHTF they would need to know them all. To keep it simple, they defined the skills the group would need and agreed to divide and conquer. Each family would become knowledgeable and perhaps proficient in a skill that would benefit the group. They would then become the teacher and "go-to" person, if needed.

The only skill required of all group members was firearms training. The families attended Front Sight Firearms Training Institute near Las Vegas, Nevada twice a year every year. Every fall, the families attended the four-day handgun course. They felt that the handgun was the one weapon that each member needed to be highly proficient in. Every family member needed to have basic, and eventually advanced, skills with a handgun. The families standardized on the Springfield XDM® 9mm with a 4.5″ barrel. This was for several reasons. First, it standardized the type of ammunition used between the two families — the 9mm round. Second, standardizing on the XDM gave any member of the group instant familiarity if they had to borrow someone else's handgun. Third, they could exchange parts from one gun to another with no issues. And fourth, it allowed the families to standardize on equipment such as magazines, sights, trigger groups, holsters, and tactical lights. In the spring, the families would rotate their firearm training between shotgun and rifle courses. They had a well-rounded understanding of weapons.

Oz and Nicki had a personal interest in gardening and were eager to learn everything they could about natural remedies, plant identification, composting, soil enrichment, seed saving, canning, salting, pest control, and water purification. Not only did they practice these skills, they also maintained a fully stocked library of books on all topics at both the Bug Out Location and their residence.

3. WHEN TO BUG OUT

THE BUG OUT LOCATION was an important part of both families' preparations, but it would only be useful if they were able to actually reach it when the Stuff Hit The Fan. This meant that there had to be established criteria that would trigger both families' Bug Out Plans. Basically, they needed a "Go/No Go" decision point. The families agreed that there were two plans: Shelter-In-Place and Bug Out. The families would shelter in place if the natural or manmade disaster appeared, based on current information, to be short-term, meaning that it would last less than two weeks. Examples of events that the families agreed would require sheltering in place and not bugging out would include tornado, hurricane, localized epidemic (avian bird flu, etc.), drought conditions, contained wildfires, localized terrorism (9/11, Boston Marathon incident, etc.), and temporary loss of the power grid (electricity, water, sewer). To effectively shelter in place, the families had a standardized list of items that were always kept on hand. Items included iodine tablets, nuclear, biological, chemical (NBC) suits, and masks due to a local nuclear facility, pre-cut boards for windows and doors, gas masks to protect against chemical spills from the local fertilizer plant, blackout curtains, backup heat sources, backup lighting, an emergency food supply to last a minimum of six months, a minimum of 100 gallons of stored potable (drinkable) water, and first aid supplies.

With sheltering in place, the families would stay in contact utilizing shortwave radios. Each family had unique call signs and cryptic vocabulary that would allow updates to each family, as well as the actions each family was taking. To the normal person listening, the conversation would be uninterpretable and appear as if both parties involved in the conversation were drunk.

Bugging out was just as important. Examples of when the families would head to the Bug Out Location would include categories such as pandemics (H1N1), large-scale terrorism, economic collapse, loss of the power grid, and chemical/ nuclear threat or release. With the bug out categories set and agreed upon, the families further defined the specific action levels that would automatically trigger the Bug Out Plan. They are:

❖ **Epidemic**: May lead to bugging out if extended. Examples of recent epidemics include Avian Flu, Crimean-Congo Hemorrhagic Fever, Ebola, Influenza, Lassa Fever, MERS, Meningitis, SARs, Smallpox, Yellow Fever, and Zika.
   o ACTION: Shelter in place with weekly reassessment of situation.
   o BUG OUT IF THE FOLLOWING CRITERIA IS MET:
      ▪ If epidemic officially becomes PANDEMIC with the following criteria:
         • > 20 deaths within a five-mile radius or 50 deaths within a twenty-five-mile radius of your house.

- o Monitor CDC, local health department, news, and police scanner for up to date information.
- ❖ **Terrorism**: Examples of recent domestic terrorism include: Pittsburgh synagogue shooting (2018), Congressional baseball shooting (2017), Orlando night club shooting (2016), San Bernardino shooting (2015), Charleston church shooting (2015), and Boston Marathon bombing (2013).
  - o ACTION: If localized, shelter in place for a minimum of two days.
  - o <u>BUG OUT IF THE FOLLOWING CRITERIA IS MET:</u>
    - If terrorist event continues to affect localized area for > 5 days.
      - Assess daily and bug out sooner if necessary.
    - If infrastructure is affected: water quality, loss of power, limited food supply, sewer backup.
    - If terrorist event leads to societal breakdown in your area: looting, stealing, rape, violence, damage to property, martial law, and imposed curfews.
- ❖ **Economic Collapse**:
  - o ACTION: Monitor triggers that may indicate an economic collapse is coming.
    - Triggers include:
      - An inverted yield curve: occurs when the yield (the return an investor in bonds receives on bonds with a short duration)

exceeds the yield on bonds with a longer duration.

- The VIX: an index that is tied to market volatility using S&P 500 index options. Also known as the Chicago Board Options Exchange Volatility Index (CBOE VIX), it is used as an indicator of the stock market's anxiety and concern over short-term future market performance.

- Market Cap to GDP: Logic dictates that the worth of a company should be related to the output of an overall economy. As such, this is one of several indicators of a potential market collapse if metrics become skewed. Use this as an indicator only in combination with the above and be aware that market capitalization comes from companies that are global; therefore, there may not be a 1:1 correlation to the U.S. GDP.

- Wealth to Income ratios: An indicator of a potential recession. Given strong stock market conditions, forecasters are generally blindsided by recessions because they tend to be preceded by economic strength.

- Other observable/reported indicators: political infighting (domestic and international), trade wars, strained international relationships, international selling and buying of United States bonds, Treasury issuing additional debt, ever-increasing national deficit, and local gas and merchant prices.

❖ **Loss of the power grid**:
- ○ Action:
  - ▪ Solar Activity: Monitor Coronal Mass Ejections (CME) and Solar Flare activity via phone app found at *http://www.spaceweather.com*.
  - ▪ Manmade: Monitor *https://alertsusa.com/* via phone app, local news, shortwave radio communication, and internet.
- ○ BUG OUT IF THE FOLLOWING CRITERIA IS MET:
  - ▪ Incoming X Class solar flare or CME:
    - • You may only have 10-24 hours to bug out before all power is lost for an extended period (maybe years).
  - ▪ Incoming M Class solar flare or CME:
    - • Monitor to find out area of impact. May not need to bug out but be ready.
  - ▪ Incoming nuclear (EMP – Electro Magnetic Pulse) threat from nation states.

❖ **Chemical/Nuclear Threat**:
- ○ Action: Monitor *https://alertsusa.com/* via phone app, local news, shortwave radio communication, and internet.

- o <u>BUG OUT IF THE FOLLOWING CRITERIA IS MET:</u>
    - Incoming or confirmed chemical or nuclear threat from nation states.
    - Imminent concern from local nuclear power or chemical plant.

With the Bug Out Plan in place and agreed upon by both families, the families continued to live their lives, working and living in separate states and practicing their survival skills as time allowed. It was always the hope of both families that the plans, skills, and bug out location would never be needed, but their confidence in the world and that of the world's governments were ever waning.

4. NORMALCY: THE DEADLY BELIEF!

OZ SAT IN HIS LIVING ROOM with Randall reflecting on 2017. Randall McTatey was a scraggily sixteen-year-old and the youngest of Oz and Nicki's three children. He was intelligent and yet your typical Millennial. He didn't answer or talk on a phone but wouldn't hesitate to text you even if you were in the next room. His enjoyment came from staying up late playing video games and sleeping late into the afternoon. However, Randall had a passion and that passion was flying. At the age of fourteen, Oz introduced the youngster to a Cessna 172. Since that day, the sky was where he found peace and purpose. As Randall approached his seventeenth birthday, he was excited to be able to complete the last step in the process of becoming a full-fledged pilot, the check ride. Though he was confident in his flying, Randall was naive, as most sixteen-year-olds are, and given his limited time on earth, he had only known the world as it had been; peaceful and perfect with very few true disasters.

"It's been sixteen years since 9/11, fifteen years since we met Brian and Elizabeth, and ten years since we purchased our joint Bug Out Location," Oz said to Randall.

"Why did you just mention Brian, Elizabeth, and the Bug Out Location? Oh yeah, in today's world something like the

Spanish Flu could never happen." Randall asked after they just finished watching a documentary on the 1918 Spanish Flu.

"I was just thinking how lucky we are to have good, like-minded friends, and a Bug Out Location," Oz said.

He paused for a second before saying, "Randall, what do you mean it could never happen?" Oz said as he realized this was an opportune time to teach his sixteen-year-old son that life and the events that occur in life are not predictable.

Randall was convinced that a pandemic of that proportion would never occur again due to modern technology.

Oz took a few seconds before stating, "Randall, the Spanish Flu of 1918 infected around 500 million people worldwide. It's estimated to have killed 20 million to 50 million people including 675,000 Americans."

Randall countered, "But Dad, with today's technology we could quickly create a new vaccine and prevent a pandemic from occurring. Oh yeah, don't forget that the United States government has millions and millions of vaccine doses in warehouses throughout the U.S., just in case."

Oz explained, "Son, I'm going to read directly from the Centers for Disease Control and Prevention (CDC) website. This is what our own government is telling us that you need to know about the flu."

"There is still much to do to be ready for the next flu pandemic. There's a need for more broadly effective vaccines that can be made quicker. The global infrastructure to produce and distribute flu vaccines also must be improved. More effective, and less

costly, flu treatment drugs are needed. It is also important to improve the surveillance of flu viruses in animals." (Prevention, 2018)

"Basically, your U.S. government is telling you several things. First, they can't predict when the next flu outbreak will occur, but they know it will. Second, there is no perfect vaccine to help prevent or mitigate flu symptoms; and if there was, they could not be manufactured quick enough. Third, the ability to distribute them where they are needed is in question. Finally, there is no way to predict when and how the virus will mutate," Oz stated.

Randall was quiet while Oz continued.

"Son, I understand you're only sixteen, but you need to understand a little word called 'normalcy.' Normalcy is defined as 'the state or fact of being normal' (Merriam-Webster, 2018). To make it easier on you I'll use big words you can understand."

Randall gave a quick smirk, but Oz continued, "Status quo, normal, no change, every day is the same. Let me give you a great example. Remember when we lived in Illinois and I bought three different types of portable heaters? I was in trouble with Mom because she didn't understand why a family would need additional heating sources when the house had electric heat."

At this stage, Nicki chimed in, "No dear, I was upset at you because the three heaters weren't in our budget. You have a thing about spending money when you want to, yet I get in trouble when I do it."

Oz countered, "Not true, my love. Everything I do, I do for you and the family."

He turned his attention back to Randall and explained, "Randall, I realized that Illinois was notorious for extremely cold winters, and even though we rarely lost power, the possibility existed. Having power is normal, and because it's normal you, your brother, sister, and mom always think it's going to be on. I don't think that way. I'm practical and understand that there exists the possibility that the grid could go down for hours, weeks, or even years."

Randall thought for a moment and then said, "You're right, Dad, because we did lose power in the middle of winter last year. I believe it was -20°F and you simply smiled and brought out the heater. We had nothing to worry about."

"Well, while you're talking about this, let me give you a little more detail about that comment," Oz stated and continued. "I knew we would be okay for the short term because power normally comes back on; hence the word 'normalcy.' But in the back of my mind, I wondered what we'd do if it didn't come back on. How would we stay warm? That's why I bought three heaters each with a different fuel source. First, there's an old saying that goes, 'Three is two, two is one, and one is none.' It simply means always have redundancy in everything you do. Using the heater for example, if one heater failed, I had two others. If I had two heaters and one failed, I still had one available as a backup."

"Dad, I can do the math and understand the concept," Randall stated.

"Of course, you can. I want to be clear on the point of redundancy as it relates directly to 'normalcy.' "Many of our friends will buy one of something and think it will always work and never fail. Why do they think that way, you might ask?"

"No, I wasn't thinking that at all," Randall said.

Oz raised his eyes and continued. "They think that way because of normalcy. Most things you buy in life do work for a long time and, therefore, you begin to think it will always work and that becomes your mindset or expectation. But what do you do when it quits or breaks, and you can't find another one or something similar? Many people would panic. In the case of heat, we won't panic because we know that the power can and will go out, and if it does, we have three backup heat sources."

Nicki replied, "Once again, those three heaters were unbudgeted. You didn't even talk to me about buying those. Stick to the budget, Oz."

Oz quickly dismissed his wife's comments and looked at Randall, "Final lesson on normalcy and redundancy, Randall. If the power had stayed off for a week or even a month, we were prepared not only because we had three heaters, but each of those heaters ran on a different type of fuel: propane, kerosene, and wood."

"Let me see if I understand," Randall stated. "If you run out of propane you have plenty of kerosene, and, of course, our house is surrounded by trees, so that's easy enough; plenty of wood to burn."

"Absolutely correct," Oz stated. "But in addition, by having multiple types of fuel for our heaters, we won't panic if, say, we can't get propane. Why? Because we still have kerosene and wood that we could barter or trade for."

As they finished their conversation, Oz realized that his biggest concern was that his family would most likely not act when an SHTF disaster occurred. He feared they would react like the masses and have the mindset that everything would be okay; help would arrive. He did his best to point out SHTF events as they occurred throughout the world and used them as training and learning exercises. He would highlight how everyday people were physically and emotionally affected by life's events and how their comfortable lifestyle never prepared them for the unexpected. It was a challenge, but Oz never gave up on his family.

5. GETTING ORGANIZED

OZ FELT "TRAPPED" AT HIS CURRENT JOB. Every day was the same thing. Wake up, shower, drive forty-five minutes, work twelve hours, come home, eat, and repeat. He was looking for . . . well, he didn't know what he was looking for, but it wasn't what he was doing. In the early spring of 2018, Oz quit his job, and because he and Nicki had a six-month emergency fund, he was able to take three months off and explore new opportunities.

"Oz," Nicki yelled. "To be clear, you get three months off and then back to work. We have tuition, a house payment, and retirement to save for. We've worked hard to get to where we are, but we still have some ways to go before the finish line."

"The finish line," Oz thought to himself. "The finish line is death and I'll be working until that day. There has to be a better way."

"Nicki, we only have Randall left at home and he's a junior in high school. Why can't we just sell everything and homestead? Let's significantly downsize and change our lifestyle. We've always talked about living off grid. It will be cheaper, and we can finally live 'as one with the land.' We have the skills to garden, preserve food, hunt, collect, store, and treat water. Our house has a septic system which isn't tied to the grid. As far as electricity, we can look into solar and wind options."

"Oz," Nicki said with a scowl on her face. "We have two kids in college and one getting ready for college. We committed to help our children through their bachelor's degrees. We have a mortgage, rent, food, tuition, car maintenance, insurance, cell phones, and a ton of other expenses we pay for. When we had children, we committed to give them the tools to be successful. The finances are our burden, not theirs. What I will tell you is that we need to continue to prepare. Though I'm not a 'prepper' like you, I've always supported you. You have three months off. Why don't you organize and catalog our existing supplies? As of right now, they're everywhere; in the garage, in the shed, in the house, and I believe you even buried some. What did you call them? A cache? Once you have that list, we can quickly identify any gaps and create a budget. Over time we can purchase more of what we need. And yes, you must continue to look for a new job. It has to remain at the top of your list!"

Oz knew Nicki was right. Though he dreamed of living 100 percent off grid, it was simply not a possibility at the time.

After prepping for almost sixteen years, Oz was amazed at how unorganized he had been. He and Nicki had collected years of preparations with absolutely no organization. They didn't know how much of each item they had or where it could even be found.

During Oz's first week off he took inventory of all his medical supplies. It was most definitely a challenge as there were medications and supplies everywhere. He first started in the garage where he went through all his bins and boxes. He placed the medications and medical supplies on his workbench and began to sort the supplies.

"How should I sort them," he thought to himself. "Do I do it by the name of the medication or what it treats? How do I classify medical equipment such as an otoscopy or suture kit?"

Even though his wife was a nurse and would easily know what to use, the kids or other family members would only know the symptoms. He made it foolproof and made two lists: a list of medications and medical supplies that he would sort alphabetically, and a list of symptoms that would correspond to the necessary medication(s) or medical equipment.

As Oz read one of the medication labels, he observed that its expiration date was quickly approaching. Oz knew of a 2012 study involving the California Poison Control System and the University of San Francisco School of Pharmacy that studied medications found in a pharmacy that expired 28 to 40 years prior to analysis. These were old medications. The study found that there was sufficient evidence that many prescription drugs and over-the-counter medications, "retain their full potency for decades beyond their manufacturer-ascribed expiration dates" (Lee Cantrell, Jeffrey R. Suchard, Alan Wu, & al, 2012). As a matter of fact, many of the expired medications still had the fully declared dosage available after the 28- to 40-year expiration date.

"Now," he commented, "to properly store the individual medications for long-term storage."

As he had in the past, Oz now needed to take all medications that came in a plastic bottle, either from a pharmacy or over-the-counter packaging, and preserve each individual medication for long-term storage.

As Oz and Nicki's children grew up, many years prior, they loved drinking Capri Sun® fruit drinks which came in pouches. They were a quick and easy drink for the kids, but Oz took careful notice of the silvery packages the drinks came in. Upon careful inspection, Oz realized that the drinks came in mylar pouches, the same material used to store other food for long-term storage, including oats, corn, rice, flour, and sugar.

He knew that the pouches, once cleaned and dried, could be used to store smaller quantities of items such as medicines. These mylar pouches would protect the medication from Mother Nature's wrath that made all supplies go bad.

"Light, temperature, humidity, and oxygen are the key drivers that make medications and food spoil," Oz said to himself.

If the mylar pouches could be stored in a temperature-controlled environment, for example, in a cache underground or air-conditioned shed, and an oxygen absorber was placed in each pouch, he knew that these medications could potentially be good for 50 years. Over time he had collected hundreds of mylar drink packages and knew that one day they would come in handy. Today was that day.

To properly store the medications for long term storage, Oz cut the tops off several dozen Capri Sun pouches and washed them. Once dry, he placed the contents of the medicine bottle in the silvery pouch while being careful to never mix medications even if they were of the same type. He would then carefully remove the label with the prescription directions and placed it on the mylar pouch.

The next step was to seal the mylar pouch. To do this he carefully pressed a hot iron on the top of the mylar pouch which instantly created a heat seal, thus preserving the medication until needed. Though this was a time-consuming exercise, he had high confidence that his medications would be good for decades to come.

"After all, you never know when you'll need them," he said to himself.

Now that he knew exactly what medical supplies he had, and they were properly protected for long-term storage, Nicki questioned him on how to best categorize their location. Her concern was they needed to be easily found.

"Nice job Oz, but in an emergency, we will need to have quick access to the medications and supplies. I'm not sure how you plan on storing them, but they need to be easy to find. Oh yeah, don't forget that we need to know how much we have of each medication. It does us no good to have a list of medications if we don't track its usage," Nicki said inquisitively.

Oz just smirked and stated, "Just like a woman to show up when I'm finishing and tell me what to do."

Nicki patted him on the butt and quipped, "That's why I married you!" With a quick smile, Nicki left the garage and headed back into the house.

While trying to determine the best way to categorize their location, BJ popped in and asked, "What ya doing Dad?" and quickly realized his father was doing that "prepper" thing.

BJ was the oldest son of Oz and Nicki. At twenty-four years old, he was a graduate student at Southern Illinois University (SIU). Of all the subjects in the world to study, he, of course, would choose biology, and more specifically, marijuana. Though Oz never asked, he knew that in high school BJ partook more than once of the forbidden fruit, weed. But he also knew that BJ was a very responsible young man and that he would never drink or smoke and then drive. Later Nicki and Oz would learn that medicinal marijuana was the only solace BJ had to help him sleep at night when the intense pain of Crohn's disease would affect him. It relaxed him and helped with the pain. Within the family, and several friends, he became jokingly known as 420.

"Dad, you really think we'll need to use those medications down the road?" BJ said.

"BJ," Oz started but before he could continue BJ interrupted him.

"I know, normalcy, the same thing you've told us for years, yet nothing has happened."

Oz said loudly, "Let's not go down that road right now. I need help figuring out an easy way to categorize the medications and medical supplies so we have quick access and it doesn't become a manhunt."

Without missing a beat, BJ explained, "First, you go out and buy bins that will fit on your storage racks. It's best to use bins that fit the dimensions or width of your shelves. You want to use the same bin size but don't want them hanging over the edge off the shelves. I would tell you the smaller

45

the bin the better because Mom will have a hard time moving them to and from the higher shelves if they weigh too much. Second, buy bins that are a solid color. In our dorm, I have the clear bins which make them easier to see in, but it also makes it easier for others to see in them which you don't always want. Third, buy those smaller plastic containers that can be placed inside of the bigger bins. You'll probably end up with something like four to five smaller containers per bin. I would recommend that these containers be clear plastic so you can easily see the contents. These will be in the bigger non-see through bins, so you're protected."

Oz interrupted, "Protected from what?"

BJ answered, "We'll get to that in a minute."

Oz was perplexed. His son, who had no interest in prepping, suddenly became an expert on how to organize long-term storage items and categorize them.

"Where is all this coming from?" Oz thought to himself as BJ continued.

"Place a large label on each bin with something like Christmas supplies, mementos, baseball cards, family pictures, automotive parts; you get the picture. This is where your question of protection comes in. It's not really protection as much as it is camouflage. Let's say we're in an SHTF and someone breaks into the garage or shed or we're not home and someone breaks in. Whoever breaks in is going to be looking for the obvious quick things to steal. If you see a bin labeled Christmas supplies, you'll never know it contains medication unless you open it. Someone who is looking to move quickly will not open it and move on to something easier. You've heard of a 'gray man', well this is a 'gray bin.'" BJ smiled and continued, "Next, place like items in the clear plastic containers by name or type. For example, place all acetaminophen medications in one container and all codeine medications in another separate clear container. This will help you track where and how much you have of each item. Next, place a label on each clear container. The label should contain two things: a sequential number and the contents of the container. For example, let's say our bin labeled 'Christmas supplies' holds four of those smaller clear containers. Each of the smaller containers has its own label with either a 1, 2, 3, or 4. The contents of each container are also listed on the label. It's yet another way to quickly identify what you're looking for, but the most important part is that it will help anyone who understands this simple code find what they're looking for."

Oz stood in amazement at his twenty-four-year-old son and asked, "What code, I'm not following you."

"Dad, you create a master list in a binder of all items by name and location and hide it somewhere no one would find it, but yet the family knows where it is. So, if Mom is looking for acetaminophen because she has a headache, she would go to the master list and on the alphabetical listing look up acetaminophen. The list would show 'Garage - Christmas Supplies – Bin 1.' Mom would then go to the garage, find the bin labeled 'Christmas supplies', open it, find Bin 1, and there she would find her acetaminophen," BJ explained.

"BJ, where did all this come from? That's an outstanding idea, but I would never have thought it would come from you. Where did you learn or hear of that?"

BJ exclaimed, "I read a book called *The Prepper's Handbook* by Zion Prepper. It's pretty good. It gives you an overview of prepping and how to prepare. I know you've been teaching us our whole life but sometimes you need an outside influence."

"Better late than never," Oz thought to himself.

After Oz recovered from his son's outstanding idea of how to store items, he took his handwritten list of supplies, bin description, and container list, and created a table in Excel. He alphabetized the list by medication first and then by symptom, and then printed out two separate tables. He placed the list of medications and medical supplies in a protective plastic sheet and then into a three-ring binder. The three-ring binder would be hidden in between the bins of medical supplies with the location known only to the family.

Now that the garage was complete, Oz continued to do the same with the contents of the shed. The task of sorting became easier using the labeling and storage method BJ recommended. The only change is that some supplies would be stored in the garage while others would be stored in the shed. It was simple enough. Oz simply denoted 'Garage - Christmas Supplies – Bin 1' if in the garage, or 'Shed – Christmas Supplies – Bin 1' if in the shed. Oz found this method so useful that he did the same for his Nuclear, Biological, and Chemical (NBC) Suits and masks, lanterns, Meals Ready to Eat (MREs), water filtration devices, long-term food stores, batteries, canning supplies, light sources, knife collection, and other prepping supplies.

6. BUG OUT BAGS

NOW THAT THE GARAGE and shed were organized, Oz turned to preparing his family. He had prepared Bug Out Bags (BOBs) or Get Home Bags for the family before. He even had the family help him prepare the bag and its contents, but soon the bags were simply thrown into their cars and forgotten. Over time the emergency supplies in the BOBs were missing, damaged, or expired. This frustrated Oz, but he knew that one day his family would depend on the Bug Out Bags and even if his family didn't have an interest in taking care of them, he would.

Oz started with Cali's BOB. Cali was Oz and Nicki's middle child and the princess of the family. She had beautiful long blonde hair and a perfect smile that cost Oz and Nicki $6,000. She was smart, good looking, and dangerously witty. Her quick retorts and sense of humor created a beautiful woman. At nineteen years old Cali was a sophomore studying Health Care Administration at Middle Tennessee State University. She was in an awkward phase of life where she was trying to "figure her life out", and her grades often reflected it. To boot, she had minimal survival and preparation skills which scared Oz. He showed her how to shoot a gun yet wasn't confident she would remember any of the training. He showed her how to start fires but knew she would be challenged. He kept this in mind as he went through her BOB. He had to make everything, from food preparation to first aid as simple as possible.

Oz took Cali's BOB out of her car and began to go through it. For the most part, everything was there but several items needed to be replaced or updated. The first task was to examine the BOB itself to ensure there were no tears or holes. He examined each pocket, zipper, and all the seams. They looked good. He then started with the medical supplies by taking all the contents out of the front pouch and laying them on the workbench.

Each BOB had a standard first aid kit with supplements recommended by Nicki. After examining and ensuring good expiration dates, he added additional packets of acetaminophen, ibuprofen, Quick Clot to stop excessive bleeding, burn gel, Benadryl for allergic reactions, emergency blankets, and an IDF Israeli Army bandage which can be used to stop bleeding as well as being used for a tourniquet. Oz reassembled all medical supplies and placed them back in the compartment.

Oz then examined the fire making supplies. Cali had the essentials: waterproof matches, blast match, two lighters, cotton balls with Vaseline, charcloth, twine, and several candles. Oz continued and made sure she had extra clothing that included a pair of camouflage pants, a long-sleeve shirt, socks, undergarments, a hat, and hair ties. He made sure she had four Mountain House® freeze-dried food pouches, four U.S. Coast Guard Emergency water pouches, and a Life Straw® for water purification.

For communication, he included a Baofeng® UV-5R radio that was vacuum sealed. On the outside of the BOB were her SOG® survival knife, Morakniv® Companion backup knife, headlamp, flashlight, and two military glow sticks. Oz then wrote a letter to Cali outlining what to do in an emergency, placed the letter in an envelope, and the envelope in a plastic Ziplock® bag to protect it. The letter was then placed in the main compartment of the BOB which was the first place she would look in an emergency. The letter read:

Cali,

If you are reading this letter the Stuff Hit the Fan. I know you well and there would be no other reason for you to use the contents of this Bug Out Bag.

First, let me tell you that your safety is priority one. Be aware of your surroundings and constantly, I mean constantly, scan your immediate area for danger. Head home!!!! If it's safe to travel during the day do so but be cautious. If you question your safety, only travel at night and hide during the day. IF TRAVELING AT NIGHT, PUT ON THE CAMOUFLAGE PANTS AND LONG-SLEEVE SHIRT. I want you to put the hat on and use the hair ties I've included to put your hair up. This is one time I don't want you looking like my beautiful angel. I want you to blend in or be a gray woman.

Second, get home. I've included maps in the Velcro compartment on the very back of the Bug Out Bag. These are just in case your car doesn't run or the highways are impassable. ALWAYS use back roads where possible.

Third, if possible, find your cousin and both of you travel together. If you can't find him, recruit another male friend who can help escort you home. Only use someone you trust. You have several good friends so I'm hoping this is not an issue. DO NOT bring home an army of your friends. We do not have enough food to feed everyone if this disaster last for years. If your friend needs a little persuasion, and the Stuff truly hit the fan, tell him we will take care of him and to the best of our ability get him home.

Fourth, your Bug Out Bag contains many things to keep you safe, warm, and fed. You have:
- *First aid kit with many different supplies including feminine products*
- *Baofeng radio (when you're close to the house contact us on Channel 1)*
- *3 flashlights*
- *3 Mountain House freeze-dried meals*
- *4 U.S. Coast Guard water pouches*
- *Life Straw® (use to filter water from a creek or a questionable source)*
- *Waterproof matches, blast match, cotton balls, char cloth, lighters, twine, and candles*
- *Two knives (on the outside of your BOB)*
- *Light (headlamp, glow sticks, and Stream Light™ flashlight)*
- *Emergency blankets*
- *Writing tools (Sharpie™ and Fisher™ Space Pen) with notebook*

Fifth, if you are the first person home, go to the safe in the garage and grab the Red Binder that is labeled "__SHTF – Elevated Threat Manual.__" Read it, then re-read it and FOLLOW all directions. This binder contains directions on how to secure our house.

If you get in a bad situation, I want you to FIGHT FOR YOUR LIFE. Do not give up. Pull hair. Kick or hit guys in the nuts. As hard as you can, push your finger through someone's eyeballs. Punch someone in the throat as hard as you can. Get your finger in your attacker's ear and push as hard as you can. FIGHT FOR YOUR LIFE!!!!

I love you very much, now GET HOME!

Love, Dad

In all, the BOB weighed ten pounds but contained everything Cali needed to get home in an emergency. Oz repeated this task for Nicki, Randall, and BJ, making each letter unique to the family member based on skills and distance from home. Oz also ensured that each BOB was identical to the next except for color. This was by design. The color of the BOB denoted which family member it belonged to. He standardized and used the exact same model of BOB for each family member and each pocket and compartment on them contained the exact same items. Regardless of which BOB you were using, you always knew where the item you were looking for was located.

With the BOBs now prepared, Oz took Nicki and Randall into the garage and showed them where important items were. He showed them how to put on a Nuclear, Biological, Chemical (NBC) suit and how to wear the NBC mask. He demonstrated how to install the NBC filters and they discussed how long they could be worn before being changed. Oz showed them where the flashlights could be found and even showed them how to light an old-fashioned white gas Coleman® lantern. He showed them where the backup heaters were and explained why he had kerosene, propane, and butane heaters. He placed the Baofeng UV-5R handheld radio on his workbench and went over the basic functionalities of the radio. He also pointed out that there were five pre-programmed channels that were labeled and would be used by the family in an emergency.

He was showing them where the multi-fuel generators were stored when Randall asked, "Dad, why do you have some many generators? They're still in the box. Looks like they're new."

Before Oz could respond, Nicki quipped, "Because your dad has more than he needs. They're sitting there wasting away."

"No, ma'am," Oz stated. "They're for bartering. I got them on sale and know they will be the perfect barter item."

"Oz, why is it that everything you buy is always on sale? That's what you tell me," Nicki half serious, half laughing said.

"Because it always is," Oz said without making eye contact with Nicki. In his heart, he knew he was doing the right thing to make sure his family was prepared.

7. RELOCATION

THE DREADED THIRD MONTH had finally arrived. Oz knew that he had to get back to work and was thankful to have had the time off to prepare and organize things for his family. It was early in February of 2018 when Oz accepted a job in Georgia. Oz was excited about the opportunity, but he would be going alone. Randall was only a junior in high school and Oz knew to move him to a new city in a new state would not be fair to him. Kentucky was Randall's home. Nicki and Oz agreed that she and Randall would stay in Kentucky while he finished high school.

The first thought in Oz's mind was the safety of his family, and the second thought was how he would get home in an SHTF situation while in Georgia. He knew that they had a Bug Out Location that Nicki, Cali, and Randall could easily get to, but it didn't help Oz who would be 458 miles away from the house and over 600 miles away from the Bug Out Location. He found comfort knowing that if it was bad, Brian and Elizabeth would bug out and would be there to support Nicki, Cali, and Randall.

"Thank God I have confidence knowing that the family will have the supplies and equipment if a SHTF happens. However, the skills to survive is most concerning," Oz said to himself.

Being 458 miles away from his family weighed heavy on Oz's mind. "What could possibly go wrong," Oz stated out loud with deep concern. "Viral pandemic, financial collapse, solar flare, electromagnetic pulse (EMP), cyberattack." As he thought, Oz realized he needed to prepare for the worst case scenario; that would be an EMP. "Ok, I'll make contingency plans to get home if there is an EMP. Worst case, the sun ejects a solar flare or North Korea or Iran launches a nuke and detonates it above the United States. There we have it; no power, no car, no electronics, no gas, no way home; 458 miles and 24 days from my house."

Oz knew he needed multiple plans to get home. After all, there is no way of predicting when or how an EMP could happen. The three plans would be Plan A: Car, Plan B: Bike, Plan C: Walk.

If the U.S. lost power because of a cyberattack, he knew there was a reasonable chance he could get home by driving his car. Cyberattacks would affect only systems plugged into the electric grid. Banks, hospitals, grocery stores, gas stations, commercial businesses, emergency responders would all be affected, but not his car. He knew he would be able to jump into his car, which was fully stocked with the necessary supplies, and drive home. The challenge would be access to fuel. He planned on only having the fuel in his tank and that was it; no ability to stop and refill. With this in mind, Oz always kept his gas tank full and, as a backup measure, purchased two five-gallon gas cans, which he kept full. He added fuel stabilizer to extend the life of the fuel and stored the containers in his apartment. This gave Oz over thirty gallons of fuel to get home. This was more than enough fuel to get home and still leave him a half tank.

As he continued to plan his way home, he knew having a car would be the easiest and fastest way to get there. He would throw his Bug Out Bag and the two five-gallon gas cans in the car and head home. He wouldn't travel the main highways unless he could leave early enough before the rest of the sheeple realized their world would be forever changed. The plan would be to travel throughout the night and only use backroads. Backroads would take more time, but they would help him avoid the masses. If all went well, he would be home in seven hours.

"Plan A complete. Now on to Plan B," Oz told himself.

Oz knew beyond a cyberattack there existed three other options. They were a solar flare, Coronal Mass Ejection, or an electromagnetic pulse created by a nuclear weapon. Regardless of the source of the EMP, cars would stop, satellites would fail, thereby rendering GPS and cell phones utterly useless, and the lives of many millions of people would ultimately end in death. Oz knew there were only two reasonable transportation choices should any of the three EMP types affect the power grid or electronics of any type. He would either have to walk home or ride a bike. Walking home would be his last option. His Plan B was a bicycle, but what type?

Like most people, he was only familiar with the two most common types which were a ten-speed and a mountain bike — neither of which would work for his purposes. He knew he needed a portable, lightweight, and compact bicycle that could be easily stored in or on his car. The bike needed the ability to carry not only himself but his equipment as well, so it would need some type of storage rack, too.

Oz immediately began researching the available options and was overwhelmed at what was offered. Ultimately, he purchased an eighteen-speed, black, Columba twenty-six-inch folding bike. This was a good choice for Oz. The bike could easily be folded in half and only weighed thirty-six pounds. Being a mountain bike with eighteen speeds, he felt comfortable that it would be the best option of traveling home with his equipment in the event of a solar EMP. The bike was not the most rugged option, but it was cost effective and functional for what he needed. With a bike, Oz conservatively thought he could ride an average of forty miles per day. Whether he biked or walked, he had to take into consideration that he would be traveling through some steep terrain and elevation changes. This would most definitely slow him down. Other obstacles would include weather, possible injuries to himself, finding water sources, hunting or scavenging for food, scouting routes ahead of him, taking alternate routes away from or around main roads, and even helping others along the way.

He relaxed a moment and then muttered to himself, "Plan A and B complete. Now, onto Plan C: walking home."

The numbers 458 and 24 kept reminding him of his challenge.

"That's a lot of food to carry. What about water? How will I protect myself? What shoes do I wear? How do I dress? Do I travel through major cities or take backroads? Do I travel at night or during the day? So many questions to answer," he thought.

The first and most important task was for Oz to map out the route he would walk. If he could leave Georgia at the beginning of the SHTF event, he knew his travels and route would be easier. He knew that most people would simply stay home and wait for the power to come back on. Even though their cars wouldn't start, their TV and computer wouldn't turn on, and their cell phones didn't work, they would have faith that everything would be fine and working within hours. After all, the power had always come back on within hours and, in a worst-case scenario, days. Oz would use this mindset to his advantage. It would take days but definitely less than a week before the unprepared realized they and their families were in trouble. During their period of ignorant bliss, he would travel home.

As Oz mapped his travels, he determined it would be best to walk an average of twenty miles per day. Over twenty miles per day was a stretch given he would need to eat, sleep, and rest, but somewhat realistic given that professional hikers walked thirty to forty miles per day in all types of terrain. Oz was in shape but not the greatest of shape and it was safe to assume that a pace of two to three miles per hour was reasonable. This was a relatively slow pace, but given the unknown obstacles he would encounter, it was a starting point.

He also considered the gear he would take. If he had to use Plan C, then he needed to consider the amount of weight he would carry. First and foremost, he would carry his Bug Out Bag which contained most of what he would need for his journey. Black in color, it contained Datrex® emergency food bars, six Mountain House freeze-dried food packages, two Life Straws, a modified first aid kit, multiple means of starting a fire, maps of his routes, an extra set of clothes, several knives, four flashlights of various size, types, and lumens, extra AA and AAA batteries, emergency blankets, gloves, duct tape, $25 in pre-1964 silver coins, $500 cash in small bills, six extra magazines (fully loaded) for his Glock 17, and six extra magazines (fully loaded) for his Ruger PC Carbine 9 mm takedown. He also carried a desert brown fanny pack that contained several Datrex emergency food bars, one Life Straw, a night vision monocular, compact binoculars, a first aid kit, $10 in pre-1964 coins, $200 cash in small bills, two small flashlights, a Swiss Army® knife, an extra set of AA batteries, a small notebook, and a Space Pen®.

As Oz left his family for this new opportunity, he knew he had prepared the best he could. He knew that he would see his family on a regular basis but had confidence that when, not if, the Stuff Hit the Fan, he would make it home.

8.QUIET BUT DISGRUNTLED

HIS NAME WAS ZAYDEN POOLER and though he was a United States citizen, he was born in Mexico. His parents, both of whom were from California, were young adults in the 1960s and felt strongly that the war with Vietnam was an atrocity, that the United States was the "baby killer" of the world. They saw the United States as the world's police and resented how the country had influence throughout the globe. They never appreciated the fact that everything they had, everything they earned, the healthcare, the house, the cars, and the education all came from the country they hated. Though his parents gave him the freedom and room to grow into his own individual, their resentment of the United States could not help but affect the way Zayden saw the world.

At eight years old he and his mom returned to California while his dad stayed in Mexico. Zayden felt uncomfortable leaving the Mexican country of his youth only to return to the land of hate, the United States. Soon enough he enrolled in school and became an excellent student. He was never in trouble, never late to school, completed all homework on time, and was always obedient. However, in the back of his mind, he felt he had to display those characteristics or there would be some type of penalty. After all, he lived in the country that was the world's police. He felt trapped and a need to right the wrongs as he saw them. After high school, he was accepted into the University of California, Berkley.

He attended three semesters before being kicked out for illegally hacking into the university's system. Not only did he change his grades, but he also diverted grants and endowment funds into an offshore account. After an FBI investigation, it was determined that there was not enough evidence to prosecute and Zayden was released from custody; however he was suspended from ever attending the university again. This further stirred the hate and discontent within Zayden. He questioned why he was targeted; why the FBI investigated him. He knew other students were doing the exact same thing, yet they weren't investigated. "They" had targeted him, he sighed.

Zayden justified being kicked out of college and investigated by the FBI as a setup. The United States had set him up for failure and one day, in the very near future, he would get his retribution.

"This country will not tell me what to do or who I'll be," he thought to himself.

With only $500 dollars and a motorcycle, Zayden dropped out of college and pondered what his next steps would be.

"Thank God I have dual citizenship," Zayden thought. "At least I can come and go from Mexico as I please. That's it. I'm going back to the country that doesn't put boundaries or expectations on me and that I call home. I refuse to live in a country that is quick to judge and rules with an iron clad military."

And so, he returned. After spending several years in Tlaxcala, Mexico and low on funds, Zayden realized that he would have to return to the United States yet again. The computer job he had while in Mexico had been outsourced to India and while he dreaded the decision he had to make, he knew if he wanted to have a career, save for retirement, raise a family, or simply get healthcare, he would have to return to the land he hated.

Zayden settled in Phoenix, Arizona. With a new job, healthcare, and a 401K, Zayden relaxed slightly, but seething in the back of his mind was how much he hated this country.

Now in his early forties, Zayden's hatred for the United States continued to grow. Everything he saw or watched he would attribute to the country heading down a "rat hole." The economy was booming but Zayden believed that to be at the expense of other countries. He saw support for the Second Amendment continue to grow and only thought that it was a matter of time before the U.S. was a military state. He saw the deportation of illegal immigrants who had committed crimes against the U.S. and its citizens as a sign of discrimination which would eventually lead to genocide. He saw Obamacare overturned and deemed illegal and attributed that to the master plan to weed out the poor and helpless.

Zayden thought to himself, "I have to do something about this. How can the United States continue to go on as a nation that only bullies and takes control of other people and countries? Enough is enough."

9. THE PLAN

AFTER WORK ONE DAY, Zayden sat down and poured himself a glass of chardonnay.

"A fancy wine for a simple person," he confessed to himself as he took a moment to reflect before opening his computer browser to the day's news. "More of the same boring crap going on in the world," he exclaimed to himself. "The U.S. deciding who does what and how they do it. Who gets support and who doesn't? It's wrong," he thought.

He scrolled down through several articles before something caught his eye:

"Federal prosecutors in Mississippi charged Yan, 41, in September with leading an empire built on the manufacture and sale of drugs related to fentanyl, one of the world's deadliest and most profitable narcotics. So strong that it's been studied as a chemical weapon, the drug has saturated American streets with breathtaking speed: It kills more people than any other opioid, including prescription pills and heroin, because it's so easy to overdose. Authorities say they have linked Yan and his 9W Technology Co. to more than 100 distributors across the U.S. and at least 20 other countries. Investigators expect scores of arrests as they dismantle his alleged network." (Esmé E Deprez, 2018)

"Fentanyl," Zayden thought. "Isn't that the drug they give mothers during pregnancy to help control pain? And now dealers have found a way to integrate it into the drug pipeline. A chemical and weapon of mass destruction. Brilliant!"

This intrigued Zayden and he began researching its uses, dosages, forms, how it's prescribed, how it's administered, and who manufactures it. The need to know about fentanyl overtook him and he spent the next week understanding this "chemical weapon."

Zayden quickly discovered that:

"Fentanyl is a synthetic opioid that is 80-100 times stronger than morphine. Pharmaceutical fentanyl was developed for pain management treatment of cancer patients, applied in a patch on the skin. Because of its powerful opioid properties, Fentanyl is also diverted for abuse. Fentanyl is added to heroin to increase its potency or be disguised as highly potent heroin. Many users believe that they are purchasing heroin and don't know that they are purchasing fentanyl – which often results in overdose deaths. Clandestinely-produced fentanyl is primarily manufactured in Mexico." (Enforcement)

Zayden continued his research and learned that clandestine fentanyl recently killed a police officer in Kentucky. Zayden read the article with interest:

"After arresting two men who were transporting clandestine fentanyl from Mexico, Franklin police officer Justin Bosch returned to the police department headquarters to fill out the necessary paperwork. When another officer pointed out a white, powdery substance on Bosch's shirt, he wiped it off without giving it a second thought. An hour later he passed out and was transported to the local hospital. Bosch had overdosed on fentanyl, an opioid so potent it can be absorbed into the body by simply

contacting the skin. The drug is 80 – 100 times stronger than morphine. Because it's cheaper than most other opioids, the drug is often used to cut cocaine and heroin. The officers called an ambulance for Bosch, who was given multiple doses of Narcan, an emergency nasal spray that blocks the effects of opioids. Hours later Officer Bosch was declared dead due to an opioid overdose. Police Chief Tom Balgemann and the entire police department are mourning the loss of Officer Bosch but are thankful the tragedy wasn't compounded. As Police Chief Balgemann explains "If he goes home and takes his shirt off, his wife, mother, aunt, whoever does the laundry could grab it, get it on her hand, and that could kill her. Or let's say he goes home, his kids run up to him, 'Daddy, daddy!' and jump on him to give him a hug. It can get on their body and kill them just as it did him. It can just go on and on."

In another article, Zayden learned that Nebraska State troopers seized 118 pounds of fentanyl which is enough to kill 24 million Americans. By simply touching granular fentanyl, the size of a two-milligram salt grain, you could be killed from an overdose.

Zayden thought to himself, "The size of a salt grain. Who can see one little salt grain? Nobody, unless you have a magnifying glass. Maybe this is the way to correct some of the wrongs done by society? It would be difficult to kill millions but maybe we start with hundreds of thousands?"

Zayden then realized that he had changed. That he had reached the breaking point; the fact that he was willing to covertly kill innocent people and it didn't bother him was deemed acceptable. He felt his attitude, beliefs, and actions were the fault of the United States.

"They drove me to this," he silently said.

He needed to act. He was determined to see if these small fentanyl grains, smaller than a grain of salt, would truly kill someone like the articles suggested. He needed to know and see what he was capable of doing. Could he truly kill hundreds of thousands and perhaps millions of Americans for their wrongdoings? Could he be the one to lead and plan the destruction of society as we know it? Would he emotionally be up to the task at hand? He needed to know.

Zayden needed access to fentanyl, but not street fentanyl. The articles he read discussed pure, unadulterated fentanyl.

"The good stuff," he thought.

He was perplexed on how he would get a few grams of pure fentanyl when his best friend, Luis Hernandez, came to mind.

Zayden and Luis were best friends growing up in Mexico. As far as he could remember they had known each other since birth. They remained close friends up to the day Zayden and his family moved back to the United States. Over the years they never lost contact. While Zayden found a career to suit his purpose, Luis lead a different life. Luis had always been into computers and eventually became self-taught on how to write computer code. His claim to fame was his work with the Mexican government who enlisted Luis's help to hack into 12,000 email accounts across the U.S. government. Luis introduced a virus that spread prolifically, and instead of collecting 12,000 email accounts, he ended with access to over 50,000 accounts including classified, personal, and private information.

Unfortunately for Luis and the Mexican government, the United States detected the cyberattack and two days later a drone had mysteriously destroyed the building from which the cyberattack was launched, killing nine, but not Luis.

Luis eventually earned the attention of the Sinaloa Cartel who made him an offer he couldn't resist. In exchange for protection and a nice salary, he would be responsible for helping them launder money. His sole job was to move Sinaloa Cartel money across multiple accounts, financial institutions, and countries without being traced. He was extremely successful.

Zayden reached out to Luis and without questioning him, Luis was able to smuggle Zayden two grams of pure fentanyl.

One month later, after careful planning, Zayden went to work as normal, with the exception that he went two hours early, and entered via the front office area. Zayden knew that the building's camera system hadn't worked in years and he had high confidence he would not be seen. After all, employees typically didn't show up until 8:00 a.m. and it was only 6:30 a.m. He took the door key out of his pocket and slipped it into the lock. The door opened.

With a villainous smile, he told himself, "Can't believe they give all exempt employees keys to get in. Guess they expect us to work overtime and weekends. That will all change today!"

He immediately walked into the men's bathroom, rubbed Derma Shield Skin Protection™ on his hand, opened the small baggie that contained the fentanyl, and placed a small amount on his hand. Zayden knew that the Derma Shield Skin Protection would prevent the fentanyl crystals from being absorbed through his skin. It was the same lotion used by scientists in laboratories to prevent chemical acid burns. Now prepared, Zayden placed a few crystals on all of the toilet seats as well as the bathroom faucets. He then walked into the women's bathroom and repeated what he did previously in the men's restroom. He walked to the front offices where he found almost all office doors open. Without any thought or sense of remorse, he placed fentanyl crystals on keyboards, mice, chairs, and desk phones. He knew not everyone would come in contact with the fentanyl, but some would. That would be enough to satisfy him. He then headed to his car and left the building and was home by 6:50 a.m. He would return back to work later in the morning.

"It's 7:55 a.m. and time to begin the workday," Zayden said to himself smiling as he stepped out of his car to walk into work.

Somewhat surprised, Zayden saw an ambulance parked near the front building office. They had Judy Ledford on the stretcher being placed into the ambulance. Judy was the plant's financial accountant. Zayden noticed that the paramedic was doing chest compressions and saw an AED defibrillator attached to her chest. There was an IV attached to the stretcher that led into Judy's arm.

"Did Judy come in contact with the fentanyl?" Zayden murmured to himself.

He took quick notice of Paul Shelby standing by the front door.

"It must have been Paul who called 911," Zayden thought to himself. "He came in early today."

Paul was the plant's HR manager who, one month earlier, lost his wife to cancer. Paul and Zayden watched as Judy was quickly placed in the ambulance and swiftly driven off.

Stunned by what he had just witnessed, Zayden thought to himself, "Had it worked? Was that all because of the fentanyl? Will Paul be next?"

Zayden took a minute to reflect on how he felt. He felt numb. He didn't feel upset that Judy may die. He didn't care that Paul had lost his wife one month prior and that he, Paul, may die today. He didn't care that Paul's children, ages 5 and 12, could be parentless at any moment. Instead, Zayden felt relief. Relief that no one knew he was in the plant earlier that morning. Relief that he didn't feel bad because Judy or Paul may die. Relief that the United States would soon get what it deserved. Without Paul taking notice, Zayden turned and entered the side entrance of the building and headed to his cubicle.

It was 9:10 a.m. when Zayden and the rest of the team in the cubicles heard multiple sirens. Before they knew it, the emergency alarm was activated, and the team immediately evacuated the building. Each team member made their way to their assigned location where supervisors took roll call to make sure everyone was accounted for.

"What's going on?" Zayden asked Bob Sherrill. Bob was the first shift supervisor as well as the Incident Commander when an alarm was activated.

"I'm not sure. I was up front when I saw Scott passed out and leaning on his keyboard. At first, I thought he was sleeping but when I shook his shoulder there was no response. He wasn't breathing. I immediately went to get Jim in the next office over to help me out. When I stepped in, I saw the phone in his hand, and it looked like he was passed out. I checked his airway and he wasn't breathing. At that point, I screamed for help and told Paul to call 911. I began CPR on Scott and Paul began CPR on Jim. When the paramedics arrived, they told us to evacuate the building. It's hard to imagine that within minutes Scott and Jim collapsed. I don't think it's a coincidence."

Zayden didn't look at Bob but inside he was glowing with satisfaction at what he had accomplished. He was happy. He didn't feel remorse.

Several days later there was a story on the incident by the local news agency. The report read:

"Two days ago, Harber Industries experienced what a confidential source called 'domestic terrorism.' Within minutes of one another three employees, Judy Ledford, Scott Bowman, and Jim Ni, were pronounced dead upon arrival at Albany Medical Center. Though city, state, and federal authorities aren't releasing any information, our source states that fentanyl may have been the cause of death. The medical examiner has disclosed that toxicology reports will be available within the next six weeks and will provide additional information that may contribute to the cause of death for all three. Authorities are not releasing any new information at this time and ask the public for any help that will bring the killer, or killers, to justice."

Satisfied with the results, Zayden felt confident he would never become a suspect but didn't want to chance that he could end up serving a life sentence in a United States prison.

"I'm already a prisoner in the United States. I can't imagine what it would be like to be a caged prisoner in a country I hate," he thought.

And with that Zayden packed his belongings and headed to the one true country he'd only known, Mexico.

As Zayden sat at the U.S. – Mexico border, he thought to himself, "All the research and time spent understanding fentanyl tells me I need to do something, but not this. No, this won't work. The difficulty of getting, buying, and transporting the fentanyl is too risky. I need something that is silent. Something that is untraceable. Something that can be rapidly deployed from anywhere in the world." Then it came to him....

10. ZERO DAY – A NEW PUZZLE

AFTER SETTLING DOWN in Mexico, Zayden began to plan his next project. He knew that the world had previously experienced computer viruses that wreaked havoc and chaos, but they had always, at some time, been detected and never finished the job for which they were intended. Zayden had done it before, and he knew he could do it again. He could create the perfect virus but this time; he would not get caught and the effects would bring down the United States.

"So, what is the purpose of this virus?" he babbled to himself. "Easy—to bring the electrical grid down and watch the United States implode from within. Cyberattack."

Zayden knew that if the power grid could be destroyed there would be no power, and without power, all electronics tied to the grid would eventually cease to function. He also knew that eventually trucks would stop delivering goods and services because of the lack of fuel. This, in turn, would cause people to panic, and eventually brother would attack brother. Those who had not prepared would die of starvation, but before they died, they would do anything they could, including kill, to get food and water.

He needed and passionately wanted to create a virus that would carry out the destruction he desired, but he also knew that it would be best to write the virus using code that had already been created. He needed to do deep analysis and pick apart the binary code to make it undetectable and perfectly executable.

"One byte at a time," he laughed to himself.

In Zayden's experience, most virus computer code could be easily deciphered in minutes, days at most. But his code would not be like that. His code would have depth, secrecy, and most important, functionality. That function was to disable and bring the United States to its knees. Zayden knew from his college days that he had to use a zero-day exploit.

"Perfect!" he yelled. "Create code that spreads without the user having to do anything. No thumb drive, no USB connection, nothing. It will spread like wildfire and they will have no clue what hit them."

Zayden had been fascinated with the zero-day malware called Stuxnet. He recalled that Stuxnet was malware covertly designed by the U.S. and the Israeli government to disable nuclear centrifuges in Iran. Stuxnet infected a very specific Iranian Siemens Programmable Logic Controller (PLC) which are very small computers that control motors and pumps that ultimately affect telecommunications, financial infrastructure, health care, power plants, and power grids.

Zayden began talking to himself as he was mentally seeking a solution to his goal, "In essence, the PLC tells the motors and pumps how fast to run and for how long. At the wrong speeds, the motors and pumps fail. Those suckers never knew what hit them. Had the Israeli's not gotten greedy and modified the code, Stuxnet would still be causing those Iranian centrifuges to implode," he finished.

Zayden needed to make sure his virus left no signature, no clue, no trace of the origins of the malware and, just as important, no bugs. But where to start? Creating a virus of this type from scratch could take years, and with no help maybe a decade.

Yet again Zayden thought of Luis. "From drugs to computers, he's the best friend a man could have," Zayden said to himself.

Throughout his years with the Sinaloa Cartel, Luis had developed a network of underground contacts from across the world. He could pick up the phone and within minutes talk with his Russian counterparts. He could easily email Iranian hackers and move millions across continents. In the U.S., he had reliable contacts who worked at the National Security Agency and Cyber Command Headquarters within the U.S. government. In Britain, he had contacts in the Government Communications Headquarters and in Israel at Mossad Headquarters, Unit 8200 Israeli Intelligence. Luis was well connected. Zayden contacted him and scheduled an in-person meeting for the following month.

The meeting took place inside a building housing the city hall for the Azcapotzalco municipal government, located in the northwest section of Mexico City, Mexico. Luis chose this site as it was the location used by the Sinaloa Cartel when they wanted to "influence" the Mexican government. The town was loyal to the cartel who provided supplies, labor, and housing when needed. After a handshake and hug, Zayden and Luis began discussing the true purpose of the meeting. Zayden spent the next hour telling Luis his plan, and why the United States needed to be taught a lesson.

Luis interrupted and stopped Zayden. He placed his hands on his shoulder and explained, "Zayden, you and I have been brothers my entire life. I would sacrifice my life for you if I had to. I would do anything for you. You don't owe me an explanation, but since we're talking about it let me share my thoughts. I agree with everything you say. To make matters worse, the United States has done nothing to support Mexico other than spew threats and acts of aggression. We do their menial work for them. We pick lettuce, collect their garbage, clean their offices. They see us as an inferior race, a third world country whose sole purpose is cheap labor. We're the next door neighbor nobody wants. I will help you any way I can," Luis concluded.

Zayden smiled and quietly said, "Real world physical destruction caused by a virus. That's what we need Luis."

As they began to design the virus, they had to make sure they understood how it would be deployed, the effects they hoped it would have, and how it would remain undetectable and complicated to decipher. It had to be invisible to software virus companies such as Norton®, McAfee®, and Kaspersky®. They further agreed that a zero-day exploit would be used. As a matter of fact, up to six zero-day exploits would be incorporated into their code. They liked the fact that zero-day exploits occur on the same day a weakness is discovered in software. In other words, they would introduce a virus before a fix becomes available. This was the ultimate project. They both understood that zero-day exploits were extremely rare, and instead of creating them from scratch they would have to turn to the black market and incorporate the help of other countries.

As they continued to explore the design of the virus, Zayden asked Luis, "Should we put in a kill date? A date to stop the attack?"

Luis responded, "You want to end the United States as we know it. Let it happen in its own time, not our time. No kill date!"

The biggest challenge Zayden and Luis discovered was how they would cross the "air gap."

"In geek talk," Luis explained. "Computers that run sensitive, highly secure programs have their own network. They're not tied nor do they have access to any outside network. Take a nuclear power plant, for example. None of those computers will have access to the outside world. They can only talk to systems and computers within the nuclear facility. To infect those systems it would require a physical means, like a USB drive or something similar, to introduce the virus. We can't simply hack into their systems and upload the virus unless we have access to their network. Technically, we don't need access. We need to know someone who has access and utilize them. For example, let's say a utility company uses a local computer company to help program or update their PLCs. We need to introduce the virus to the service technician's laptop. Once he connects to the nuclear power plant network, the virus will unknowingly be transferred, and the chaos will begin."

"Understood," Zayden said and continued. "The virus solves one part of the problem, but it doesn't prevent cars, semi-trucks, generators, or other things that are not tied to the grid from running. That's when we can truly expect the end of the United States. Imagine, no fuel, no food, no medical supplies, no access to money, no water, no deliveries. Their society completely collapses," Zayden said with a smile.

Luis responded, "I'm one step ahead of you, Zayden. In addition to the virus, we need to create a manmade EMP as insurance that their world is forever changed. Zayden, have you heard of a Marx generator?"

"No," he responded.

Luis looked down and showed Zayden a YouTube® video of a Marx generator before explaining. "Its purpose is to generate a high-voltage pulse from a low-voltage DC supply. Marx generators are used in high-energy physics experiments, as well as to simulate the effects of lightning on powerline gear and aviation equipment."

"So?" Zayden blurted.

"The government has a number of these generators across the United States," Luis said. "The biggest being at Sandia National Laboratories. The government claims the generators are only used to test government equipment against EMPs but my source in Iran says it can create a manmade EMP unlike anything ever seen. It was created to disable Russia's infrastructure during the Cold War. The U.S. government never shut it down but instead continued to invest and upgrade the generator with new, more effective technology."

Zayden was very excited when he interrupted Luis and interjected. "So you're saying we're going to use the government's own equipment against itself. The U.S. government will bring down the entire country and not even realize it."

"That's the plan," Luis exclaimed. "We also need to introduce software into the HAARP mainframe and take control of it."

"HAARP. That's the government research facility in Alaska, right?" Zayden asked.

"Yeah," Luis affirmed. "It's another one of those programs the government has lied to its citizens about. HAARP is the world's most capable high-power, high-frequency transmitter that the government claims is being used to study the ionosphere. The reality is that HAARP is a high-power transmitter facility operating in the high-frequency range used to temporarily excite a limited area of the ionosphere. This, in turn, can generate a highly controlled EMP. Simply put, Zayden, we tell HAARP to create an EMP which will destroy the grid on the West Coast, and we'll use the Marx generator at Sandia National Lab in New Mexico to destroy the power grid on the East Coast! With my network of contacts throughout the world, I'm highly confident we can unite on a plan and enlist the help of resources in Iran, Iraq, Russia, China, Cuba, Mexico, and, yes, even in the United States!"

11. FOREVER CHANGED

AS OZ WRAPPED UP his seminar entitled "Prepping 101", he told the participants, "In closing, we'll end with where we started the seminar. We prepare because we don't know when a Stuff Hits the Fan (SHTF) event will occur, how long it will last, or the impact it will have on our families or society. Being prepared prevents us from becoming victims to the 'Rule of Threes.' Remember what they are?"

Several seminar participants raised their hands. Oz called on them and they said, "You can only live three seconds without the desire to live, three minutes without air, three hours without shelter or fire, three days without water, three weeks without food, and three months without hope for the future."

"Absolutely correct, and thank you for your time and support and may God bless each one of you," Oz stated.

Oz stopped for a moment as he watched the crowd leave and reflected on how he had arrived at this time and place teaching the obscure subject of "prepping."

"It will be eighteen years since that terrible day. September 11, 2001," he thought to himself as he came out of his trance. "It's hard to believe that's why I'm here today" he sighed.

His mind immediately switched to one of concern for his family. For the last eighteen years his wife and three kids had grown up in a household where prepping was practiced yet they themselves never really participated or practiced it themselves. Nicki fully supported him when he wanted to buy bulk food or buy 250 pounds of AA and AAA batteries, but she was not involved in the hands-on portion of prepping. She and the kids didn't see the urgency, need, or purpose of having so much "stuff." Oz simply accepted this fact and continued to store the essentials and develop his skills. He prayed that he would never need to use his supplies or skills and was even more concerned that if he did, how would the family fare given their lack of participation and skill building.

Seminars were something Oz did on the weekends several times a month, but his full-time job was working as General Manager for a chemical plant. Oz worked for a great employer and he absolutely enjoyed his team.

"They truly are the best team," he noted when his computer began acting funny. He quickly glanced at the clock that read 2:30 p.m. when he first noticed the fan on his laptop was making a high-pitched whining noise almost like a small jet engine. The fan soon quieted. He immediately noticed a burning smell coming from his laptop. As he released the laptop from its cradle, he felt the back of the laptop. It was extremely hot. As he continued to hold the laptop it became hotter and hotter and eventually caught on fire. The plastic casing burned with a distinguishable black smoke and produced a terrible smell.

"What the ..." Oz thought.

He had seen lithium batteries catch on fire before and destroy equipment, but it had never happened to him.

"Was this caused by the batteries? Why did the fan whine and then suddenly quit?" He questioned himself.

Before he could answer his own question, his monitor and printer produced the same black smoke and smell, but without the fire. Oz immediately stood up in his chair and headed down the hall to grab the fire extinguisher. As he turned into the hall, he was shocked to see black smoke and the very noticeable smell of burning plastic coming from all the offices. Not only were computers, monitors, and printers being destroyed, but so were UPS power backups, USB connected devices, and computer connected phones. It seemed like anything that was connected to the internet was self-destructing.

Without hesitating, Oz walked to the factory floor to see if they were experiencing the same thing. As he opened the door to the factory floor, he saw his teammates with fire extinguishers in hand putting out fires. Every piece of equipment on the factory floor had either quit or was on fire. Oz immediately grabbed Jake, his Operations Manager, and told him to call 911 and explain the situation.

"Tell them that we have small localized fires and the concern is that they could spread to the main building structure. Tell them it appears to be an EMP..."

Oz stopped short of finishing the sentence. Really, was he going to tell emergency services that an EMP had just hit his plant? Yes, it was something he studied for the last eighteen years but he had only read about it. He knew what to look for, but would they think he's crazy? After all, it's probably just a power surge.

"A large power surge! You can't question what you're seeing. You must react. Don't be one of the sheeple," he said to himself.

Oz then looked Jake square in the eyes and finished his sentence, "Tell them it appears an EMP has hit the plant."

"You mean a power surge, don't you boss?" Jake said with confusion.

"No. I mean an EMP. I'll explain later. Get on the phone now," Oz finished.

As Jake turned away to make the call, Oz continued to survey the damage. He could see his Emergency Response Team in action putting out fires. He could see the confused look on their faces as they quickly extinguished the fires.

Within seconds, Jake returned with a look of concern and stated, "Oz, I've tried ten different times to call 911 but with no luck. Each time I call I get nothing. It's like it won't dial out."

"Let me try," Oz stated.

Oz pulled his phone from his pocket and noticed that everything looked fine. The phone and screen lit up just as it should. All the phone icons were in the right place. Every screen appeared as it had the last time he used it. Oz dialed 911 and pushed the call button. Nothing. He repeated the process two more times with the same result—nothing. Oz then rebooted his phone and dialed 911. Nothing.

"Jake!" Oz shouted. "Get in your truck and drive to the fire station. Tell them what's happening and to hurry."

Jake turned and ran to the parking lot, jumped into his truck, and drove away. Oz then turned and walked to the main office area he had just left to survey the damage and make sure everyone was safe. He looked around and his team was accounted for. He returned to the plant floor to make sure all teammates were accounted for. They were. Oz told the team to unplug all equipment from any outlet and make sure all computers connected to ethernet ports were disconnected as well. With the plant secure and all employees accounted for and safe, Oz returned to his office and slowly sat down in his chair. He closed his eyes. After several seconds he opened his eyes and was staring at a melted laptop that absolutely smelled. He had that tingly feeling inside that yelled, "Go home!"

Fifteen minutes later Jake ran into his office and exclaimed "Oz, the fire department says we're on our own. A low priority. They've lost all communication. They're unable to make contact with anybody — police, ambulance, Department of Transportation — nobody. They have no idea where to begin. I drove by the police station and it's the same. Officers were standing in the parking lot talking; almost like they too didn't know what to do."

Everything he had prepared for, everything he taught and told others what to look for had just happened. Oz knew what he needed to do; he needed to react, but he couldn't, not at that moment. He was paralyzed, but then he thought of his family. He quickly snapped out of his daze as he noticed the lights slowly dimming. As he looked around his office the emergency exit signs were doing the same thing. The lights would go dim then bright, dim then bright and then nothing. No lights, no emergency exits glowing, no computer lights blinking — nothing. Only silence. He walked into the hallway and saw nothing. The power was completely out.

He heard the voices of his teammates and by the tone in their voices knew they were confused and scared. Within seconds he could see faces peering from the office entrances. Despair—that's what he saw on the faces staring back at him.

Oz panicked and reached for his phone to call Nicki. He quickly realized that his phone didn't work. This time there was no lit screen. Absolutely no power. He hit the power button several times before realizing the phone was dead. His mind shifted to Nicki and the kids. Had they experienced the same thing? Were they scared? Would Cali and BJ realize they needed to head home? Would Nicki and Randall shelter in place until he arrived home? Many questions, no answers. Oz knew he had to rely on his training. It was time to act.

12. BUGGING OUT

OZ KNEW BEFORE HE BUGGED out that he needed to have a conversation with his team. His mind was made up. He was going to bug out no matter how crazy it sounded. But first, he needed to let his team know what he saw happening and explain why he was leaving. He needed to say his final farewell just in case this event was truly as bad as he imagined. He had his supervisors gather the team in the main conference room. The conference room was next to large windows that allowed the sun to freely shine through. With a thoughtless stare, Oz took notice of employees entering the conference room with their heads down. No smiles but an occasional handshake to show there was still civility.

"At least for the next week or two," Oz thought.

He saw looks of confusion and knew there would be many questions. And so, he began his unprepared, unplanned end of the world speech.

"First, like many of you, I can't reach my family. I thought my computer catching on fire, the lights and power fluctuating, and then the loss of power was scary — and it is — but not as scary as not knowing about my family. I don't know if they're going through a similar event or if they're fine. The same questions I'm sure you have. I want to give you my thoughts on what's happening and share how you need to act.

"First, I strongly feel that we've been hit by some type of electrical event. I hope I'm wrong, but I feel I'm not. I have no idea if it was a cyberattack, EMP, or a combination of the two. The equipment in the plant failed followed by the power grid. This was a deliberate attack and not a coincidence. Cell phone services are down to the point where our local emergency services can't contact one another. The fire department told Jake they can't contact anyone.

"After this meeting, I encourage each of you to go home and make sure your family is safe. After you know they're safe, you and they will need to shelter in place. In other words, stay in your house for as long as you can before you venture out. If these events last more than two weeks people will be completely unprepared. Unprepared people will need water and food. When they don't have food, they will come to your house and ask you. As harsh as this sounds, I encourage you to NOT give them food or supplies of any type. I've thought about this answer for many years and here's the reason why: if these events last longer than one week you and your family will need that food. You'll eventually run out unless you've prepared. The moment you feed others they will keep coming back to you and asking for more and more. They will tell others you have food, and before you know it you're feeding more people than you realize.

"Next, after you leave our parking lot, head immediately to stores such as Dollar General®, Dollar Tree®, and yes even auto part stores. Auto parts stores will have water and even snacks that you can load up on. Your grocery stores like Walmart, Kroger's®, and Publix® will be packed with unprepared people. It will be chaotic. You don't want or need to be a part of that. People won't necessarily head to the smaller dollar stores. Load up on the basics like beans, rice, flour, peanut butter, canned vegetables, medical supplies, feminine products, toothbrushes, toothpaste, baking soda, salt, and bottled water. Buy what you can afford. If you go to these stores and there's no power, add up the cost of the items your buying on a piece of paper, add nine percent for tax, and then add an additional ten percent for the person behind the register. Tell them to keep the extra ten percent when the power comes back on. This ensures you get what you need and compensates them for their troubles. From there, head to the lumber store and purchase sheets of wood which you can use to secure your windows and doors. This won't be the greatest security but it's something.

"Then, sit down with your family and discuss how you plan to survive, yes survive, if the power outage lasts more than three weeks. Why three weeks? Because you can only live for three weeks without food. Again, people will be hungry and will act in ways you've probably never experienced. That's when I expect neighbors to turn against neighbors. The neighbor you've known for twenty years will do absolutely anything to get food for his or her family. This includes killing you and your family.

"Next, secure your house to the best of your ability. Use the wood you purchased or any other material you have on hand to barricade all entrances. Then, take inventory of your guns and ammunition. Know exactly what you have and use it wisely. Gather your medical supplies in one location and take an inventory of those, too. Know what you have and what you can and can't treat.

"Set up a security detail next. To the best of your ability set up a 24/7 watch detail. This will give you and your family advanced notice if something or somebody could jeopardize your safety. And finally, be aware. Every time you step out of your house be aware of your surroundings. Always and constantly check your environment. Put your head on a swivel. Know your environment.

"My hope is that the power will come back on. My hope is that you and your family will not need to implement anything I have discussed. I don't mean to scare any of you, but I want you to be prepared. God bless each and every one of you and your family; be safe."

As Oz stared into the crowd, he only saw blank faces. No expressions. No further words needed to be spoken. No one knew how to respond. One by one they exited the conference room and headed to the parking lot. Oz turned to his leadership team, shook each of their hands, and wandered back down the hallway to gather his personal belongings before heading to his car. As he exited the side door he wondered if he would ever be back in Georgia, let alone this job. After all, he just scared the hell out of his team. He would probably be fired if the lights came back on.

Standing in front of his car he pushed the door-unlock button on his key fob, but nothing happened. He pushed it again; still nothing.

"No big deal," he thought. "The battery is probably dead."

He inserted his key into the door lock and stepped inside the vehicle. He immediately noticed that there was no dinging. No overhead or dash lights. Nothing.

"Oh, no," he stated to himself.

He sat in the driver's seat, closed his eyes, fumbled to insert the key into the ignition, and turned the key. Nothing happened!

Oz was now at a point in his training that he had never experienced. He had mentally prepared for this moment in time but to physically be sitting in a car that wouldn't start after experiencing a power outage and some type of cyberattack was crazy.

"The stuff you only read about in books," he laughed.

He was now scared. He turned his head to look at the back of his car where he saw his folded bicycle. Was it time to start riding home? Should he give it one more day? Maybe the power would come back on. After all, he didn't want to look like a fool riding a mountain bike down the highway.

As he was staring at the mountain bike, he heard a knock on his window. It startled him. He saw Jake and Susan. Susan was the second-shift supervisor. They were desperately trying to get his attention.

Oz stepped out of his car but before he could say a word Susan exclaimed, "They won't start. None of the cars in the parking lot will start. We've checked the batteries and nothing. Oz, it's like you said. At first, I didn't want to believe you. I didn't want to hear what you had to say. But it looks like it's true."

Oz looked at Susan and Jake and gave them a look of sincerity and understanding. Jake and Susan, just now, at this moment, realized what Oz knew for years, that something major was going to happen to the United States. The only piece of information Oz didn't have was when or how it would happen. Now he knew. Oz walked to the employee parking lot and saw small groups of his employees huddled together. He wondered what they were saying. He wondered what they would do. He knew that most of them were not prepared.

"They probably don't have money to go to the store. They lived paycheck to paycheck," he thought to himself.

Some of them were so out of shape they would most likely not be able to walk home. He turned to Jake and Susan and told them to leave the plant open for those who choose not to walk home.

"It's better to give them an option as opposed to not having one," he told Jake and Susan.

As Oz stared at his team huddled in the parking lot, he wondered if he should approach them and talk to them. After all, he was the Plant Manager. That's what good leaders do; take care of their team. He couldn't bring himself to do it. He knew that there were no more words to be spoken. He had said his goodbyes in the conference room and there was literally nothing he could do. He knew that he had priorities just as they had priorities. The difference was he was acting on his priorities. He was leaving to be reunited with his family. He was heading to Kentucky where he had everything he needed: food, water, heat, shelter, and protection.

Oz turned and walked away. It was now time to begin his journey home.

13. THE JOURNEY HOME

OZ LIFTED THE HATCHBACK on his Subaru Outback™ and pulled the Columba mountain bike out. He paused for some time before he pulled the release on the bike. He was pondering what his journey would be like. Would he run into trouble? Would he have the endurance to ride or walk 458 miles? Would he be able to find water along the way?

"Too many questions," he thought to himself. "Time to get back to reality."

Upon pulling the frame release lever, the bike frame swung open and the front and rear tires were now in their proper position. He tightened the frame release lever which locked the frame in place. He then loosened the handlebar lever that allowed the handlebars to rotate 90 degrees to the proper position. He turned to the seat, loosened the lever, raised the seat, and locked it into position. His last task was to flip the pedals 90 degrees to a normal position. He pressed on each tire to check for inflation.

"Who would have ever of thought to make a mountain bike that could fold in half? Pure genius," he sighed.

Without thinking he took the reflectors off the spokes on each tire and removed the reflector on the front of the bike. He fully inspected the bike for anything that would reflect light. The last thing he wanted was to be riding at night and be discovered because of light reflecting from the bike. He wanted to be silent and stealthy. With the mountain bike fully assembled and inspected he changed his shoes. There was no way he would survive in his loafers on a trip that could take up to one month. He opened a small tote stored in the back of the car that had critical supplies. He removed a pair of Danner® tactical boots. He put the boots on and zipped them up. He then reached back into the car and took his SOG Seal Pup Elite tactical knife and a magazine pouch with two extra 9mm Glock magazines and slid them through his belt loops securing them on his right-side belt. He opened his Bug Out Bag and grabbed his Glock 17 which he removed from the inner waistband holster. He placed the holster on the left side of his belt. Oz knew that being left-handed gave him a slight advantage. That's why right-handed boxers often struggle against left-handed boxers; they never see it coming. Oz then picked up the Glock and chamber-checked the gun to verify it was unloaded. He immediately racked the slide which loaded a round in the chamber. He chamber-checked for a second time to visually verify the gun was loaded. He removed the magazine and made sure it was topped off and there were no signs of visual damage. He reinserted the magazine and holstered his weapon.

"Glock, knife, magazines," he said to himself as if he was going down a mental checklist.

He then took everything out of the back of his hatchback to gain access to the spare tire compartment. That is where he stored his Ruger PC Carbine 9mm takedown. He took both halves of the Ruger, the forend assembly and action, and carefully twisted the two sections together until he heard a "click." As he had done with the Glock, he verified the rifle was empty. He verified yet again that the rifle was empty and dry fired the weapon in a safe direction. He was testing functionality. Everything worked as expected. He then slapped a Glock magazine into the magazine well and racked the slide. He checked the breach to make sure the rifle was loaded, and when he saw a Hornaday® Critical Defense round chambered, he smiled. He removed the magazine and made sure it was topped off and there were no signs of visual damage just as he had done before. He reinserted the magazine, pressed the gun's safety and carefully placed it on the passenger's rear seat. Oz loved the Ruger PC Carbine 9mm takedown. It was easily hidden in his car with the true advantage being that it came with an adapter for Glock magazines. Oz had confidence knowing that if he were to get into a firefight he could transition between handgun and rifle and use the same magazines in each weapon. To finish the task, he retrieved the Meprolight® 21 sight from the car's center console and placed it on the rails of the rifle. He took the cover off and made sure the reticles illuminated as they should. The Meprolight 21 used a fiber optic collector system during the day and a miniature self-powered tritium light source at night. This meant no batteries. Oz took a brief minute to admire the weapon he just assembled. In less than two minutes he went from rifle pieces to a fully functional self-defense weapon.

"Now, the fanny pack" he whispered.

Prior to placing the fanny pack around his waist, he did a thorough inspection to make sure everything was accounted for.

"Datrex emergency food bars, Life Straw, night vision monocular, binoculars, first aid kit, pre-1964 coins, cash, flashlights, Swiss Army knife, AA batteries, notebook, and a Space Pen. Check," he said out loud. He placed the fanny pack around his waist, facing forward, and tightened the straps. He then grabbed his Bug Out Bag and did a quick but thorough inspection to make sure everything was in its place. He double checked to make sure items were evenly distributed. Bulky gear and items not needed until he stopped were stored in the bottom zone. Heavier, dense items were stored in the core zone. Bulkier items he may need while riding his bike were stored in the top zone. Essential items he would urgently need were stored in the accessory pockets while he used the tool loops and lash-on points for oversized or overly long items. He pulled six Glock magazines out of his Bug Out Bag and loaded them with ammunition that was stored in the tote in his car. He placed the six fully loaded magazines in a front pocket of the bag which would allow for easy access. He placed it across his back, snapped the support straps in place, and removed any slack in the straps.

He retrieved his North Face® all-weather jacket from the car and secured it to his Bug Out Bag. He jogged in place for ten seconds to ensure nothing was moving, making noise or would fall off.

"Good," he said as he sighed a breath of relief.

Oz now had a decision to make. He could jump onto 75 North which would take him directly to Atlanta. Once through Atlanta he would continue north to Chattanooga, Tennessee where he would get on 24 West. From there it was straight to the Kentucky border. This was the easiest and most direct route. He knew if he took this route the possibility of finding food and water along his journey would be easier since stores along the highway might still be open. If they would not take money, he had items he could use to barter. Though this was a quicker route, in the back of his mind he also knew that the next three days would be a true test for society. With no communication from the federal, state, or county governments, there were many questions. The main being would people remain calm or would the panic start early? He bet on the later and that with no power or cars there would be no law enforcement. Those with lower morals or those in gangs would see an immediate benefit in a world with no power and law enforcement. If he could get through Atlanta with no issues, the rest would be easy.

"Ok then, the main highway it is," he told himself.

Oz jumped on his bike, turned down Gardner Street and within a mile was on the overpass to 75 North where he stopped before entering the highway. In both directions, he saw individuals and families surveying their surroundings. Some were looking at their car hoping they would mysteriously start. Some had the hoods up and were inspecting their vehicle. Others had their hands on their hips and eyes closed, looking down as if praying.

Oz could only imagine what they were saying, "Please God, let me get home," he thought.

A chill ran down his spine. All those people, stranded. They had no clue. His heart sank as they too would have to make a hard decision. Do they wait for help or do something else? And if they did something else what would it be?

Wanting to be able to see further in the direction he was headed, he reached into his fanny pack and took out his collapsible binoculars. As he peered in the direction of the northbound lane all he saw was stalled vehicles as far as the binoculars would allow. Several minutes later he saw a vehicle driving on the outer part of the highway used by emergency vehicles.

"Now that's a beast!" he blurted.

As he looked at the vehicle, he noticed it was a Chevy Suburban. As he looked closer, he noticed the winch on the front bumper and that the Suburban was lifted two to three inches. The Suburban had a roof rack with four, five-gallon gas cans on top, in addition to two more mounted on the back bumper. Oz estimated the Suburban to be from the 1980-1984 era.

"No wonder it's running. It has no electronics. It's 100 percent mechanical," he said as his lips moved but no sound came out.

He continued to watch the Suburban drive away and took notice of how many stranded individuals were trying to flag the driver down; some nearly getting run over before they realized the driver was not going to stop.

"At least somebody was prepared," he said out loud.

Oz placed the binoculars in the fanny pack, zipped the pouch, and turned ready to begin this part of his adventure.

Oz jumped on his bike and drove down the ramp to enter 75 North. It was only a matter of minutes before he was forcefully stopped by a man who jumped in front of him. The man, appearing to be in his fifties, was overweight but wore professional looking clothes. It was obvious he used hair spray to hold what little hair he had remaining in place.

"Hey, I need information on what the hell is going on?" he said with anger.

As the man spoke, Oz could tell he was a smoker. Every time he opened his mouth Oz felt putrid vapors entering his nose. As if the world ending was not bad enough, he had to now smell the breath of a desperate, unprepared pain in the ass.

"What's going on? What happened to the cars?" the man demanded.

"How would I know?" Oz said briskly.

"Because you look like you're ready for the world to end," the man snapped and continued. "You have your backpack on and you're carrying a rifle. What the hell?" he finished.

"Get out of my way and don't touch me if you value your life," Oz commanded.

"I just want answers and you look like you were prepared for something. So, tell me what's going on," the man said as he stepped closer to Oz.

With his left hand ever so slightly touching his Glock, Oz said, "This will be the last time I tell you to move and get out of my way."

Oz immediately saw a glimpse of fear in the man as they stared at each other eye to eye. The man raised both hands in the air and slowly backed up as he stuck his middle finger up at Oz. Neither man spoke another word. Oz quickly assessed the situation and rode back up the ramp to the overpass.

"Two minutes on the highway and my first confrontation," he silently thought.

With one eye still on the man he had just confronted, Oz looked at his map yet again. It was clear that he would have to use secondary and back roads to get home. If people were scared and confused now, he knew it would get worse as the hours passed by.

The facts were straight forward. People can only live three seconds without hope, three minutes without oxygen, three days without water, and three weeks without food. If the man he just confronted was like most people, they would be dead in less than a week which meant it was only a matter of days before the survival instinct innate in humankind turned on. Once the survival instinct kicks in, people have no boundaries. They'll do whatever they have to do to survive and ensure the survival of their loved ones, which includes killing with no remorse.

"First," Oz thought to himself "I need to disassemble the Ruger. That was the first thing that man saw. I need to be a gray man and blend into my environment. I need to do my best to not stick out." Oz ensured the rifle safety was on before pressing the release mechanism on the rifle and twisting, the rifle separated into two parts: the forend assembly and action. They could now be easily carried in his Bug Out Bag out of sight of others. If needed, he could quickly assemble the two pieces and the rifle could be back in action within ten seconds.

Oz chose to take Highway 41 until he reached the city of Ashburn, Georgia. Highway 41 ran parallel to the main highway separated by a fence and significantly fewer cars. Though the fence was easy to jump over, it would at least be a barrier of sorts. Once at Ashburn, he would decide to either stay on Highway 41 or find an alternate route.

Oz chose cities as "waypoints" along his route. By using cities as waypoints, it would ensure he was traveling in the right direction as well as give him a rough understanding of how long he had been traveling. Ideally, he would follow

Highway 41 to Atlanta and detour around the city, head to Chattanooga, and straight north to Kentucky.

Mentally, Oz reviewed the plan again and noted the advantages of following Highway 41. One major advantage was that it was a small two-lane highway used by local commuters and, therefore, in theory, he would have limited interactions and avoid what he had previously encountered. In addition, there would be plenty of woods, fields, and ponds along the way; after all, this was the country. Woods meant cover for hiding as well as hunting, whereas ponds meant water and even fishing. Open fields would allow him a line of sight in the direction he was headed. He would still pass houses and people, but once in the country he felt he had more options as compared to traveling in the open. He could stay low and move with caution. Without over complicating the situation, Oz jumped on his bike and headed down Southwell Boulevard for a few miles where he turned north onto Highway 41.

He stopped, brought his binoculars to eyes, and scanned the road ahead.

He saw cars stopped on the highway, but not nearly the amount he experienced on north 75. He would have to ride through the town of Tifton, Georgia on his way to Ashburn, but given the time and the fact that people were still digesting what happened, he felt comfortable that he would not experience trouble; at least for tonight.

As Oz rode through the town of Tifton, he could see people gathered in groups talking. Men were angry and women were crying. Kids, being kids, just played. They had no knowledge of what happened, or more importantly what was about to happen.

As Oz drove past the buildings, he thought to himself, "Those are the ones who will survive. The kids; they have the best chance of surviving. Once they get over the fact that there will never be Xbox® and Fortnite™ again, they will adapt and overcome. They don't have the mental roadblocks adults have."

Oz noticed a few candles and lanterns being lit as the town was being consumed by the night. It was an eerie feeling. As early as eight hours ago he was working on a computer and enjoying hot coffee. Now there are no computers and he would have to start a fire for hot water and, hell, he didn't even have coffee. Eerie! Once past the town, Oz rode for two hours before deciding to make camp. Of all the things to forget for a bike, a headlamp shouldn't be one of them. He had his flashlights but needed something brighter; something with more lumens that would be easy to mount to his bike.

"How stupid could I be?" he said as he looked down at his feet. "I could be riding now and instead I have to stop. No light means no travel. Not even the moon to help."

This was upsetting to Oz as his plan was to sleep during the day and travel at night. He wanted to remain hidden as much as possible during his travels. With no options, he moved his bike fifty yards into the woods and pulled his hammock out and hung it between two nearby trees. He pulled an emergency blanket out of his Bug Out Bag and placed it on his hammock. He cut two twenty-foot lengths of paracord and threw them over a tree limb. He then tied his Bug Out Bag to one rope and his fanny pack strap to another. He hoisted each of them up so they were sufficiently off the ground where an animal could not get them, and a human would not see them. He then tied the other end of the ropes off on a tree. He checked his left side for his Glock and smiled upon touching it. Regardless of where he headed or what he did, the Glock would be his companion for life.

He slowly leaned back in his hammock, covered himself with his emergency blanket, and tried to relax. It was hard to relax. There was nothing but quiet and noises that he didn't recognize. Sure, the crickets were easy to identify, but what about the other high-pitched noises he heard.

"Are those cicadas?" he thought. "What are the noises wrestling in the leaves?" It would be a long night.

14. MEDICAL FAILURE

AS A CHARGE NURSE at Hubbard County Hospital, Nicki was always on the move. It wasn't easy work, but it was rewarding. She enjoyed working with geriatric mentally ill patients, and early in life knew it would be her calling. Her schedule was balanced with family life and working three, twelve-hour shifts — 2:00 p.m. to 2:00 a.m. — working every weekend which was convenient. Her schedule gave her time during the week to keep the family affairs in order as well as to attend all of Randall's sports events.

With Oz working out of town, Nicki not only had to contend with her daily routine, but she now had to make sure that the bills were paid on time, all financial affairs were in order, do the shopping, coordinate repairs to the house if Oz wasn't in town, and make sure she attended all family events in his absence. With no family of her own in Kentucky, Nicki felt fortunate to have Oz's family to visit every weekend. They had adopted her as if she was one of their own. Nicki missed Oz and it was hard coming home to an empty bed, but knew his absence was only for the next couple of years. It was simply something they as a family had to do.

"He would do anything for our family," Nicki said to herself as she picked up the medication for Mr. Johnson in Room 204. "I love that man," she whispered.

As Nicki picked up the medication and scanned the barcode label into the computer, she noticed the computer screen flicker before going blank. Not thinking much of the situation, she moved to the workstation to her left and continued where she left off.

"Funny," she said as she placed the medication bottle down. "This computer isn't working either," she sighed.

She picked up the phone to call IT but there was no dial tone. She walked around to two other workstations when she noticed the lights begin to dim. Within seconds the lights returned to full brightness.

"Holly," Nicki said in a loud voice, "did we lose power? It looks like we're running on generator power. And by the way, the computers aren't working. Can you run down to IT and get help?"

"Yes, ma'am," Holly said as she briskly turned the hallway corner and headed to the IT cubicles. Holly was a Certified Nursing Assistant who had worked with Nicki on the same shift for several months.

Nicki took a moment to peer out the window.

"None of the fluorescent blue security light beacons are blinking and the streetlights are all off. The hospital never turns off the streetlights. They're on 24/7," she thought.

As she continued to look out the window, it appeared that the entire surrounding area had lost power; but thanks to a generator, the main hospital had power. She picked up her phone to call Randall when she quickly realized she didn't have cell service.

She immediately thought of Oz and knew he would say something like, "It's the end of the world. Aren't you glad we're prepared? I told you it was coming!" but she quickly dismissed the thought.

She headed back to check on Mr. Johnson when Holly appeared.

"Nicki, IT has lost all systems," Holly said. "Every computer system in the hospital is down. The IT Supervisor told me that they had bigger fish to fry than our problem. She said the mainframe computers were smoking. As if that weren't enough, I saw John from the Admin area with a fire extinguisher in his hand pointed at his computer. I can only assume his computer was on fire. Doesn't make sense, does it?"

"Holly," Nicki said. "I'll be right back. Watch the patients for me and tell them there's nothing to worry about if they ask."

"Will do," Holly responded.

Nicki headed down the hall, took the stairs to the first floor, and went out the side door. She unlocked her phone and tried to call Oz. Nothing. She rebooted her phone and called again. Nothing. No signal. Beginning to get somewhat worried, Nicki remembered Oz describing EMPs to the family. She wished she had paid more attention. Worry set in. She walked to her car and pushed the fob to unlock the door. Nothing. She pushed the fob again. Still nothing. She removed the key from the fob housing and opened the car door. No lights, no dinging noises, nothing.

Nicki put her foot on the brake and pushed the button to start the car. It was dead. Nicki's worry now turned to fear — fear for her family. The moment she could use her cell phone she would call Oz and the kids to make sure everyone was fine. For the first time in her life panic set in. She became sick to her stomach and understood why Oz had spent so many hours trying to train and prepare them for a SHTF. Slowly, she regained her composure and knew her only option was to go forward and remain focused.

As Nicki was sitting in her car, she was glancing at the hospital's main entrance when she saw the lights shut completely off. She stepped out of the car and couldn't see one single light on the inside or outside of the hospital. What before was a well-lit hospital, even in the day, was now void of all lights. Nicki closed her eyes and listened. She didn't hear one single car, or the hospital generator which was running thirty seconds ago. There was only silence.

Before she returned to work, she grabbed the Bug Out Bag Oz prepared for her. She never opened it before but knew Oz had put a lot of thought into what items were placed in the backpack. She opened the main compartment and found a letter protected in a Ziplock bag. She opened the bag and pulled the envelope out. On the front of the envelope it read:

"To the Love of My Life, open only in an emergency. I Love You. Oz."

Just reading that brought some relief to Nicki as she opened the envelope and read the letter:

Nicki,

If you are reading this letter, then I know you're scared and in a bad situation. I just hope the Stuff hasn't Hit the Fan. I want you to read this letter in its entirety and then re-read it. It's the exact same letter I placed in each of the kids Bug Out Bags. You know how I like to be consistent.

First, let me tell you that your safety is priority one. Be aware of your surroundings and constantly, I mean constantly scan your immediate area for danger. Head home!!!! If it's safe to travel during the day do so but be cautious. If you question your safety only travel at night and hide during the day. IF TRAVELING AT NIGHT PUT ON THE CAMOUFLAGE PANTS AND LONG SLEEVE SHIRT. I want you to put the hat on and use the hair ties I've included to put your hair up. I want you to blend in or be a gray woman.

Second, get home. I've included maps in the Velcro compartment on the very back of the Bug Out Bag. These are just in case your car doesn't run or the highways are impassable. ALWAYS use back roads where possible.

Third, if possible, travel with a buddy from the hospital or wherever you are (no men!). Only use someone you trust. You have several good colleagues you work with so I'm hoping this is not an issue. DO NOT bring home an army of people. We do not have enough food to feed everyone if this disaster lasts for years. If your friend needs a little persuasion, and the Stuff truly hit the fan, tell them we will take care of them and to the best of our ability get them home.

Fourth, your Bug Out Bag contains many things to keep you safe, warm, and fed. You have:

- *Keltec® PMR-30 with four magazines fully loaded with .22 Magnum*
- *Outer Waist Band holster for Keltec PMR-30*
- *Belt (for holster)*
- *First Aid kit with many different supplies including feminine products*
- *Baofeng radio (when you're close to the house contact us on Channel 1)*
- *3 flashlights*
- *3 Mountain House freeze-dried meals*
- *4 U.S. Coast Guard water pouches*
- *Life Straw (use to filter water from a creek or a questionable source)*
- *Waterproof matches, blast match, cotton balls, char cloth, lighters, twine, and candles*
- *Two knives (on the outside of your BOB)*
- *Light (headlamp, glow sticks, and Stream Light flashlight)*
- *Emergency blankets*
- *Writing tools (Sharpie and Fisher Space Pen) with a notebook*

Fifth, if you are the first-person home, go to the safe in the garage and grab the Red Binder that is labeled "__SHTF – Elevated Threat Manual.__" Read it then re-read it and FOLLOW all directions. This binder contains directions on how to secure our house.

If you get in a bad situation, I want you to FIGHT FOR YOUR LIFE. Do not give up. Pull hair. Kick or hit guys in the nuts. As hard as you can, push your finger through someone's eyeballs. Punch someone in the throat as hard as you can. Get your finger in your attacker's ear and push as hard as you can. FIGHT FOR YOUR LIFE!!!!

Nicki, I love you very much, now GET HOME!

Love, Oz

Nicki began to cry as she read the letter and truly knew Oz loved her. Although she hadn't paid as much attention to prepping as she should have, Oz never gave up. He took care of her. At that moment she found the courage and strength to get home safely but first felt it best to return to work and hope the power and cell phones turned back on before the end of her shift.

As the end of Nicki's shift approached, she looked at her phone with hope. She was disappointed when she saw the "no signal" icon appearing, but was not deterred from calling Oz. As she pushed the button to call, her heart sank when nothing happened. The situation became direr when her colleagues who would relieve her and her team did not show for their shift. It was a rough shift without power and when Nicki next saw them, she would have a story for them. She would share with them the challenges of running a medical floor with no power, especially in the evening as darkness set in. Luckily, Nicki's floor did not have critical care patients or any patients on life-saving equipment. A small relief given the situation.

Angie, Nicki's supervisor, approached Nicki and asked if she would stay over until the night crew showed up. Nicki knew that they most likely would not be showing up any time soon.

"Nicki," Angie snapped. "I really need you to stay over until we get relief. As a nurse, you can't leave the patients in a time of need. No one from the night shift has shown up," she finished.

Nicki, unsure of what to do, asked Angie if she could take a quick break; she wasn't feeling well.

"Of course," Angie said.

As Nicki walked to the breakroom her mind was running a million miles a second.

"What would Oz do?" she thought to herself.

She knew Oz would not wait. Even if he was wrong, he would act in a manner that would ensure the safety of the family. He would not wait for others to act. He knew that if the Stuff Hit the Fan, the sooner you reacted the safer you would be. Nicki knew exactly what to do.

She walked back to Angie and with a voice of confidence said, "Angie, I do not want to leave the hospital short staffed, but I have to get home. I need to make sure my family is safe. When and if my phone works again, I'll make it a priority to call you."

"You'll probably lose your job," Angie retorted.

"I understand. You have to do what you have to do, but my family is my main priority," Nicki stated as she turned around and began the walk to her car.

Nicki thought through her plan and knew she would have to walk home. It took her about forty-five minutes by car and that was only because of traffic. Walking, without traffic, would take around seven to nine hours depending on her pace. She felt confident that the walk would be straightforward and that she probably would not encounter any danger, but she was not going to take a chance.

Nicki inserted her key into the car door lock and opened the car door. She reached in and placed her Bug Out Bag on the driver's seat, opened the bag, and took out the set of clothes Oz had placed in the bag. She was wearing her nurse's uniform and knew she would stick out, or worse yet, be a target; and that by changing her clothes she would blend in with the locals. She would be a gray woman.

"After all, it's Tennessee. Everyone wears camouflage clothes," she said as she smiled.

Next, she took out the hat and removed the hair ties Oz had taped to the hat. She put her hair in a bun and put the hat on. She then took out the belt, Keltec PMR-30, and four magazines for the gun. She placed the belt through the loops on her pants and ran it through the holster.

"Time to go hot," she whispered to herself as she removed the pocketknife attached to the Bug Out Bag.

She grabbed the PMR-30 and slowly began cutting the plastic bag that encased the gun. Oz had placed the gun in a vacuum sealed bag to protect and keep it dry.

"He's a smart one," Nicki said as she removed the gun.

Nicki ensured the safety was on and chamber-checked the PMR-30. Once cleared, she placed a magazine in the magazine well and racked the slide. She double checked that the safety was on and pulled the slide back ensuring a round was properly seated. It was. She removed the magazine and checked to make sure it was loaded in addition to looking for any mechanical issues. She was satisfied and slapped the magazine back in the magazine well and holstered the gun. She placed her shirt over the holster which provided some concealment for the gun.

"The shoes," she said disappointed. As she looked down, she realized the only pair of shoes she had was the shoes that matched her nursing outfit. "Not the best but they'll have to work," she sighed as she placed her hands through the straps of the Bug Out Bag. Once across her back she secured the straps across her chest and waist and clipped them together. She would walk home.

Her route would take her down Rivergate Boulevard to 2 Mile Pike. From there she would head to Highway 174 – Long Hollow Pike in Goodlettsville, Tennessee, to Highway 41 – Dickerson Pike, to Forks Road, to 31 West (Blue Star) – Louisville Highway. Once in the town of White House, Nicki had two routes she could take depending on the situation. She could continue on 31 West to Kentucky or take Portland Road which would ultimately end up at the same place. She was relieved to know that she had options. With a spare flashlight in her pocket and one in her hand, she headed into the darkness.

Nicki never thought she would have to ever walk home from work in the dark. Furthermore, she never thought she would have to use the Bug Out Bag Oz prepared for her.

"I will kiss that man as soon as I see him. I just need him home," she thought.

Nicki began her walk down Rivergate Boulevard and noticed how many people were out. They were just walking, almost as if they were looking for something, but she had no idea what. It was about 2:30 a.m. and as she walked it was hard to not notice the cars that just seemed to have stopped. The streets resembled the scenes in the video games Randall played. In the video games, there were always streets filled with disabled vehicles and fires burning in 55-gallon barrels. Minus the burning 55-gallon barrels, this is what she saw.

As she passed the Rivergate Mall, Nicki heard what sounded like a "thud." When she turned in the direction of the noise, she saw six people with sledgehammers and crowbars trying to get into the main doors of the mall.

One of the men in the group saw Nicki and yelled, "Hey, come help us. Free stuff inside!"

Shocked at what she just heard, she simply raised her hand in a waving motion and now more than ever would focus on getting home.

Thirty minutes later Nicki approached Highway 174. Though it was dark, she could make out stranded vehicles in both directions. Cars everywhere. As she looked around, she could detect motion and assumed it was stranded drivers and passengers. She quickly touched her hip to make sure she still had her PMR-30.

"Yep, it's there," she whispered as she checked her pocket for the spare magazines.

She would walk using the emergency lanes. This allowed her to stay as far off the highway as she could, always ensuring to stay in the shadows, if possible. Nicki never let her right hand leave the holstered PMR-30. It was the only comfort she had.

The walk on Highway 174 was long but easy. While walking, she noticed that there seemed to be more activity as the night went on. Instead of sleeping, albeit, in their cars, people were milling around.

"It must be the stress," she thought.

Nicki saw the sign for Highway 41, and she felt relief knowing she was closer to home. She was glad to be going on Highway 41 because the highway was surrounded by forests on both sides. It could provide cover if she needed but she also realized it could be used to ambush her.

The comfort she felt immediately went away when she heard a voice say, "You're going to put out rather you like it or not."

Nicki could hear the crying and whines of a woman. Without thinking, Nicki lifted her shirt and positioned the PMR-30 in her hand. She brought the gun to the low ready position as the adrenaline began to flow. Her heart was racing, and her senses were on high alert.

"Calm, calm, calm," she repeated to herself.

Though she could hear the woman struggling she couldn't see where the crying was coming from. Nicki had never been in this position in her life. Though she had extensive handgun training, she had never pulled her gun with the intent to defend her or someone else, let alone to kill someone. It had only been used for training and practice.

She had two choices—she could keep walking and ignore the situation or help the woman. Nicki knew that Oz would tell her to keep walking, that her safety was the priority. But Nicki was a nurse. She was trained to help others in need. If she didn't help that woman, she would regret it for the rest of her life; but if Nicki died, Oz would never forgive her.

As Nicki stopped to listen, she could tell that the screams and crying of the woman were coming from below the underpass. Nicki slowly walked down the highway ramp and with her back against the concrete wall, walked toward the screams and crying woman. It was a dark night, and with camouflage clothes it would be hard for her to be discovered. She needed to pick up her pace as more and more thoughts raced through her mind. "What if those animals kill the woman?" she thought to herself. She knew she would not allow that to happen.

"Who's next?" said the man who had the voice Nicki originally heard.

"My turn. I'm gonna hurt her," another voice said.

"There's more than one," Nicki thought.

Her mind ran rampant. What if there was a gang waiting to rape that woman. There was no way Nicki would be able to take them all out. And hell, if they were armed, Nicki knew she would be killed. Before Nicki could finish her thought a man smoking a cigarette approached to within eight feet of her. He was looking around but didn't notice her. She immediately noticed he was wearing an orange jumpsuit with the words "Kentucky Department of Corrections."

Fear hit Nicki when she saw that he was carrying a holstered handgun on his right side. The black belt and handgun were out of place around the jumpsuit. Things had just changed. Without so much as moving, Nicki reviewed her options yet again. Take the man hostage and hope the others let the girl go, shoot this man and catch the others off guard, or do nothing and simply don't move. "No more thinking," she thought. It was time to act.

Nicki could tell the woman was in pain by the groans she was making while the man raping her was enjoying himself.

Nicki focused on the man in front of her and as best as she could, said, "Put your hands up or I'll shoot."

The man was caught completely off guard and instinctively reached for his gun.

Nicki, in a more forceful voice, yelled, "Please don't do that!" He did not stop.

Nicki lifted the PMR-30 and with a smooth trigger pull fired two rounds center mass at the man standing by her. He had no idea what hit him as he instantly fell to the ground. Nicki turned to the underpass, and with her left hand pressed the button to the flashlight. The area was illuminated when he saw a woman pinned down on the hood of a car and a man in an orange jumpsuit hovering over her. The man turned and started running toward Nicki. Nicki was in a daze. She had just killed a man, making it hard to focus on the man running toward her. Before she knew it, the man was standing in front of her and the last thing she saw was a fist headed directly toward her face.

As Nicki slowly came to, she felt a sharp pain near her left eye. She touched the area and felt an even sharper pain. She couldn't open her left eye, but vision slowly came back to her right eye. Her head was spinning. She slowly sat up and looked around her. The PMR-30 was still in her right hand as she immediately noticed two dead men in orange jumpsuits; one to her left and one behind her. Confused, she noticed that her magazine was empty. She must have emptied it in the man charging her right as he lunged at her. She quickly glanced, searching for the woman whom she had just saved; she was nowhere to be found.

"Some thanks that is," she thought.

She looked at her mechanical watch and realized she had been unconscious for over two hours. She wanted to cry but knew she couldn't. She needed to be quiet and focus on getting home. The last thing she wanted to do was attract other people, even if they wanted to help.

Nicki took the Bug Out Bag off her back and took out the first aid kit. She took out a package of Tylenol® and searched for a U.S. Coast Guard water pouch. She opened the water pouch and swallowed the two Tylenol tablets. She took out a cold compress, activated it, and placed it over her eye. She wrapped gauze around the cold compress and her eye holding the compress in place. She slowly stood up making sure to keep her balance. She replaced the magazine in her PMR-30 with a fresh magazine and holstered the gun. She did a 360-degree assessment of the area, turned, and continued her walk home. With pain in her left eye, a major headache, and one good eye, she had to be cautious and focused. After what seemed like days, when in fact it had only been hours, Nicki began walking on 31 West. If she continued to follow this route, it would take her into Kentucky and she would soon be home.

15. PREPPING SKILLS KICK IN

RANDALL WAS SITTING IN ENGLISH CLASS when he heard the fan on the smart projector begin to whine. At the same time, the projector light began oscillating between bright and dim. Several seconds later he could see black smoke coming from the projector before it shut down. At almost the same time, he saw his teacher, Ms. Hale, jump up and scream. The entire class watched as she grabbed the fire extinguisher, carried it to her desk, aimed it at her laptop, and pulled the trigger. The class sat silent as a white fog filled the classroom.

Everyone was stunned when they heard similar commotions coming from the other classrooms. Randall was quick to realize that what had happened to Ms. Hale probably happened in other classrooms, too. As Ms. Hale tried to figure out what happened, Randall noticed the lights acting funny. They were pulsing from dim to bright before they turned completely off. Without thinking, Randall looked immediately at the Emergency Exit light which was located above the main classroom door. It was out. Not a flicker of light could be seen. Randall remembered his dad telling him time and time again that if the power went out, the Emergency Exit lights would turn on. Usually, nothing to worry about. If the power went out and the Emergency Exit lights didn't illuminate, it was time to go to your car and drive home; or if the car wouldn't start, walk home. Oz told Randall that it wasn't a free pass to leave school whenever he wanted, but if he felt an SHTF had happened, he should have confidence knowing that Oz would defend and support his decision.

"We're probably going to go into lockdown," Joe said to Randall. Joe had been Randall's best friend since tenth grade. They were two peas in a pod.

"Do I or do I not," Randall contemplated?

"Joe, you need to go home. This sounds crazy, and trust me my dad is crazy, but the Emergency Exit light isn't working. We have no lights. I'm willing to bet that the entire town has no power," Randall said with a look of concern.

"So what?" Joe retorted. "The lights have gone out many times and they'll go out many times in the future. Don't freak out, Randall."

"You don't understand, Joe," Randall explained. "The Emergency Exit lights are only hardwired to make sure the batteries stay charged. The actual lights themselves operate off the battery. They should be on but they're not. The lights short-circuited. Only a strong power surge could cause that," Joe looked stunned as he tried to understand Randall's explanation.

"Joe, you need to get home. I'm leaving now," Randall said as he stood up, grabbed his backpack, and stopped by Ms. Hale's desk.

"Ms. Hale," Randall said in a soft voice. "I have to go to the bathroom. Something I ate is not agreeing with me."

"Hurry back. We need to make sure everyone is accounted for," Ms. Hale said.

Randall turned and began to walk out the door when he heard Ms. Hale say, "Randall, why are you taking your backpack?"

"Sorry, Ms. Hale. It's a habit," he said as he took his backpack off and sat it by his desk before leaving the classroom.

As Randall turned into the hall, he saw a group of teachers huddled together.

"That doesn't look good," he thought. He could hear them saying things like, "Do we need to go into lockdown?" "My phone's not working," "Was your computer smoking?" "I can't reach my husband" and "I hope that Walmart has power."

Without making eye contact, Randall walked past them, made a right turn down another hallway, and headed out an emergency door. Where there would normally be an alarm going off when Randall pushed the door bar to exit the building, there was only silence followed by the door opening. Randall walked briskly to his car. As he approached the door, he took the car key out of his pocket and unlocked the door. He quickly sat down, inserted the key in the ignition, and turned it. Nothing. He turned the key a second time. Nothing.

"Dad was right," he said out loud. "My dad is actually right. Oh man, I'm never going to live this one down."

Randall stepped out of the car and opened the hatchback. He pulled his Bug Out Bag out and opened the main compartment. Like the rest of the family's bags, there was a letter in a plastic protective bag. Randall unzipped the plastic bag and pulled the letter out. On the front of the envelope read "I told you so, Love Dad." Randall laughed. Was his dad ever predictable? He opened the envelope and pulled the letter out, and read it:

Randall,

If you are reading this letter the Stuff Hit the Fan. Like your sister, I know you well and there would be no other reason for you to use the contents of this Bug Out Bag.

First, let me tell you that your safety is priority one. Be aware of your surroundings and constantly, I mean constantly scan your immediate area for danger. Head home!!!! If you're at school, you'll walk home will only take four to five hours and it will most likely be in daylight hours. If you can, jog home. You're in great shape. If you question your safety only travel at night and hide during the day. IF TRAVELING AT NIGHT PUT ON THE CAMOUFLAGE PANTS AND LONG SLEEVE SHIRT. Remember when I taught you about a gray man (fitting into your environment and not sticking out like a sore thumb)? Now is the time to be that person.

I've included maps in the Velcro compartment on the very back of the Bug Out Bag. These are just in case your car doesn't run or the highways are impassable. ALWAYS use back roads where possible.

Second, your Bug Out Bag contains many things to keep you safe, warm, and fed. You will most likely not need them because of your distance to our house. Just in case, you have:

- *First aid kit with many different supplies*
- *Baofeng radio (when you're close to the house contact us on Channel 1)*
- *3 flashlights*
- *3 Mountain House freeze-dried meals*
- *4 U.S. Coast Guard water pouches*
- *Life Straw (use to filter water from a creek or a questionable source)*
- *Waterproof matches, blast match, cotton balls, char cloth, lighters, twine, and candles*
- *Two knives (on the outside of your BOB)*
- *Light (headlamp, glow sticks, and Stream Light flashlight)*
- *Emergency blankets*
- *Writing tools (Sharpie and Fisher Space Pen) with a notebook*

Third, if you are the first person home, go to the safe in the garage and grab the Red Binder that is labeled "__SHTF – Elevated Threat Manual.__" Read it then re-read it and FOLLOW all directions. This binder contains directions on how to secure our house.

If you get in a bad situation, I want you to FIGHT FOR YOUR LIFE. Do not give up. Pull hair. Kick or hit guys in the nuts. As hard as you can, push your finger through someone's eyeballs. Punch someone in the throat as hard as you can. Get your finger in your attacker's ear and push as hard as you can. FIGHT FOR YOUR LIFE!!!!

Randall, there's a chance I may not be home, or it may take me some time to get home. If that's the case, you're the man of the family. Your mother and sister will rely on you and will need you more than you can imagine. Be strong in everything you do. Be strong for our family.

I love you very much, now GET HOME!

Love, Dad

Randall was sad as he thought of his dad. Oz was in Georgia, and without a car, Randall knew it would be weeks before his dad made it home. Of all people who would make it home, it would be Oz, and Randall knew it. Randall put the letter back in the backpack, zipped the compartment, and placed the backpack over his shoulders. He locked the car doors, turned, and began his walk home.

The walk home for Randall was surreal. The first thing he noticed was how quiet everything was. There were no sounds of engines roaring or airplanes flying overhead. There was no sound of his high school friends revving their car engines. There was no music blaring. There were only droves of now useless cars blocking the road along his route. What was strange for Randall was to see the different reactions of the people he passed. He saw women comforting their children who had grown impatient from sitting in the car. He saw an older couple looking aimlessly at an oxygen bottle before turning to look at one another. He saw a woman crying as she threw her phone on the ground. He saw a young couple having sex in their car as he walked by. He saw an overweight man profusely sweating as he walked to some unknown destination. Randall reflected on some of the lessons his dad had tried to teach him. When Oz explained the behaviors of how people would react in an SHTF, he focused on the fact that over time most people would turn into animals and become predators. He never mentioned that there would be sadness, concern, crying, lack of hope, or even the possibility that someone in his family could be killed.

"I'm not ready to be the man of the family," he groaned.

16. LISTENING TO THE VOICE IN YOUR HEAD

AS WAS TYPICAL FOR CALI, she woke up for her 8:00 a.m. class, attended class, and then headed back to the apartment for a nap.

"The life of a college student," she thought as she rolled around to see what time it was after waking from her nap.

She pushed the side button on her phone to check the time and noticed it didn't light up. She pushed the power button and nothing.

"Dang it," she said. "I forgot to charge my phone." As she roused herself out of bed, she plugged her phone into the cord on the nightstand and looked to make sure it was charging. She was perplexed when she still saw that the phone wasn't charging.

"I'll take a shower instead," she said talking to herself.

She walked into the bathroom and turned the light switch on.

"The power's out," she said when the light did not turn on.

Cali would not be defeated and instead took a shower in the dark. Out of the shower and dressed, it was time to head to her 3:30 p.m. Anatomy and Physiology class. As she left her apartment, she noticed other students milling around. She gave a friendly wave and headed to her car. As she approached her car, she pressed her key fob to unlock it but noticed the car's lights didn't flash as was customary. She pushed the key fob again and surrendered to the fact that the battery had died.

"Irony," she thought to herself. "My cell phone battery dies, my key fob battery died; let's hope my car starts."

She unlocked the car door with her key, inserted it into the ignition, turned the key, and nothing. If Cali learned anything from Oz it was to always be aware of your environment. She stepped out of the car and saw her friend, Autumn.

"Cali, I need some help. Can you jump start my car? It won't start," Autumn said.

"That's weird," Cali said. "My car won't start either."

Autumn was excited and yelled, "No class! Time to party! Let's head back to the apartment and let the fun begin."

Cali just smiled. She knew in the back of her mind something was wrong. None of what she experienced added up.

"Autumn, I'm going for a quick walk. I'll be right back," Cali said as she headed up the street.

Cali took notice of the shops, traffic lights, cars, construction equipment, and noticed one thing in particular: nothing was working. Anything with a motor had stopped. Anything requiring electricity had just quit working. She stopped to think for a moment. She thought back to a time when her dad insisted that the entire family shelter in place at the house. Three convicts had escaped from a nearby prison and as fate would have it, search helicopters could be seen hovering above the McTateys' house. With law enforcement searching their residential area, Oz made sure that the house was secure and that he and Nicki were armed. The search lasted several hours before law enforcement moved on, but with three criminals on the FBI's Top 10 Most Wanted list on the loose, Oz was not taking any chances. The safety of his family was his priority. Sure enough, the escapees were found and captured within five miles of their house after killing a family of four.

"He listened to the voice in his head," Cali said.

Cali went back to her car and pulled out her Bug Out Bag. She found the letter her dad had written and took several minutes to read it. With Bug Out Bag in hand and a new sense of purpose, she walked back to her apartment.

Once inside she said, "Autumn, something's not right. The power's out but it's different this time. I'm not sure why. I feel like I need to get home. Why don't you come with me? Worse case is we walk four hours for no reason at all."

Autumn was quick to respond, "Cali, we're going to party. Everything will be fine. Now, grab the vodka and let's go next door."

Cali knew what she had to do. She looked at Autumn, gave her a hug and said, "My dad would want me home. I'll see you in a couple days."

Cali turned, picked up a few things from her room, and headed to her car. There was still plenty of daylight left and she took note that no one was panicking. Getting home would take no more than four hours and using the highway she felt the walk would be uneventful, in addition to being the quickest route. She placed her Bug Out Bag across her back and headed toward the highway. Once she was about ten miles from her house, she would take the back roads to their doorstep.

17. 4:20 PM

IT WAS 4:20 P.M. when BJ woke up. The life of a graduate student in Biology was difficult; so he thought. For the last eight hours, he had been stuck in a greenhouse measuring, recording, and analyzing plant data. As part of his thesis research, he had to crossbreed different species of marijuana plants with a focus on breeding plants that would maximize the production of cannabidiol (CBD) oil.

BJ was part of a new breed of scientists focusing on the medicinal and healing properties of this illegal plant and, more specifically, CBD oil. Having Crohn's disease, BJ personally knew the powerful effects of CBD oil and knew it would benefit others. He sat up in bed and looked around. Slow to open his eyes, he immediately reached for his cell phone to check the time. When the screen didn't immediately light up and display the time, he thought nothing about it; after all, he would run the battery down to the 1 percent level before plugging it in to charge.

"BJ!" Scott yelled. Scott was BJ's best friend and roommate.

"The power's out," he said frustrated.

"Well, then," BJ yelled back. "Time to get more sleep." BJ threw the blanket over his body and closed his eyes, quickly falling back to sleep without realizing he would wake up to a completely different world.

18. NEIGHBORS – BE CAUTIOUS

RANDALL HAD BEEN WALKING for about five hours when he made a right turn onto the long drive that led to their house. As he did, he noticed their neighbor, Frank, standing outside with a beer in each hand. Frank Zire was the nearest neighbor to the McTatey's house. Not only was Frank their nearest neighbor, but he was also a person Oz had been leery of. Frank was in his mid-forties, married, and had one son. Frank was about 6'5", in relatively good shape, a chain smoker, and was often seen drinking. Even though Oz never had a reason to not like Frank, he was always weary and paid attention to where his neighbor was at all times.

Nicki, Randall, BJ, and Cali didn't even notice him as far as Oz knew, but Randall always wondered if Frank worked. Not that it mattered, but he was always home. When Oz was mowing the front half of his property, he would frequently talk to Frank. Oz was continually feeling Frank out and would often ask off-the-cuff questions to see how Frank responded.

Over the years Oz determined that he and his family didn't need to fear Frank, but they did need to be aware and perhaps at times cautious. Oz never saw aggressive or challenging behaviors from Frank, but his behaviors and answers to his questions highly suggested there was more to the man than could be seen. Oz would often loan Frank tools and even allowed Frank to go into his garage when he wasn't home. Though Oz was protective of his prepping endeavors, he still needed to be a good neighbor. Oz felt that if he didn't occasionally allow Frank onto his property, Frank would become suspicious and even question Oz on his activities. After all, Oz was constantly bringing in construction materials, water containers, generators, and other odd equipment that was visible to his neighbor.

The garage was a "normal" garage but was well stocked with tools of all kinds. The one visible concern Oz had when Frank entered the garage was the gun safe. Larger than most, the safe weighed 1,200 pounds and contained a few shotguns and one AR-15. The saving grace was that Frank wasn't aware that Oz had stored most ammunition and guns throughout the house in various locations. Oz was smart enough to know you don't put all your eggs in one basket.

19. RANDALL HOME ALONE

AS RANDALL WALKED UP THE DRIVE, the only thing he could hear was the sound of Benny. Benny was the sixth member of the family — a Maltipoo who weighed a mere twelve pounds.

Randall opened the front door to let Benny out. Benny was excited to see Randall who was confused and sad at the same time from the day's events. Randall took a quick glance at the driveway and noticed there were no cars. On any normal day, the driveway would have at least three parked cars and someone yelling that they were blocked in. But today there were no cars, and no one was yelling. There was only him and Benny.

Randall sat down on the front step and pulled his dad's letter out of the Bug Out Bag and reread it again.

"If you are the first-person home, go to the safe in the garage and grab the Red Binder that is labeled '*SHTF – Elevated Threat Manual.*' Read it, then reread it and FOLLOW all directions. This binder contains directions on how to secure our house," Randall read out loud.

He stood up, unlocked the garage door and walked to the safe. He punched in the security code and the door didn't open. Maybe he made a mistake? He punched the code yet again and nothing.

"Well, the electronic combination lock was hit as well," he said as he looked at Benny.

His dad made sure the family was aware of the location of the hidden skeleton key to the safe. Randall walked to the back of the garage and moved a sheet of plywood propped up in the corner. Oz had cut out a small section of the concrete floor which he used to hide small important items. Randall knelt down, and with a pry bar lifted the cutout concrete block from the floor. Sure enough, there was a plastic Ziplock bag full of keys. The safe key was easy to identify because it was about four inches in length and looked different from all the other keys.

He stood up and walked to the safe where he removed the electronic combination lock by lifting it straight up. Once the electronic lock was removed, Randall saw a slot that the key could be placed in. With the key inserted, Randall twisted the key and the safe unlocked. He returned the key to the plastic bag and replaced the concrete slab. He put the sheet of plywood back and walked back to the safe. His dad was very well organized, and Randall immediately saw the red binder which was in between several other binders. He pulled the binder out, grabbed a chair, and sat down. In big font, the words "*SHTF – Elevated Threat Manual*" was plastered on the front cover of the binder.

"Benny," Randall said. "You definitely can't question what this manual is. Our dad thought of everything."

Randall opened the binder and began reading out loud as if he was telling Benny a story:

<u>SHTF – Elevated Threat Manual</u>

To whomever in my family is reading this, use these instructions when the SHTF or there is an Elevated Threat. It could be anything from riots in Nashville to a disaster in South Dakota that could affect the family.

If you're reading this manual, it's because you're afraid or scared and you want security. Let that be enough to ACT and NOT wait. TAKE ACTION. Don't talk yourself out of taking action. Don't let NORMALCY set in!

There are two parts to this manual:
- *1 – 5 are tasks to complete immediately; within hours of the SHTF and only if possible and if safe.*
- *6 – 14 are items to complete to secure the house.*

1) *Arm yourself - At a minimum, you need to carry a handgun with four extra magazines. Use an outer waistband holster (one that goes on the outside of the belt). Rack the gun and make sure it's loaded. Never carry a gun that is not loaded. Carry the extra magazines in a front pocket so that you can easily and quickly get to them.*

2) *Cash - If possible, go to the bank and withdraw $2,500 - $3,000 in small bills. If the bank is closed or you're unable to withdraw money, go to an ATM and try to withdraw the maximum amount. I think there may be a $600 limit. As a backup plan and prior to leaving the house, take $2,500 cash from the safe and place it in your front left pocket. Yes, your front left pocket. Take small bills ($5,*

$10, $20). Use this cash only if you're unable to take money out of the bank or ATM.

DRIVE THE SUBURBAN! It is 100% mechanical, no electronics.

To start the Suburban, push the glow plug button for 10 seconds. The glow plug button is located on the lower panel to the right of the steering wheel. To find it, place your finger in the middle of the steering wheel and run it down past the steering wheel and on to the beige panel. Now, move your finger to the right where there will be two switches. The glow plug switch is the one that requires you to push it in. A red light on the dash will come on. Push and hold the button for 10 seconds then start the Suburban.

*****GO WITH 2 PEOPLE IF POSSIBLE (2 is safer than 1) ******

3) *Supplies - If there are no crowds, go to Walmart and get as much as you can from the attached inventory list. Use a credit card or debit first. If credit or debit cards cannot be accepted, use the cash you got from the bank first, the cash from the ATM second, and the cash from the safe last.*

SAFETY ALERT: If it's NOT safe to go to Walmart for whatever reason, go to Dollar General, Walgreen, and CVS. Use the same attached inventory list to purchase what you can. If it's not safe, don't go, and DON'T WORRY. We're prepared. Getting additional items is just a bonus.

IMPORTANT NOTE: If you go to Walmart, Dollar General, Walgreen, and CVS and the power is out (meaning the cashiers can't accept credit or debit), you will use cash. Purchase the items on the attached list and help the cashier manually add up the total cost of the items. To the total cost, add 9.5% for tax Plus 10% for the cashier to keep (it's like a bribe). Tell the cashier to keep the extra 10% for inconveniencing them.

4) *Gas - Fuel - While the Suburban is warming up, LOAD ALL GAS CANS INTO THE BACK OF THE SUBURBAN. You will fill them up on your return trip with gas, diesel, and kerosene (red, blue, and yellow plastic containers).*
    * *Red containers are for unleaded gas*
    * *Blue is for diesel*
    * *Yellow is for kerosene which can be found at many gas stations and smells like diesel*
        o *The kerosene fuel is used for the kerosene heaters which are in the garage.*

    When you get home, add fuel stabilizer that you purchased at the store (if you couldn't find it, I have some in the garage) to each gas and diesel container. The gas and diesel should now be good for about one year.
5) *You'll need to get grandma and grandpa if they haven't arrived at our house within two days. As I've said before, go in pairs and take the Suburban. Take the route that goes past Beech High School. There are more backroads and fewer houses and people. Use your judgment, but it's probably the safer route.*

While at grandma and grandpa's, take as much as you can

carry in the Suburban. Take all construction material, wood sheets, nails, drills, screws, electrical wire, tape, glue, tools, food, medicine, blankets, pillows, all guns and ammo, batteries (including car batteries and lawn mower battery), and whatever you think will benefit the family.

IMPORTANT NOTE: *Once complete with the above, <u>do not leave the house</u>. Be prepared to Shelter-In-Place while determining if it's necessary to Bug Out. It's going to be tough. People will get desperate and hungry. EXPECT people to steal and take what they want by any means that are available to them.*

I need you to understand that our friends, neighbors, acquaintances, and people we trust will not be the people we knew. When people are scared, hungry, thirsty, and afraid for the welfare of themselves or their family, they will do everything up to and including killing to survive. Always be cautious of everyone. The only ones you can trust is family. I will say it again. If they're not family, be on the alert. Behaviors to look for: failure to make eye contact, shaking hands, hands in pocket, hands reaching inside the waistband or jacket, telling you one thing but contradicting themselves, looking around all the time, nervous behaviors, wearing a tactical or bulletproof vest, carrying a weapon, including a knife, even wearing camouflage clothes. Behaviors <u>YOU NEED TO HAVE AT ALL TIMES</u>: be aware of your surroundings, keep a weapon on your person, use the buddy system when leaving the house or property, silence, be discreet in all your actions, blend into your environment (gray man or gray woman).

6) *Weapons - Go to the garage and bring all rifles and handguns in the house. No need to secure the ammunition. It's located in the safe in the house.*

    a. *Grab all rifle and handgun magazines which are also located in the safe in the house.*

    b. *Load all magazines with the appropriate ammunition.*

    c. *Place a magazine in the magazine well of each rifle and handgun BUT DO NOT LOAD A ROUND IN THE CHAMBER.*

    d. *Double check to ensure the safety is on for each weapon.*

IMPORTANT Place and hide a weapon in each room of the house. Makes sure all family members know what weapon is in what room. Place four extra magazines or extra ammunition with each weapon. The purpose of hiding a rifle or gun in each room is to ensure we always have access to a weapon.

7) *Food - Move the food from the shed and garage into the house. The shed can be broken into and items stolen without you knowing.*

    a. *Place food in each room of the house. In other words, spread it out. This is a precaution so if it's stolen from one room, you'll still have food hidden in other rooms.*

8) *Security - Set up a security detail. It will be hard until the entire family is together, but set up a schedule where someone is always on security detail (24/7). It's a pain but it could save your life.*

   a. *Setup a security perimeter. I have 30 tripwire security alerts in the garage with instructions. Place them around our property and they will give you advance notice of intruders.*
   b. *LISTEN to Benny. Benny has very good hearing and hears things we can't at distances we can't. If he barks, at a minimum, scan the area.*

   c. *We have two night vision monoculars as well as binoculars. They're located in the garage in the Communications bin.*
   d. *Cover all windows with blackout drapes. The drapes block all light (candles, flashlights, etc.) and movement that could be seen by others who are looking into the house. You need to be discreet in all of your actions.*

9) *Power – We have a whole-house generator that will provide power to the house.*
   a. *Considerations when using the generator:*
      i. *We only have 1,000 gallons of propane. Use it wisely.*
      ii. *The generator is housed in a soundproof structure (at least as soundproof as I could make it) but it will still make noise that will attract the attention of unwanted people in the area.*

1. Be cautious and ensure everyone is on High Alert when running it. At a minimum, post 2 security details.
2. Before running the generator, make sure to check the oil level. Oil can be found in the garage if needed.

10) Light – Caution: When using lights at night, be aware that neighbors will take notice. Use the blackout curtains.
   a. Honey candles - Can be found in the garage. Use the Inventory manual to find them. Use the honey candles for the following reasons
      i. They're organic.
      ii. They emit significantly less smoke than commercially produced candles.
      iii. They're fragrance-free.
      iv. We save on batteries.
      v. We have a ton of them.
   b. Lantern – LED and very efficient.
      i. Operate off AA or AAA batteries - We have a limited supply of batteries so use sparingly.
         1. Batteries are in the garage.
   c. Lantern (12 volt) – LED and very efficient.
      i. Operates off a 12-volt battery which is in the garage.
         1. A 12-volt battery is simply a car battery.
   d. Lantern – Coleman.
      i. Operates off of White Fuel – in garage.

1. Limited supply of white fuel – use sparingly.
2. Spare parts (wicks, pump rebuild kit) in garage.

11) Heat – Be aware of Carbon Monoxide with any heater.

If the SHTF occurs in the winter and there is no power, don't worry, we have multiple sources of heat.

a. Big Buddy® heaters - We have two. They're in black carry bags.
    i. They operate on the small propane canisters that are stored in the garage and shed.
    ii. Use this heat source only until you can get the Yukon M-1950 wood stove installed and in place.

b. Yukon M-1950 - Stored in the garage. About 10" tall and 36" long. The stove is rectangular in shape.
    i. Uses wood as the fuel.
        1. The stove needs to be placed on the living room floor on top of the fire bricks.
            a. The fire bricks are stored in the same area as the stove in the garage.
        2. I've made wood cutouts that will fit in the window and can be found in the garage.
        3. The double-walled flue piping will be routed from the back of the

> *Yukon M-1950 through the precut board which will then vent to the outside.*

ONCE AGAIN: You need to be aware of carbon monoxide poisoning. Make sure the stove is properly vented.

c. *Coleman Heater – about 8" tall and circular in shape.*
    i. *Uses white fuel, same as Coleman lanterns, as a fuel source.*
    ii. *Will not produce a ton of heat but could supplement any of the heaters above.*

12) *Communication – We have several means of communication.*
    a. *Baofeng UV-5R radio*
        i. *We have eight of them and they all have pre-programmed channels.*
            1. *The main channel will be 'McTat1.'*
        ii. *There are headsets for each radio to make sure communications are not heard and remain secure. Use them!*
    b. *Shortwave radios*
        i. *More complex to setup but reach a longer range.*
    c. *WWII field phones*
        i. *Used if a Listening Post/Observation Post is established (below).*
    d. *NOAA Dynamo radio*
        i. *Emergency weather radio that can be cranked by hand to provide power.*

e. *TV – 12 Volt*
   i. *TV can be connected to a car battery which can be found in the garage.*

13) *LPOP (Listening Post/Observation Post) – This is a location on our property from where we can watch and listen for (enemy) activity for the security and intelligence of the family. It needs to be a location that has a complete overview of the property yet remains hidden. Below are things to take note of when establishing an LPOP.*
   a. *Consider the following:*
      i. *The LPOP should take advantage of natural cover and concealment to provide protection.*
      ii. *Within rifle range of the house.*
      iii. *Select a covered and concealed route to and from the LPOP.*
      iv. *Avoid obvious terrain such as hilltops.*
   b. *Communication*
      i. *You must be able to report what you see and hear.*
         1. *We have two WWII phones and telephone wire that can be used for communication between the LPOP and the house.*
            a. *Run the telephone wire underground, if possible and allowable, from the LPOP to the house and then connect to the telephones.*
   c. *Manning*

       i. *If possible, always use two-(wo)man teams.*

  d. *Equipment to have in LPOP*

       i. *Binoculars, maps, compass, monocular (night vision), field phone, paper and pencil, a watch.*

14) *Uniforms – All family members, while at the Kentucky house or Bug Out Location, are to wear Italian military Vegetato battle dress units (BDU).*

  a. *Consider the following:*

       i. *The Italian BDUs have a uniquely different color pattern when compared to U.S. BDUs.*

      ii. *Allows us to quickly identify a person on our property as friend or foe.*

           1. *If you are wearing the uniform, your friend. If not, your foe.*

      iii. *The Italian BDUs cannot be easily purchased and are hard to find. Hence the reason it's our standard dress when on the property.*

FOOD	MEDICINAL	PERSONAL CARE	COMFORT	MISC
Alcohol - Any type	Acetaminophen, Ibuprofen, Aspirin	Dental Floss	Hand Warmers (sporting goods)	Aluminum Foil
Beans (pinto, white, black)	Alcohol Wipes	Allergy Relief medication	Batteries - Any type	12 Volt Car Batteries (Deep Cycle)
Coffee - Any Type	Bandages (Any)	Contact Solutions	Blankets	Bleach (UNSCENTED)
Cooking Oil	Benadryl	Feminine Products - Any type	Candy - Any type	Bottled Water
Electrolyte Powders (Gatorade or similar)	First Aid Kits	Hand Sanitizer	Games - Any type - Toy department	Cast Iron cookware (Camping section)
Flour	Hydrocortisone Cream	Heartburn medication - Zantac	Lantern Mantles (for lantern - camping section)	Flashlights - Any type
Garden Seeds - Any type	Hydrogen Peroxide	Lip Balm (Burts Bees - Carmex)	Pillows	Fuel Stabilizer
Honey	Ibuprofen	Soap	Propane canisters (camping department)	Gas Cans - Any type
Mountain House freeze dried food (camping department)	Imodium	Soap - Any type	Propane Lantern (camping dept)	Lighter Fluid
Rice	Isopropyl Alcohol - Any %	Toilet Paper	Propane stove (camping dept)	Lighters of any type
Spaghetti - Noodles in general	Nasal Mist	Tooth Paste	Rain Gear	Matches - Any type
Spices of all types - Grocery Section	Orajel (mouth care)	Toothbrush	Sleeping bags	White Fuel (camping section) 1 Gallon containers
Sugar	Triple Antibiotic Ointment	Vitamins - Any type	Clothing - Various	Ziplock bags®

After reading the manual, Randall paused for a second and looked at Benny.

"This is one time we should listen to Dad," Randall told him.

Benny looked up only hoping to hear the word "treat" but instead, Randall continued.

"He said re-read the manual and that's what I'm going to do."

After re-reading the manual, Randall went to the safe and took out $2,500 in small bills. For reasons only known to his dad, he placed the money in his front left pocket. He felt uncomfortable when he noticed his pocket bulged after placing the money in it.

"That's noticeable," he whispered.

To make sure nobody saw the bulge he would wear either a sweater or light jacket to cover his pocket. Against his better judgment, Randall decided he would go by himself to the stores. He had no idea when Cali or his mom would be home. He knew that he had the best chance of getting the supplies his dad had listed if he were to leave now before the sheeple realized how bad it was about to get.

"Benny, you're my partner. Let's do this," Randall excitedly told Benny.

Randall grabbed the Suburban keys and being familiar with how to start it, pushed the glow plug button for 10 seconds. He then turned the key causing the big diesel engine to rumble before shooting black smoke from the exhaust. As

458 Miles and 24 Days

the diesel engine warmed up, Randall opened the back swing-out doors of the Suburban, hustled to the garage, and carried fifteen gas, diesel, and kerosene cans to the vehicle. Once they were loaded, he shut the doors and then had a decision to make. He was confident the power was out, so why would he go to the bank or ATM? He knew it would most likely be a waste of time and instead decided to use the cash in his pocket to purchase goods if anything was even open.

His first stop would be Dollar General which was about two miles away and literally in the middle of nowhere. Randall lifted Benny into the Suburban, slammed the door shut, and began driving down the drive. As he approached the end of the drive, he was flagged down by Frank.

20. TESTY NEIGHBOR

"WHAT THE HECK. Power's out. Cell phones not working. Randall driving Oz's Suburban when my car won't start," Frank said rather bitterly.

With few neighbors and most having at least five acres, he wasn't worried that someone might be listening. And even if they were, he still wouldn't care. Randall noticed that Frank seemed to always be looking down their drive. It didn't matter what time of day or night. It was creepy. As Randall drove down the drive, Frank waived for Randall to stop.

"Where you going, Randall?" Frank said while looking Randall directly in the eyes and placing his hands on the Suburban door. "I saw you walking up your drive. Did your car quit? I can help you fix it. I know your dad's out of town."

Chills ran down Randall's back. He responded, "No Sir. No help needed. It quit right up the road. Dad is having it towed to the repair shop sometime today. Appreciate it though."

"Weird. We lost power and my damn cell phone isn't working. Any idea what's going on?" Frank said as he tried to look into the Suburban but was unable to due to the 6-inch lift kit and tinted windows; a thoroughly thought out security detail by Oz.

Randall acted as if he knew nothing and respectfully responded, "Sorry, sir. I'm not sure what you're talking about. I didn't even notice the power was out. I'm sure it will come back on shortly. Apologize, but I have to head to the store for my mom."

Frank looked puzzled before asking Randall one last question, "Can I go in your dad's garage and borrow the battery charger? I think the battery in my car died."

"Best not to sir. I'll call my dad and ask him and let you know when I get back. I have to head to the store. I really need to go or I'll get in trouble. Take care," Randall said with haste.

"That was not good," Randall said as he petted Benny. "We're going to have to be on the lookout."

Frank turned and looked down the drive while talking to himself, "I wonder where Randall is going? There's something about that family. I have no idea what he does but Oz is always building something. He's always taking his Suburban and trailer and coming back with crap no one else wants."

With Randall gone and Nicki and Oz not home, Frank looked around and walked down the drive. He stopped in front of the garage door and checked the door. It was locked. He walked to the side of the garage and looked in the window.

"Damn, Oz. Just like him to put cardboard in the windows."

Upset and beginning to get angry, Frank walked over to the 10 x 36 shed that was tucked away within the trees next to Oz's house. Frank noticed that Oz kept the overhead door locked with an industrial lock. It wasn't worth Frank's time. He turned and tried the door on the side of the shed. It too was locked. Because the ground surrounding the shed was uneven, Oz had to use cinderblocks to level the shed. This presented a problem for Frank when he tried to look into the only window on the shed. It was too high for him to see through. He would need a ladder at a minimum.

"Wonder what's in there," Frank said while trying to open the door again. "Must be something important to keep all the doors locked."

Without another thought, Frank turned and began walking home. He stopped and admired Oz's raised bed gardens and noticed that all the trees on the property were well mulched. The mulch around the trees was about three feet high and about six feet in circumference. What he didn't know was that Oz would grow plants in the mulch that helped to prevent insects from destroying the tree and the fruit it produced. This was his approach to natural insecticides. Over time the mulch also broke down into soil which benefited the trees in addition to retaining water which provided constant moisture to the tree.

The real secret was the survival caches buried under most of the mulch piles. Oz stored food, medications, and ammunition all over his property and had maps showing the location and contents of each cache. He was a firm believer in the philosophy that you don't store everything in one location. Frank continued his walk home, went in the house, grabbed a beer, and sat outside on the porch. He stood up, crushing the beer can in his hand, and with a scowling look stared in the direction of Oz's house.

21. DAD'S MANUAL

RANDALL PASSED SEVERAL CARS that had stalled on the highway but the drive to Dollar General was uneventful. As he parked the Suburban, it was easy to notice that the power was off. The store doors were wide open where he could see movement inside but no lights. He rolled the front driver side window halfway down for Benny and exited the vehicle.

As he walked in the store, he was greeted by a young woman who said, "Sorry, but we're closed until the power comes back on."

Randall's first impression was not the words she said but how cute she was. She had long black hair which made her blue eyes stand out. She was slightly shorter than him and her smile was absolutely beautiful.

It seemed forever before Randall said, "I understand. I can pay with cash."

"Sorry, but I can't make change. Cash registers are electronic, and electronics need power," she responded.

"Not a problem," Randall said. "I will write down everything I buy, add 9.5% for tax and then add an additional 10% on top of that."

The young woman looked confused and questioned Randall, "Why would you add an additional 10%?"

"That's for you. I know it's inconvenient to have to record everything and then when the power comes on manually enter it into the computer system. It's no fun, I'm sure," Randall said as he stared into her beautiful blue eyes.

She stared back at Randall and with a smile told him, "Well, I'm not doing anything anyway. Let me get some paper and we'll get what you need."

Randall started with over-the-counter medications, checking the items off the list one at a time.

"My name is Stacey," she said. "I haven't seen you around here before. Are you new to the area?"

Being somewhat coy, Randall responded, "No, we've lived up the road for several years. I go to Beech High School."

Stacey was intrigued and responded, "So you're one of those."

Randall looked perplexed.

"Our high school is not good enough, but our town is?" she said as she smiled at him. "I'm playing with you," she continued. "Why are you buying all this stuff?"

Randall's goal was to quickly end her questioning when he responded. "I have no idea. My dad told me I had to do it. You know parents. Half the stuff they make you do doesn't make sense."

"Looks like you need a second cart. I'll go get one for you," she said.

"Thanks," Randall said.

Fifteen minutes later Randall had purchased as many of the items on the list that the store had. He would need to try another store for the other items.

"I told you my name, but you never told me your name," Stacey said in a shy tone.

"Sorry about that. My name is Randall," he said.

"Well Randall, your total is $420.42 which includes tax," she said.

"Don't forget to add 10%. That's for you," Randall responded.

With her eyes looking at the bagged groceries she said, "No. I don't want the 10%, but I would like you to take me on a date."

Randall was caught off guard and tried to respond, but no words came out. After several seconds he said, "Stacey, would you go out on a date with me?"

She immediately responded, "We'll see," then quickly changed her answer saying, "Of course. I would love to go on a date."

Stacey grabbed a piece of paper and wrote her phone number down, handed it to Randall, and said, "Call me. Well, you're going to have to wait until the power is on. I need to charge my phone."

Randall was confused. He didn't know her, but he liked her and felt compelled to help her. Of all the times in this world to find a beautiful young woman who had an interest in him, of course it would happen at the beginning of the apocalypse.

It looked like Randall was in deep thought when he did something he knew he shouldn't have done. Something that would get him in trouble with his dad. He asked Stacey for a piece of paper and started writing. He handed her the piece of paper, looked at her beautiful eyes, and said, "Thank you for everything. I can't wait to go on our date."

Stacey quickly looked at the note and with a look of confusion looked at Randall wanting to ask a question.

Without hesitation, Randall turned, pulling the two carts behind him and headed for the Suburban. As he opened the suburban door to place the groceries in the back, he took one last glance at Stacey and waved goodbye.

"Benny, let's drive by Walmart and see how bad it is," Randall said as Benny jumped on his lap.

Randall passed four gas stations on his way to Walmart and quickly noted that without power it was useless to stop. Several miles later Randall turned the Suburban into the Walmart parking lot and was amazed to see the store was just as busy as any another day. The only difference was that today people were walking and not driving cars.

Randall was about to get out of the Suburban and head into the store when he saw several Walmart employees trying to stop people from entering the east door. People were pushing their way in while the Walmart employees were desperately trying to close and lock the doors.

Eventually, the Walmart employees were successful and locked the set of sliding doors. The crowd of people instantly ran to the west doors. The Walmart employees followed suit and rushed to the west doors and tried to shut and lock them. This proved to be a challenge since the crowd was growing larger by the minute. The crowd demanded to be let in. Randall saw arms waving and heard voices screaming. He saw grabbing and pushing and within seconds the crowd simply overpowered the Walmart employees and forced their way in.

Suddenly, Benny began to bark, but something was different. It was a different bark; one Randall had not heard before. It was a deep bark that sounded truly menacing for a dog his size. Randall did a quick scan and realized that four men were approaching the Suburban. One man was walking toward the back of the vehicle, two were approaching from the passenger side, and one man on the driver side. The man at the back of the Suburban pushed the button on the door handle and the back door swung open. Randall could clearly see the man's face in the rear-view mirror.

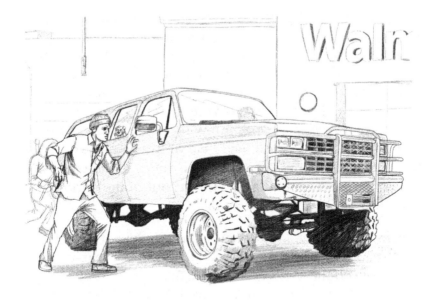

Benny was now aggressively trying to break Randall's grip and attack the man when Randall quickly glanced in both side mirrors and saw the other three men approaching. The men on the passenger side tried both the passenger and driver side door handles but they were locked. The man on the driver side tried the same, but the driver side doors were locked.

Randall immediately threw the vehicle in drive and floored the Suburban. The Suburban weighed 6,500 pounds and was not meant for speed. It was meant for power and torque and that's exactly what he got. When Randall floored the Suburban, several gas cans flew out the rear door, hitting the man in the face. Even though they were empty, it caught the man off guard forcing him to loosen his grip on the door. The man fell to the pavement and was trying his best to stand up and run after the Suburban.

Randall wasn't concentrating on what was in front of him. He was focused on the men behind him, and because he wasn't paying attention, he hit a parked vehicle. He hit the car at a slow speed and because the Suburban had an extended front grill, there was no damage to the vehicle, but it scared him. He quickly recovered, and while continuing to hold Benny in one hand, threw the Suburban in reverse and floored the vehicle. Once clear of the damaged vehicle he hit, he put the Suburban in drive and this time focused on what was in front of him. He was out of the parking lot and onto Main Street in seconds.

Several miles later, Randall pulled over in a vacant lot and felt his entire body shudder. He looked in the rear-view mirror and noticed his face had turned white. He felt cold. He was in shock, but he told himself he didn't have time to be in shock. He needed to get home. He quickly checked Benny for injuries and found none. He looked in the back of the Suburban and saw that the rear door was still open and groceries were everywhere. He quickly jumped out of the vehicle, slammed the rear door shut, and drove straight home.

After fifteen minutes, Randall turned into his drive and intently looked for Frank while driving up to the house. He didn't see Frank this time, but going forward he would always be more aware of their neighbor.

"My gut says don't trust him, so be wary," Randall said to Benny.

Randall drove the Suburban as close to the house as he could, put the emergency brake on, and turned it off. He looked in the rear-view mirror again and saw he was still pale white. He wasn't feeling good. Slowly, he opened the door and headed into the house to lie down.

"We'll unload the Suburban later, Benny. I don't feel good," Randall said as he held his stomach and headed into the house.

As Randall opened the door, he was surprised to see Cali. She had only been home for about thirty minutes and was excited to see her little brother. She could tell he didn't feel well and helped him to lie down. Before he went to sleep, Randall handed her the SHTF – Elevated Threat Manual. He told her to read and then re-read it just as Dad had instructed. He closed his eyes and quickly fell asleep.

22. HUNGER SETS IN

BUZZ, FRANK'S SIX-YEAR-OLD SON, was looking through the kitchen cabinets looking for something to eat.

"Dad!" Buzz yelled. "There's nothing to eat."

Frank stormed in through the porch door and went to the pantry. When he opened the door, he was staring at shelves that were almost empty. He grabbed the last can of chicken soup and tossed it to Buzz.

"Chicken soup?" Buzz whined.

"Eat it, boy. Mom will go shopping later this week," Frank growled.

Buzz opened the can, poured it in a bowl, and then placed it in the microwave. In his ever-continuing whiny voice, Buzz yelled, "Dad, the microwave doesn't work!"

"Eat it cold!" Frank yelled.

Frank kept looking at his watch, expecting his wife, Veronica, to drive up to the house at any moment. The sun was setting, and this was unlike her. She was almost always home by 6:00 p.m. Several hours later, Frank was on edge.

As best he could tell, it was around 8:00 p.m.

"It's hard to tell time when your iWatch isn't working," he said as he poked the watch with his finger.

With a headlamp strapped across his forehead, Frank went back to his car and started pulling at wires in hopes the car would miraculously start.

Several minutes later he surrendered yet again, but he needed to find his wife, not to mention they were almost out of food.

Frank was frustrated and turned to go into the house when he noted the reflection of the Suburban's bumper as his headlamp shown toward the McTatey's house.

"Suburban," Frank grumbled. "It runs and I'm sure if I ask nicely, Randall will let me use it."

Without thinking twice, Frank headed up the drive toward Oz's house. As he approached the house, he could hear Benny barking.

Randall was still sleeping when the constant barking woke him up. Randall peeked out the front window curtain and saw Frank standing at the door.

"Randall, it's Frank. Open the door. I need to talk to you."

Randall wasn't sure what to do. If he opened the door, it could simply be a conversation between the two, or worse, Frank could do something stupid and then who knows what would happen. Randall remained quite while Benny continued to bark.

"Randall, I know you're in there. Open the damn door. Sorry about my language. I just need to borrow the Suburban. I need to find my wife. I'm worried about her!" he yelled.

Randall knew he needed to say something; after all, Frank knew he was home. "Sorry, sir. I can't let you borrow my dad's car. I'll get in trouble," Randall said through the door.

Frank decided to take the soft approach and said, "I understand. I would probably be mad too. However, I would loan your dad my car in an emergency."

Randall thought Frank had a good point, but after everything he saw today, this was not the same world it was yesterday. "Sorry, Sir. I can't loan you the car. As soon as my mom gets home, I'll let her know and you can ask her."

"You little jerk!" Frank screamed as he began pounding on the door.

Without thinking, Frank reached for the door handle and was shocked to find the door wasn't locked. Randall fell to the floor when Frank threw the door open with a massive jolt.

"Shut the dog up before I kill him!" Frank demanded.

"Get out of our house or I'll call the police!" Randall screamed.

Frank threw his cell phone at Randall and said, "Go ahead. Call the police!"

Frank had called Randall's bluff.

"Where are the keys, boy?" Frank said.

"They're in the Suburban. I didn't feel good and left them in there by mistake," Randall stated.

Frank turned around and, once out the door, Randall stood up, shut the door, and turned the deadbolt. He had left his gun on the table and quickly ran to grab it. Cali had seen the entire event but was too scared to act. She had never seen her little brother act as brave as he had just been but knew he was scared as was she.

Randall watched as Frank went to the Suburban and discovered all the doors were locked. He had been duped. Frank's temper now flared. He ran to the front door and began punching, kicking, and pounding on the door. Randall knew the front and rear doors were security doors. They were made of pure metal and had reinforced hinges along with two deadbolts. The doors would hold Frank off long enough for him to grab the shotgun hidden underneath the couch.

"You're dead, Randall. I'm going to slit your neck and piss down your throat," Frank said as he was getting angrier.

Randall waited patiently with the handgun on his side and the shotgun in hand. Now tired, Frank realized that he would need more than his fists to break the door down. As angry as he was, he knew he wouldn't get into their house on this day. He decided to head home to see what tools he had that would make the job easier.

With the shotgun hanging down near his side, Randall listened and peeked out the window watching Frank head home. Randall was visibly shaken and had no idea what would come next or how to react. He truly wished he had paid attention when he was being taught survival skills by his dad. He wished he had taken the handgun, shotgun, and AR-15 training that his mom and dad took. But he didn't. He was going to have to deal with the situation the best he could, given what he had.

Having the shotgun made him feel better but he wasn't sure if it was loaded or needed to be loaded. He looked at the shotgun and could tell the safety was on. He reached under the couch and felt for shotgun shells. He came up empty-handed.

"It has to be loaded," he thought to himself. "Why else would Dad put it under the couch?" With Benny calmed down, Randall kept guard, constantly looking out the window. He was tired but knew he had to stay awake for both he and Cali's sake.

23. ALMOST HOME

"IT MUST BE LATE AT NIGHT or early in the morning," Nicki thought as she continued walking on 31 West.

With no concept of time, she guessed that she was now only about four hours from her house and looked forward to taking more Tylenol and crashing. Her eye was black and blue and her head was throbbing. She was scared but found the strength to continue going.

What seemed like an eternity had passed before Nicki saw the "Welcome to Kentucky" border sign. The walk along 31 West had been uneventful, and Nicki was glad. She had nothing left in her. No will. No fight. It was time to get home and sleep.

As she approached her drive, she heard a very unusual noise; a noise that you don't hear at that time of the night or morning.

Thud, thud, thud, thud

Nicki stopped and listened and heard the noise again.

Thud, thud, thud, thud

"That noise is coming from my house," she thought to herself.

Without thinking, she sprinted down the drive and stopped at the edge of the tree line. She had a good view of the house but was well hidden. As she continued scanning the area, she could tell the Suburban had been moved and she saw what appeared to be a man with a sledgehammer beating on her front door.

It was hard to tell with no light but he, or it, was breaking into her house. She slowly approached the house with her gun drawn. This would be the second time tonight that she'd have to pull her gun to save the life of another human; but nobody was going to harm her family.

Nicki was able to take a defensive position by using the Suburban to shield her body yet still have a clear view of her porch. She fired the gun which lit up the night with the muzzle flash and sent a loud thunder rippling through the air.

"That was a warning shot," she yelled. "The next two will be center mass ending your life!"

The shadow slowly walked down the porch stairs with the sledgehammer still in their hand.

"Drop the sledgehammer or I drop you!" Nicki continued.

"Nicki, it's me, Frank. You wouldn't shoot your neighbor, would you?" he retorted.

Without hesitating, Nicki said in a nice calm voice, "You bet I would. Drop the sledgehammer, Frank!"

Though it was hard to tell, she thought she could sense Frank getting mad and more upset. She knew she needed to keep her guard up. With steady hands and the Keltec aimed at Frank's chest, she said, "Get off my property. If you return, you do so at your own risk; that being the risk of your life!"

Frank burst out in a deep laugh and dropped the sledgehammer. "The power has been out all night. Cell phones aren't working. Who you going to call, Nicki? You can't call the police. You can't call Oz. Nobody's here to defend you. Even if the power comes back on, nobody's going to believe you. And you know what? You won't shoot me." Frank said in an ominous voice.

"Well, Frank," Nicki said in an *I told you so* voice. "Mr. Keltec said he would defend me, and he would like to show you what two well-placed shots, center mass, look like. Are you ready? And Frank, remember this: 'Words are used by many, wisdom by few, and the trigger by me.'"

That last phrase infuriated Frank. "I see," Frank said as he headed for home, but then turned to make one last point. "This is the way it's going to be? Me against you, Nicki? Well then, count me in," he said as he walked into the dark.

Once Nicki could no longer see the shadowy figure headed down the drive, she lowered her arms and tears began to stream from her eyes. She was careful to not make a noise. She would not let Frank see nor hear her cry. She would not give him the satisfaction of knowing he had scared her.

Now thoroughly exhausted, she walked up the porch stairs and turned the door handle. The door was locked. She thought for sure Benny would be barking, but she heard nothing.

Still holding the Keltec tight in her hand, she examined the door. Frank had beat the crap out of it, but it didn't budge. The door was solid as could be. She turned to do a 360-degree assessment of her surroundings before unlocking the deadbolt.

Once inside, she locked the deadbolt before yelling for Randall. Within seconds, she heard Benny barking and soon after he ran up the stairs where he greeted her with excitement.

As Nicki walked down the stairs, she could see Randall holding the shotgun and Cali sitting on the couch. They were expressionless, but slowly made eye contact with their mom.

"Randall, Cali, are you okay? Did that beast hurt you?" Nicki exclaimed.

Visibly upset, Randall responded, "No, Mom. He didn't hurt me, but had you not come along I know he would have tried. He may have even killed us."

Though Nicki felt weak inside and out, she had to be strong.

"Randall, Cali, he won't touch us. Your dad has prepared this house well. We have food, water, heat, shelter, guns, ammo, and communications. What we need to do is read the manual your dad prepared and wait for him and BJ to come home. The sooner we get started the better."

Randall felt better knowing his mom was home, and with relief in his voice said, "I've already started, Mom."

Nicki glanced at the shotgun Randall was carrying and knew he must have truly feared for his life to be clutching the weapon so tightly.

"Do you even remember how to shoot a shotgun? I know your dad took you out one time, but after that you lost all interest," Nicki asked her son.

"Not really," Randall replied.

Nicki picked up the shotgun, made sure the safety was on, and opened the gun port. Randall was surprised to see a 00-buckshot shell eject. It was loaded. All he had to do was push the safety off, aim, and squeeze the trigger.

"You and your sister need to be armed at all times regardless of where you go; inside or outside. Do you understand?" Nicki asked Randall and Cali firmly.

They shook their heads indicating they understood and said, "Yes, ma'am."

Nicki removed the PMR-30 and holster and placed it on the couch. She walked to the closet in Cali's room and came back with two Springfield® XDM 9mm handguns. She made Randall and Cali stand next to her as she instructed them on the basic handling of a firearm.

"Cali, Randall, first, check to make sure the weapon, in this case, a handgun, is not loaded before inserting a magazine and racking the slide. You do this by making sure there is no magazine in the magazine well and then pulling back on the slide, only slightly, to see if a round is in the chamber. See how the chamber is empty?"

After she saw the weapon was in a safe condition, she continued.

"Second, slap a magazine into the magazine well and rack the slide. Third, pull the slide back slightly to ensure a round was properly seated in the chamber. Fourth, eject the magazine and physically check for physical damage and to verify the round count. Fifth, if you're satisfied, slap the magazine back in the magazine well and holster. Now, repeat what I just did," she said as she handed both of them a Springfield XDM 9mm.

She intently watched them and made a few corrections as they went through the exercise.

"Good," she said and continued. "Your gun does not have a mechanical safety. One more time. Your gun does not have a mechanical safety. The most important safety on all guns is your trigger finger. Always, I mean always, keep your trigger finger straight and off the trigger until you're ready to fire. When you pull the gun from the holster, get your sight picture, release the tension on the trigger, hold your breath, and with a smooth motion, pull the trigger. Easier said than done. More later. Right now, we don't have time for lessons. Put your holster on and in a safe direction place the gun in the holster."

Randall and Cali did as instructed. Nicki then took five additional magazines and loaded them with hollow point self-defense rounds and showed the kids how to do the same. They were now armed.

24. 4:20 AM

AFTER SLEEPING FOR OVER twelve hours, BJ woke and once again sat up in his bed. This time it was dark, and he was somewhat disorientated after sleeping so many hours.

He grabbed his phone to check the time when he remembered it had died. Looking at his dead phone he said, "How could I forget to plug it in?".

Still trying to orientate himself, he looked around his room and noticed that his night light, which was always on, was off. He was also quick to see that the Star Wars® glow in the dark clock that he had since he was a young boy was not illuminated.

"Wait a minute," he thought to himself. "I did plug my phone in." He followed the cord from his phone to the wall outlet and realized that it was, in fact, plugged into the outlet. "The power must still be out," he muttered.

He slipped on his sweatpants and sweatshirt and slowly got out of bed. The night had a chill to it, but he was thankful that the power hadn't been lost in the dead of winter. After all, Illinois winters can be brutal; often dipping down to -30°F.

BJ knew he needed to be at the greenhouse by 5:00 a.m. but wasn't sure what time it was. He stumbled into the kitchen when he realized that without power the clock on the stove would be useless. He peeked into Scott's room. It too was pitch black with no lights and no noises except for the occasional noise made by Scott tossing and turning in his sleep.

BJ turned around and walked to the kitchen window where he peeked out and saw a sea of darkness. Darkness as far as the eye could see. No lamppost lights flicking. Not one neighborhood house with any type of light glowing. The only light that could be easily seen were the stars and galaxies above.

"How eerie," BJ whispered when his thoughts turned to his dad. "This is how it would be if the grid went down," he thought as he recalled the training his dad had tried to give him and his brother and sister.

Goosebumps ran up and down his body. "What if the power never came back on," he whispered. "I would be so screwed."

BJ was amazed at how uncomfortable he was because he simply didn't know what time it was.

"It's amazing how those digits control our life, tell us where to be and when. Unfortunately, I need to know what time it is. Can't be late to the greenhouse," he thought to himself.

The first thing he would do is take a shower and then jump in his car. "It's ironic", he thought, "that it would be the clock in his car that told him how his day would begin and end." If it was close to 5:00 a.m., he would head directly to the greenhouse; but if it was earlier, he would drive to Waffle House™ and get breakfast.

With his backpack thrown over his shoulder, BJ walked out the front door and headed to his car. He pressed the key fob to unlock the car door, and when he reached for the handle, the door did not open. He pressed the button again and reached for the handle only to find the same result. He separated the key from the key fob, inserted it into the door lock, and turned it. The door unlocked. He opened the door and placed his backpack on the passenger's seat. He placed his foot on the brake and pushed the start button. Nothing. He placed the key, which he separated from the key fob, in the ignition and turned it. Nothing. BJ's mind came back to the thoughts he had earlier that morning.

"What if the power is out across the United States?" he said quickly dismissing the thought.

He walked back into the house and grabbed Scott's car keys from the counter. He walked to Scott's car only to find out that the key fob did not work. He unlocked the door using the key and sat down in the driver's seat.

"Please, please, please," he whispered. He placed his foot on the brake and pushed the ignition button. Nothing. He didn't waste his time trying a second time. There was no need. There were no dash lights or noises of any type coming from the vehicle.

His heart sank, and for the first time in his life he thought that maybe, just maybe, his dad may be right.

"If my dad is right, I'll need to get home quickly before things get worse. But first, I want more proof the power is out everywhere," he thought to himself.

BJ went back to his car unsure of what to do when he remembered the Bug Out Bag his dad gave him. He never opened it and was lucky to remember he had one. He opened the trunk of the car and there it was. He brought the bulky olive drab green bag inside the house and opened the main compartment. He saw an envelope in a plastic Ziploc bag. He could make out the words "BJ – My firstborn." He took it out and began reading it:

BJ,

If you are reading this letter the Stuff Hit the Fan. Like your sister and younger brother, I know you well and there would be no other reason for you to use the contents of this Bug Out Bag.

*First, let me tell you that your safety is priority one. Be aware of your surroundings and constantly, I mean constantly scan your immediate area for danger. By car, your six hours from our house as well as the Bug Out Location. Assess your circumstances and determine which location is best for you. Either location will provide safety and security. The most IMPORTANT point is taking action. **DON'T WAIT**. If you can drive, then drive. If it was an EMP you'll have to find a bike or begin walking.*

There's an additional option you have. You're only a three to four-hour walk from Brian and Elizabeth's house. If you question your safety, only travel at night and hide during the day. IF TRAVELING AT NIGHT, PUT ON THE CAMOUFLAGE PANTS AND LONG SLEEVE SHIRT stored in your Bug Out Bag. Remember when I taught you about a gray man (fitting into your environment and not sticking out like a sore thumb)? Now is the time to be that person.

I've included maps in the Velcro compartment on the very back of the Bug Out Bag. These are just in case your car doesn't' run or the highways are impassable. ALWAYS use back roads where possible.

Second, your Bug Out Bag contains many things to keep you safe, warm, and fed. You will most likely not need them because of your distance to Brian and Elizabeth's house. Just in case, you have:

- *First Aid kit with many different supplies*
- *Baofeng radio (when you're close to our house, or Brian and Elizabeth's, contact us or them on Channel 1)*
- *3 flashlights*
- *3 Mountain House freeze-dried meals*
- *4 U.S. Coast Guard water pouches*
- *Life Straw (use to filter water from a creek or a questionable source)*
- *Waterproof matches, blast match, cotton balls, char cloth, lighters, twine, and candles*
- *Two knives (on the outside of your BOB)*
- *Light (headlamp, glow sticks, and Stream Light flashlight)*
- *Emergency blankets*
- *Writing tools (Sharpie and Fisher Space Pen) with notebook*

Third, if you are the first-person home, go to the safe in the garage and grab the Red Binder that is labeled "__SHTF – Elevated Threat Manual.__" Read it then re-read it and FOLLOW all directions. This binder contains directions on how to secure our house.

If you get in a bad situation, I want you to FIGHT FOR YOUR LIFE. Do not give up. You're a wrestler, use everything you learned. Pull hair. Kick or hit a guy in the nuts. As hard as you can, push your finger through someone's eyeballs. Punch someone in the throat as hard as you can. Get your finger in your attacker's ear and push as hard as you can. FIGHT FOR YOUR LIFE!!!!

BJ, there's a chance I may not be home or it may take me some time to get home. If you're not home by the time I get home, we will plan to find you. The first place we will head is to Brian and Elizabeth's. Be strong in everything you do.

I Love you very much, now get home or head to Brian and Elizabeth's!

Love, Dad

BJ placed the letter back in the Bug Out Bag and zipped it up. He grabbed the flashlight hanging on the outside of the bag before putting the bag across his shoulders. A twenty-four-hour Walmart was less than a mile away. He simply needed to see for himself if the power was truly out in the city.

His walk took him through several neighborhoods, and he noted that all the houses were consumed by the dark. Not one indication that power was available to any house; not even the sound of a generator.

As he turned the corner, he saw the Walmart 200 feet in front of him. He took a quick glance and turned around and began walking home.

"No lights and a few people milling around. No need to walk any further," he said to himself. "Time to figure out what to do next," he said out loud.

25. SUPPLY RUN

OZ WAS AWOKEN the following morning by the sounds of a group of people walking by. He was well hidden, and unless they intentionally went into the woods, he would remain undetected.

As expected, they were sharing theories on what happened and how long it would be before help arrived and the lights were back on. Oz just shook his head. Not only was their conversation meaningless but he was still upset that he wasn't able to travel at night because of not having a headlamp for his bike.

He knew he needed to travel at night and finally decided to camouflage his bike and walk twenty minutes to Ashburn. His plan was to find a shop or store and buy a headlamp. He dared not ride his bike into town for the fear that it might be stolen, or worse, someone would forcibly take it from him.

The walk into Ashburn was uneventful as he passed several people, but no words were spoken. A quick hand wave was all that was shared. Ashburn was a small town with no major retailers. Finding a headlamp would be a challenge and he knew he would most likely have to improvise.

On the corner of Hill Avenue and North Street sat Ashburn Builders Supply. Oz approached the building, somewhat cautiously, and pulled the door. It was locked. He walked around the building and found all the doors locked. He came back to the main entrance and knocked. No answer. He knocked harder, and as he peered through the door, he saw a middle-aged man approach. The man looked confused and it appeared as if he had been crying.

"What do you want?" the man yelled.

"I need a headlamp for my bike," Oz responded.

"We're closed, but it wouldn't matter anyway. We don't have bicycle parts," the man shouted even louder.

"Do you mind if I come in and look around. I'll need to improvise something," Oz stated.

"Are you alone?" the man asked.

"Yes, I'm alone. Why do you ask?" Oz answered.

The man turned the main deadbolt to unlock the door and allowed Oz in. "You look harmless enough," the man said while not making eye contact.

"Can you show me where your flashlights are?" Oz asked.

"Follow me," the man motioned.

As Oz looked at the flashlights, he noticed that the brightest flashlights were 300 lumens. Though not the greatest, it would have to work.

Oz's plan was to keep it simple. He would buy three 300 lumen flashlights, duct tape two on the handlebars of the bike for headlights and keep one as a spare.

"Three flashlights, three extra sets of batteries, and one roll of duct tape; how much do I owe you?" Oz asked the man.

"I can't accept credit cards and I can't make change because my cash register is locked. It won't open until the power comes back on. Before you ask, I lost the key to open the drawer. What—"

Before the man could finish his sentence, Oz interrupted, "The total cost of these items is roughly $50. I'll give you $4.00 in pre-1964 silver quarters. The exchange rate is typically $3.50 for every pre-1964 quarter. You don't need to make change and worse case is you now have a precious metal which you can keep or exchange later."

The man thought for a moment and looked Oz in the eyes before stating, "Who does that? In today's world, who proposes a trade for silver coins?"

The man thought for a minute before saying, "It makes sense, but you caught me off guard. I never thought I would be in a situation where I would accept silver. Deal. By the way, any idea of what happened or when we'll have power back on?"

Oz thought long and hard before responding.

"To tell you the truth the power is never coming back on as far as I can tell, and I have no idea what happened. It would appear we were hit by some sort of Electromagnetic Pulse, an EMP. Maybe even a cyber-attack. My computer, printer, and monitor were all fried. Listen to me. You have a well-stocked store which will serve you well. You'll be able to trade your goods for food, bullets, guns, and medical supplies. I highly recommend you get around-the-clock security in this place and be prepared to defend it."

Oz shook the man's hand, wished him luck, gathered his goods, and exited the store. As Oz walked back to his campsite, he was proud that he made the deal for the flashlights but sad because he knew that money would never have value again.

"Unless you need something to start a fire," he whispered.

Once at camp, Oz duct taped two flashlights to the handlebars of the bicycle.

"Perfect," he said as he smiled.

He was now ready to travel at night. It was only 1:00 p.m. and it was time to sleep if he could. His plan was to awake in the evening, about an hour before sunset, eat, and ride until sun up. At least that was his plan.

26. FAMILY FIRST

RANDALL SHOOK NICKI by the shoulder and startled her out of a deep sleep.

"Mom. Mom," Randall whispered.

Nicki quickly jumped up and reached for her Springfield XDS. Before she could unholster the weapon, Randall placed his hand over hers.

"Mom," he said. "Everything is okay; at least for now. You were startled that's all."

Nicki recovered and peeked out the window. The sun was out. She did a quick scan of the front yard looking for Frank.

Looking at Randall she said, "I can't believe I fell asleep. Randall, we can't do that. Someone needs to be awake and on security detail at all times. I'm sorry."

"Now you sound like Dad," Randall said.

"I sure hope so," Nicki said with a smile and then continued, "You said you read Dad's manual. What do we need to do next?" Nicki asked.

"He wants us to move the guns and food inside the house."

"Makes complete sense. If we don't, we stand a chance of them being stolen and a good chance it will be by our good neighbor, Frank."

Nicki pulled out four boxes of 00 buckshot and replaced the shotgun shell she had ejected earlier.

"The shotgun is one of the best weapons you can have when you're in close contact with someone. It has a wide shot pattern and will almost always hit its target. You are to never leave this house alone. Do you understand, Randall?"

"Yes, but that goes for you too, Mom," Randall responded.

"Fair enough," Nicki replied and continued, "Let's get the rifles, shotguns, and handguns in the house first. I will stand by the corner of the Suburban while you and Cali unload the safe and place everything in the house. We'll let Benny outside, too. He'll tell us right away if Frank is around," she finished.

It took Randall and Cali about twenty minutes to remove all guns and ammo from the safe and place them in the house.

"Done. Food's next," Cali told her mom.

As Nicki was standing guard, she saw movement in the trees ahead of her, but Benny wasn't growling. Being nervous, she pulled Randall and Cali over to her side and turned her back so that if someone were watching and listening, she would not be heard as she whispered to them.

She put her head down and said in a low tone, "I'm not sure if we're being watched but I recommend we stop for now. I don't want to take the chance that someone knows what we have. We'll unload the food tonight when it's dark. I can hide easier and it will be harder for someone to figure out what we're doing."

"Fine by me," Randall said.

Nicki locked the garage and the three went inside.

Nicki read Oz's manual and now understood the importance of having constant security. She sat Randall and Cali down and the three agreed to a plan. The three would pull eight-hour security details and should the one on security duty not be able to stay awake, they would awaken the next on duty who could fill in for an hour or two while they slept. They would work as a team.

"What about Grandma and Grandpa?" Randall asked Nicki.

"Yeah, I've been thinking about that too," she said.

"It's ironic that they're only forty minutes away but compared to several days ago, it's not a simple drive," Randall responded.

"Frank—we'll have to drive by his house, and as we head down the drive he'll know we're gone and most likely rob us blind," Nicki said with an air of caution.

"We have to get Grandma and Grandpa regardless. I'll stay home and you go get them?" Randall said in a questioning manner.

"No, I'll stay home, Nicki said. "You and Cali drive to their house. We need to be reasonable. If Frank tries anything, I have the most experience with a firearm; you two don't.

This is going to sound absolutely crazy, and I can't believe I'm even saying this, but the three of us need to put on one of Dad's bulletproof vests and wear those military helmets we used to make fun of." Nicki said as she rolled her eyes.

"You're scared, aren't you, Mom?" Randall said in a serious tone.

Holding Randall's hand, she explained, "Yes, I am baby. I'm scared for our entire family. We may never experience the life we used to live. We may now be living in a much more dangerous world, and the sooner we understand that the better. The power has been out for several days and we have not seen or heard from anyone at the county, state, or federal level. I shot two men last night, almost a third..." Nicki continued to say before Randall cut her off.

"You shot two men last night?" he said in disbelief.

Nicki began to cry when Randall grabbed her in a big hug and said, "If you shot them then they were going to kill you or hurt someone else. I know and love you Mom and know you did it for the right reasons. There's no guilt in what you did."

Nicki embraced Randall in an even bigger hug and continued, "Randall, our goal is to get the family together and figure out this mess—how we're going to survive together—and that means we need to have each other's back at all times."

"Grab your shotgun, Mom. I'll need cover when I start the Suburban. So you know, I'm going to floor it down the drive and we'll head straight to Grandma and Grandpa's without stopping. If Frank is in the way, then he'll become a

458 Miles and 24 Days

permanent part of the Suburban's front grill. I will not stop for anything or anyone," Randall said with determination.

Nicki went downstairs and came back with three Baofeng UV-5R dual band two-way radios and headsets. She powered them on and turned the selector on each to the channel labeled "McTat1." This was a programmed channel that Oz had placed on all their two-way radios. It was a channel that was not frequently used or monitored by others and would provide security and privacy when family members spoke to one another.

"From now on, we always have radios with us and our headsets on. Randall, leave this radio on until you leave our property and you're safely on the crossroad. Turn it back on about five miles before you get to our house and make contact with me so I can provide cover if necessary," Nicki said looking very concerned.

Nicki grabbed the shotgun, scanned the area, noticed Benny wasn't barking and gave the all-clear to Randall and Cali who jumped in the Suburban.

Randall pushed the glow plug button and started the vehicle. He let it warm up for thirty seconds before heading down the drive at full speed. Nicki intently watched as he drove down the drive and could soon hear that he made it onto the cross street.

"Mom, no sign of Frank. We're safely on the road headed to Grandma and Grandpa's. Be safe and we love you," he said into the radio.

"Love you, Randall. Love you, Cali," Nicki responded.

Randall turned the radio off and was on his way to pick up his grandma and grandpa.

27. EVER-CHANGING WORLD

WITH VERY LITTLE SLEEP, Oz awoke thirty minutes before sunset. He opened his Bug Out Bag and removed a pouch of Mountain House chili mac, his butane/propane stove, and a collapsible pan to heat water. He pulled out two four-ounce Datrex emergency water packets and poured them into the pan, lit the stove, and waited. Several minutes later, he poured the boiling water into the Mountain House pouch and waited five minutes before eating.

"Better than home cooking," he laughed.

While eating, he looked at the map and decided he would stop near the town of Perry, Georgia. In daylight, the ride was around five hours but at night it was only a guess.

"Six to eight hours," Oz murmured to himself.

At Perry, he would have three options one of which was to scope out 75 North and see how feasible it was. His last two options were to take highway 341, which ran to the west of 75 North or simply ride over the overpass and continue on highway 41 North which ran east of 75 North.

With night setting in, Oz was packed and ready. He turned on his newly-mounted flashlights and headed onto the highway.

After four hours of riding, Oz knew something didn't feel right. His eyes had sensed motion ahead of him and the hair on the back of his neck was standing straight up. He quickly turned off the flashlights and brought the bike to a stop. He could make out movement several hundred feet in front of him, but his eyes hadn't fully adjusted to the dark after accidentally glancing into the flashlight. He froze. It was silent and pitch black.

"Do I go offensive or defensive?" he thought. "Offensive wins."

He lifted his sagging shirt and tucked it in his waistline, exposing his Glock and Glock holster. He now had quick and easy access to the gun. He rolled the bike over to the side of the road and carefully set it down on its side. He felt the bike would be safe while he scouted the area ahead of him. After all, it was dark. Who would see the bike? He drew his Glock in his left hand and slowly began moving forward. He would walk forward ten feet and then do a quick check to the right, left, and behind him for any sign of movement. He moved forward another ten feet and did his checks.

In a matter of minutes, he was about 100 feet from his bike when he could make out two shadows quickly dart to the side of the road and into the woods. He could hear their footsteps as leaves crunched and twigs broke. They were running fast. Unsure of what to do, he stopped and assessed his situation. He was not about to follow whoever ran into the woods. It was most likely a trap and to make it worse he had no knowledge of the lay of the land. Running in the woods at full speed would be suicide. He would most likely injure himself and that's the last thing he needed.

Instead, he crouched down on the road and watched and listened, ready to react.

It was only minutes later that he heard someone yell, "Enjoy your walk you dumb ass!"

He could barely make out two individuals riding away on his bike. One was sitting down while the other was standing tall with his feet on the bolts of the frame.

Oz took aim with his Glock but given the distance and darkness, it was a guess. He slowly lowered the gun and realized that he would most likely waste bullets and draw attention to himself if he were to shoot. This was the second critical mistake he made in the last two days.

"At least I was smart enough to keep my Bug Out Bag and fanny pack on," he thought as he clenched his teeth.

As he reached down to touch the fanny pack, he realized he had a night vision monocular in it. He sighed knowing he should have used it and because he didn't, it cost him his only means of transportation. If he had used the night vision monocular, he could have easily seen the two thugs and prevented this incident. He needed to be smarter in his actions. Three days on the road and Oz had seen the world change bringing out the worst in people. It was time to switch tactics.

28. SAVING FAMILY

RANDALL AND CALI ARRIVED at Grandma and Grandpa's without incident just as the sun was setting. As Randall drove, he noticed that nothing had changed from the day he walked home from school. There were still broken-down cars and a few wondering people on the roads.

Randall pulled the Suburban into the driveway and felt to make sure his Springfield XDM was easily accessible. He and Cali stepped out and quickly looked around. From the windows, Randall could see the neighbor's watching them, but wasn't concerned. They were good people who would soon be desperate; but today, he would not worry.

Cali and Randall walked up to their grandparent's door and knocked. His grandma, Connie, peeked out the side door glass window before answering the door. She ushered them in the house and gave them a big hug.

"Hi, Grandma," Randall said with excitement.

"Hi, G'ma," Cali said.

"Where's Grandpa?" Randall asked.

"He's not feeling good. He's been throwing up and has a fever. We tried to go to urgent care, but the car won't start. Can you take us there, please?" his grandma asked.

"Grandma, the power is out across the city and maybe even the state," he said.

Randall had a decision to make. He could take them to urgent care, or even the hospital, but Randall felt confident it would be useless; after all, his mom worked in a hospital and had to walk home.

"Grandma, let's get Grandpa in the Suburban and take him to our house. My parents have medication and, as weird as this sounds, my mom has stuff to start IVs. I'm nervous and you should be, too. Mom walked home from the hospital yesterday. Her car wouldn't start either. It's time to be wary of people we encounter including your neighbors. Soon they'll want what we have." Randall finished.

"What do you mean people 'will want what we have,' Randall?" his grandma asked.

"Grandma, it's been three days since the power went out and people are freaking out. Our neighbor tried to break in our house and I honestly think he would have hurt Cali and I. Remember, my dad told us that when people begin to run out of food and water that they'll get desperate? Well, they're panicking, not to mention we're the only ones who have a running vehicle."

Randall looked out the window and saw several neighbors milling around. He turned to his grandma and said, "Let's get Grandpa in the Suburban and leave right away. Take only what you need and pack in the next five minutes. We need to leave."

"Randall, Grandpa's not feeling good as I said before. Let's stay the night and leave in the morning. Hopefully, he'll be feeling better," she said.

Randall knew his mother would be worried, but with night approaching, it was probably best to spend the night and leave early in the morning. Randall and Cali went into their grandparents' room where they saw him sleeping. He, in fact, was not looking good. They didn't wake him up but let him sleep while his grandma began packing their clothes.

"I'll be back in a minute," Randall said to Cali.

Randall went into the garage and opened the overhead door. He drove the Suburban inside and lowered the garage door. He looked around his grandpa's garage and began loading tools, boards, sheets of wood, and other supplies he thought they could use or would need. He then went into the pantry and loaded everything into the Suburban. He went through his grandpa's closet and found two shotguns and ammo that he placed in the Suburban. Randall knew he would not sleep that night; but instead, he would pull guard duty.

Early the next morning, Randall gently awoke his grandparents and Cali and told them it was time to leave. He and Cali helped his grandpa sit up.

Randall whispered, "Grandpa, I'm going to help you into Dad's Suburban. We're going to our house."

His grandpa acknowledged him and placed his arm around Randall's shoulders. Randall walked his grandpa to the Suburban after descending several stairs leading to the garage. He opened the Suburban door and with one hand made sure the passenger seat was fully reclined. His grandma placed a pillow on the seat as Randall and Cali helped their grandpa in.

Once their grandpa was comfortable, Randall slid the seatbelt across his lap until he heard a *click*. He placed his grandma's luggage in the Suburban, helped her into the vehicle, and opened the garage door. He started the Suburban and began to back out of the drive when he saw several neighbors opening their doors.

Without further thought, Randall positioned the Suburban in the direction of his house.

Fifty minutes later Randall was within five miles of the house, and just as his mother had requested, he turned the radio on and called for his mom.

"Mom, it's Randall and Cali. We have Grandma and Grandpa. We're about five miles away."

As soon as he finished, he heard, "Thank God. I was worried about you two. You were supposed to pick them up and come home immediately," Nicki said as her voiced quivered.

"Randall, slow down. I'm headed outside. I'm going to take up a security position and be ready for Frank just in case he decides to be a jerk. Give me a couple minutes."

"10-4, Mom," Randall said as he slowed the Suburban down.

Nicki left Benny in the house while cautiously hiding near a row of trees by the drive. From there, she could see down the entire length of the drive and, with the sun rising, she would be able to see Frank if he tried something stupid.

Within minutes, Nicki could see the Suburban turn onto the drive and, just as quickly, saw Frank open the sliding glass door located at the back of his house.

Nicki didn't take any chances and stepped out onto the drive where she placed the reticle of the rifle's scope on Frank's chest. Frank definitely saw her. He looked in her direction and flipped her off before going back in the house.

Connie could not believe what she just saw. She saw her daughter-in-law pointing a rifle at their neighbor. Connie turned to Randall and said, "Randall, what is going on? Why is your mom pointing a rifle at your neighbor? Is she okay?"

Randall looked at his grandma and said, "Grandma, I love you, but you and Grandpa will need to change your behavior. The rest of the world already did."

29. THE SCREAMS OF DESPAIR

OZ WOKE UP THE NEXT MORNING and dreaded the fact that he was now walking; at least until he found alternate transportation.

His best estimates suggested he was about four to six hours away from Perry by foot. The plan was to get started immediately but stay off the road. From now on, he would travel during the day and sleep at night but needed to remain camouflaged and concealed to the best of his ability —a much harder challenge during daylight hours.

His main concern was what would happen when others saw he had a Bug Out Bag and fanny pack. He had no doubt they would want both and would take them by force if necessary. He decided to travel in the woods that ran parallel to the highway. With downed branches and other obstacles in the way, traveling through the woods would be a challenge as well as much slower.

As Oz began walking the rough terrain, he realized that he could be heard miles away. If there was a stick in the path, he would step on it making others aware of his position. If there was a pile of leaves in the path, he would kick it.

"Lift your feet, Oz," he muttered to himself.

For the next couple of hours, he intentionally focused on how he walked, ensuring he was as quiet as possible. Though he was more silent, he had much to learn.

About 60 minutes outside of Perry, Georgia, Oz stopped and peered through his binoculars to scout the area ahead. He saw a most bizarre scene. In front of him, about a half mile directly north of his position, he saw a man kneeling with his knees firmly planted on the road. The kneeling man kept looking behind him at a woman and a teenage girl who were crying. The woman had her hands clasped together as if she was praying, but Oz could only guess she was pleading for something.

"The life of the kneeling man," Oz sighed.

Her mouth moved, but Oz could not make out the words. He knew there was despair in her words as her facial expressions were one of distress. The woman appeared to be in her early forties while the teenage girl couldn't be more than fifteen.

"A kneeling man, a woman, a teenage girl, and six dirty, scroungy looking men," Oz muttered as he assessed the situation.

Oz sat and watched the group for a few more minutes when he saw a rather tall, overweight man pull out a handgun, place it to the head of the man kneeling on the ground, and pulled the trigger. The sound of the gun rippled throughout the air as Oz saw blood and brain matter scatter all over the road. The kneeling man immediately slumped to the ground.

"What the hell just happened?!" Oz said in anger. "What the hell? What the hell?"

This was truly the first time in Oz's life he had witnessed anything like this. He felt an anger he had never felt before. He wanted vengeance. He immediately grabbed his Glock and Ruger PC Carbine 9mm and started walking toward the man who pulled the trigger when he quickly realized it would be a suicide mission. He needed to settle down and come up with an action plan. He was sick to his stomach.

As Oz sat down contemplating what had just happened, he thought he could hear the woman and child crying. Rather the cries were real or not, he knew he would confront the group. He would free both women and he would risk his life tonight to make that happen. He peered through the binoculars again where he saw the situation go from bad to worse. He saw a middle-aged man grab the teenage girl and push her into a van. Right before Oz's eyes, they both disappeared into the van as the doors were slammed shut. The rest of the men circled the middle-aged woman like a pack of hungry wolves around a wounded animal. Oz knew what came next. He knew that she would be raped and possibly killed. Before he could continue his thought, he heard the screams of the woman.

"The bastards couldn't even wait," Oz said silently. He would make his move tonight but could do nothing at this moment other than pray.

It was one hour before dark when Oz began moving silently through the woods. He needed the remaining light to get into position where his plan would be to simply catch them off guard and shoot until they were all dead or he was dead. It was not much of a plan, but Oz had little to no experience in combat. It was the best plan he had, given the fact he needed to react quickly.

Oz was now about 200 yards away from the group and had good coverage. Using the binoculars, he saw four members of the group leave together.

"Could this really be happening?" he thought. "They're separating? Two against one was much better odds."

With night setting in and the four men no longer in sight, it was time for Oz to act. Oz surmised that if he could get within ten yards of the two men, he could quickly kill them using his handgun. If he could get closer, he would. He also knew that when he fired the gun the four men who had recently left would come back to help their friends, but it would be too late. Oz would have to quickly grab the woman and girl and head back into the woods for cover where he would take up a defensive position.

He took off his Bug Out Bag and fanny pack and covered them with grass, twigs, and other material on the ground.

Anger raged within Oz, and without reservation or question, he wanted to make sure the women were freed, and the two men paid for their sins.

He began to belly crawl toward the men. It was a slow process, but it enabled Oz the silence he needed and the ability to remain hidden. He quickly peeked up one last time to make sure the four men were not returning. They were not. Oz would wait another hour before he killed the two men. This was insurance that the four men would be at least three to four miles away and would not be able to help their soon-to-be-dead friends.

The two remaining men sat next to a fire, periodically looking at the captive woman and teenager.

Oz heard one of the men say, "I sure hope they find a place for us to stay. Somewhere that has food. It sucks being in the middle of nowhere."

His friend responded, "Hell, I don't need a house. I need more women. The younger the better," he laughed.

Oz's blood was boiling. He quickly assessed his situation. It was dark and he knew he could now walk to within ten to fifteen feet of the men. He stood up with his gun in hand and inched toward the two men. Oz was now within five feet when he pulled the trigger. The man closest to Oz dropped. Oz had put two shots, center mass, into the man.

With only one man remaining, Oz shouted, "There will be no more women or children for you!" as he shot the man in the groin.

The man screamed with agony and pain, cupping his hands around his groin area. Oz shot the man two more times. One shot in each thigh. Instinctively, Oz changed his magazine assuring he had seventeen fresh rounds in the Glock. Oz intentionally didn't fire another shot. He wanted to see the man suffer. This was not the man Oz had become or the morals he believed in, but his anger turned to hatred.

Oz turned to the woman and girl who were tied up and scared.

"My name is Oz. I'm here to get you out of here. We need to hurry. I know you're scared but you have no choice but to trust me. You need to know I'm a husband, father, and man of God. You can't think right now. You can't say a word. We need to leave immediately. There are four more men who I imagine are running back to us right now. Shake your head up and down if you're coming with me. Let's go."

"Are you going to kill him?" the older woman said in a faint, desperate voice.

"No. I'm going to let him suffer," Oz said.

"I want him dead," she said.

There was no time. Oz handed her his SOG knife. "She deserved this," he thought.

After all, within the last several hours she's been through hell and back.

She had seen the guy she was with killed and then she was raped by multiple men; not to mention what may have happened to the teenage girl.

Without thinking, she took the knife and put it to the throat of the already bleeding man.

Before she slit his throat, she yelled, "He was my husband and the father of our daughter!"

She drove the knife across his throat and the man gurgled causing blood to flow onto the ground. She handed the knife back to Oz who cleaned the blade by running it across the dying man's clothes. He placed the knife back in its sheath and told the woman and girl to follow him.

The three headed back to pick up Oz's Bug Out Bag, fanny pack, and rifle. They followed Oz, who headed deep into the forest. Twenty minutes later, Oz stopped. He needed to get a pulse on the four men. He needed to know if he was being followed. He pulled out his night vision monocular, pulled the lens caps off, and turned the monocular on. He carefully scanned the area focusing on the direction they just left. Though the night vision monocular had no magnification, it gave him the lay of the land. He didn't see any light emanating from a flashlight and no movement. He then scanned the area in front of him. He pulled his map out again and replaced the monocular with his flashlight to which he added a red lens.

He crouched down to take cover and put his finger to his lips, indicating silence, making sure the ladies saw his motion. They shook their heads in acknowledgment. Oz folded up the map and motioned for the girls to follow.

After two hours of walking in unfamiliar woods, Oz quietly whispered, "We'll make camp here. We can talk, but we need to keep it to a whisper. I'll take another look but I'm sure we're not being followed. If we were, we would have heard something or seen flashlights."

Oz knew the girls had been through a lot, but he needed more information. He needed to know their names and what their plans were. He really wanted to know what happened and how they ended up in that terrible situation, but it could wait until morning.

Oz took out several emergency water pouches and handed them to the ladies. Within seconds, the water was gone. "I'm out of water for now. When the sun is up, we'll find more. Here, eat these energy bars. They taste terrible, but they'll give you the calories you need," Oz said.

"Thank you," the woman said. Oz could see that they needed to sleep. He did his best to make them a comfortable bed using leaves, grass, and an emergency blanket. The overnight temperatures wouldn't be too cold, but he recommended they sleep as close to one another as possible to conserve heat. Their eyes were shut, and they were sound asleep within minutes of lying down. As tired as Oz was, he needed to stay awake on guard duty. He felt obligated to at least see them through the night.

30. FAMILY ADAPTING

NICKI CHECKED ON LLOYD, her father-in-law and Randall's and Cali's grandfather. He was still running a temperature and was unable to keep liquids down. His fever had yet to subside and he was dehydrated. She knew he needed fluids and opted for an IV.

She walked outside and over to their shed to get the supplies. She unlocked and opened the overhead door, immediately grabbing the manual containing an alphabetical list of their preparations. She looked up "IV Kit," "Sodium Chloride flush," and "IV bags."

She went to the appropriate bin and found the supplies she needed. She opened the IV kit to make sure it had all the right components including tubing, a BD® Insyte Autoguard 20 GA needle, a microbe extension set, rubber tourniquet, alcohol wipes, and gloves. The set was complete.

"I need something for nausea and vomiting," she thought to herself.

She then looked up Zofran, opened the bin, and placed the medication in her pocket. She returned to the house and began the process of giving Lloyd intravenous fluids.

Once the IV was going, she gave Lloyd the Zofran and waited to see how he responded. Several hours later, Lloyd was feeling better and able to keep electrolytes down. Nicki gave him Tylenol for his fever and felt comfortable it would break within the coming hours.

"How's g-pa doing?" Randall asked Nicki after returning from guard duty.

"He's turned the corner. He should be up and moving in the next day or two," she said and continued. "You know Randall, in today's world, without medical facilities and access to nurses or doctors, your grandpa could have easily died. Compare that to several days ago when he could have simply walked into urgent care, been treated, and went home. Hundreds of thousands will die because of lack of medical care. Compared to the masses, we're prepared. It's ironic that we have food, medical, and other critical supplies, and yet we have to be selective in who we help; if anyone."

Randall replied by saying, "Dad had that difficult discussion with me. Mom, do you think the power will ever come back on? If Dad is right, it's going to get a lot worse. I mean people are going to become hungry and desperate. He always talked about it. He always told me two things: First, never give anybody outside of our family any of our food or medical supplies no matter how bad the situation. They'll keep coming back or tell others about your supplies. Soon, you'll have nothing left. Second, people, even friends, will do whatever they have to do to survive, including stealing and killing you for your supplies. Trust no one," Randall said as if looking for confirmation.

"Randall, I never wanted to believe what your dad thought. Being in the Navy, he saw things none of us ever did;

people killing people and people starving. In a way, he was trying to protect us from that by prepping. It's crazy that I started an IV on your grandpa. We had all the necessary supplies. How many people can do that in their house? Your dad thought of everything. By the way, someone should be on guard duty."

"No worries, Mom. Grandma and Benny are watching the front yard from the living room and Cali is watching the back of the house from the kitchen window," Randall stated.

"So, back to your question, Randall. Of course, I want to believe that things will return back to normal, but..." Nicki paused and looked down. "I already had to protect myself, you, and Cali; something that life didn't prepare me for. The reality is that whatever happened to cause the power to go out will only bring out the worst in humankind. It doesn't matter if the power stays out for two weeks, two years, or the lights come on in an hour, our life has been permanently changed. We're changed because of what we saw, and for some of us, what we did. Randall, in the last few days you've been forced to grow up quicker than any other time in your life. I'm proud of you."

"Mom, do you think Dad's okay?" he asked as if trying to change her mind.

Nicki thought before answering and said, "Of all the people in this world, your dad has the best chance to survive and get home. Not to say it won't be a struggle, because it will, but he'll make it. I'm very confident he left when the power went out and realized it wasn't coming back on. He's a smart one."

Nicki was hugging Randall when suddenly Benny started frantically barking. Both of them looked out the window waiting to see Frank when out of nowhere a deer and two fawns leaped across the yard.

With her heart beating fast, Nicki whispered, "I'll never get used to this."

31. NEW FRIENDS - NEW INTRODUCTIONS

THE NEXT MORNING the ladies woke up to a pouch of Mountain House eggs and bacon. While they slept, Oz found several plastic water bottles which he filled at a nearby pond. He filtered and then boiled the water over his portable camp stove, poured the hot water into the pouches and waited five minutes before waking the ladies up. They were hungry and ate the eggs and bacon within minutes.

"I don't even like eggs, but these are incredible," the teenage girl said with excitement.

"My name is Naomi Brennan and this is my daughter Cheyanne," the woman stated.

"My name is Oz McTatey."

Naomi's hands began to shake as she slowly explained, "They, those terrible men, killed my husband. His name was Johannes. When our car quit, we just stayed there. We thought for sure someone would come and help. The man who killed my husband and his brother, I think, pretended to want to help us. They told us that they had food and water, so we walked with them to their camp. When we got there four others appeared. The men immediately separated us and pushed Johannes to his knees. They were questioning him about where we lived and how much food we had. They didn't believe him when he said nothing. They told him that at least he had a beautiful wife, not to mention a gorgeous daughter. That's when I saw Johannes's face turn red. He was getting ready to do something when the tall, fat guy shot him in the head. And then, what they did to me — wait, Cheyanne. What did they do to you? Did he? Did he?"

Cheyanne interrupted with tears in her eyes, "No, Mom. He only touched me. He said he was going to have dinner first and I would be his dessert. Oz killed them before anything happened"

"Thank God. I don't know what I would have done if, if something would have happened," Naomi uttered and then continued. "I have no emotions right now. I can't even cry. I'm numb."

Oz needed to distract Naomi and asked, "What are your plans now?"

"I have no idea. I don't even know where we are," Naomi stated.

Oz replied, "I was just trying to put distance between us and them last night. According to the map, we're on the west side of Highway 341 and about two hours south of Fort Valley. Fort Valley is on my way to Griffin which is a waypoint as I head to Kentucky."

Naomi was shocked when she stated, "You're walking to Kentucky? Are you crazy? Five days into whatever happened to the United States and people are already crazy. You know you probably won't make it?"

Oz interrupted, "I will make it. I will return home to my family."

Naomi made eye contact with Oz and said, "That's not what I meant. I'm sorry. I meant it would be a difficult and treacherous path." She touched his shoulder and continued, "We're from San Diego, California. We were visiting family in Florida and on our way home when whatever happened, happened. So where are we headed? I have no idea now."

Before she could continue her body began shaking and she started crying hysterically. Oz could barely hear her say "They took my husband. They killed my husband. Now Cheyanne is the only family I have, and they almost took her away from me. He's gone. My Johannes is gone."

Cheyanne, also in tears, grabbed her mother and embraced her in a passionate hug. Oz didn't know how to handle the situation. He quickly looked around to make sure no one could hear what was happening. He was worried that the crying mother and daughter would give their position away.

As compassionately as he could, Oz told them, "Ladies, I know you're in pain and you don't understand why what happened to your family happened. I get it, but I need you to be quiet. I don't want to end up in the same position we were in yesterday. This is going to sound bad but there will be a time to grieve, but it's not now."

The ladies looked at Oz with red eyes but understood what he said. While he had their attention Oz made a quick, on the spot decision, and that decision was they had to travel with him. Though he couldn't guarantee their safety, he would try. He trusted them though it went against everything he taught his family. They were simply an innocent mother and daughter. He knew Nicki would welcome them into their house — if they made it. Oz committed to helping others along his journey, if possible, but he would not be inviting others to his house. He didn't have food or supplies for additional people beyond his family, but he had personally witnessed what Naomi and Cheyanne went through. He had a personal bond with them.

Oz looked at the ladies with worried eyes and told them, "I want you to travel with me. I will do my best to protect you and you're both welcome at our home. My wife's name is Nicki and we have three children — BJ, Cali, and Randall. They're waiting for me. We have food and supplies, but being open and honest, you will have to earn your keep. I can't promise you I will get you home to California, but you're more than welcome at our house."

Without thinking, the ladies embraced Oz in a hug and in unison said, "Thank you."

"Now," Oz said. "What skills do you have? Can you fire a handgun? Rifle? Have you ever camped before? Do you know how to read a map? Tell me what you can do."

While looking at her mom, Cheyanne said, "I'm on the high school archery team. I'm ranked in the top 50 in the state of California."

"Outstanding. We'll make it a priority to get you a bow with arrows," Oz said unassumingly.

Though Oz knew Cheyanne's skill would be a great addition to the group, he could not rely on her, nor would he want her to take the life of another individual. One day he knew she would have to kill someone, but for now he was hoping he could rely on her to hunt for food.

Naomi smiled at Oz before telling him, "I'm a Chief Petty Officer stationed in San Diego. I'm a Master at Arms."

"Can you please show me your military ID card?" Oz said.

Naomi reached into her back pocket and pulled out a driver's license, bank card, and military ID. She handed Oz the ID and with intent eyes, Oz compared the picture on the ID to that of the woman standing in front of him. With a big sigh of relief, and without a word, Oz reached into his Bug Out Bag and took out the rifle forend assembly and action. He handed them to Naomi who instinctively locked the two pieces together.

"Ruger PC Carbine 9mm with an Israeli MepPro reticle. Read about these rifles but never shot one. Not a problem though. As long as the MepPro is sighted in, I'm good," she said as she cleared the weapon and checked for functionality.

"Magazines, please," she said while holding her hands out.

Oz reached into the Bug Out Bag and handed her four Glock magazines fully loaded.

"A Ruger that takes Glock magazines?" she said with a puzzled look.

"Yes ma'am," Oz said.

In a very fluid motion, she inserted a magazine, pulled the bolt handle to load a round, and then double checked to make sure the safety was on and again pulled the bolt handle to visually check and ensure a round was loaded. She slung the rifle over her shoulders.

"Now, we need to get both of you Bug Out Bags and a bow with arrows for Cheyanne," Oz finished.

Both girls listened to Oz as he explained his plans. It was time to set out on the day's journey.

32. SECURING THE HOUSE

IT HAD BEEN A ROUGH NIGHT for Randall. He and Benny had pulled guard duty all night. It seemed as if even Benny was aware the world had changed overnight. He barked most of the night keeping Randall on edge, yet Randall couldn't figure out or see why Benny was being so aggressive. Nevertheless, he was glad Benny was by his side.

"Good morning, Grandpa," Randall said as his grandpa approached.

"Morning, Randall. Thank you for staying up all night. I'm back to my old self so I'll work with your mom and Cali and we'll come up with a schedule that involves the four of us. We need a rotation so you're not always on nights. We all need to pull our weight," Grandpa said.

"I'm going to bed. Benny either heard or saw something last night but I couldn't figure out what he was barking at," Randall said. He then told his grandpa, "We really need to get the food from the garage and shed into the house. It's something Mom, Cali, and I were supposed to do several days ago but, well, things happened."

His Grandpa hugged him and told him to go to bed.

Lloyd peered out the window and noticed how beautiful and calm the morning was. It was peaceful. As a Vietnam veteran, he had experienced many quiet, peaceful mornings that ended up in gunfire and death. The difference was he never thought it would happen on U.S. soil.

The previous evening, Nicki shared with him the actions and behaviors of the men she encountered and the radical behavior of her neighbor. Lloyd knew that he would have to be the one to secure the property and house until Oz returned.

Nicki approached Lloyd who appeared to be going somewhere. He was caught off guard when she said, "Lloyd, Randall, Cali, and I have a rule. You can't go anywhere without a buddy. And you have to tell someone where you're going. So where are you going?" she finished.

"Headed to the garage. Oz and I made some perimeter security devices several years ago. I thought I'd go find and set them up tonight. It's not much but they'll at least give us a heads-up," Lloyd said.

"Ok, but the buddy system. Benny is your buddy while you're outside. When he barks, you listen and take a defensive position until clear. Second rule, you go nowhere without a handgun at a minimum and a radio for communication," Nicki said before handing him a Springfield XDM 9mm handgun and a Baofeng radio with a headset.

"Here's your holster and four extra magazines. Remember how to shoot one?" Nicki smirked.

"Smart ass," Lloyd said. Lloyd placed the holster on his belt and inserted a fully loaded magazine into the handgun. "Let's go, Benny," Lloyd said.

It took some time to find the perimeter security devices, but Lloyd smiled when he saw them. Oz had purchased thirty hand grenade heads with springs and pins.

In the military world, the grenade head is the triggering mechanism for the grenade. When the grenade pin is pulled and the spoon separates, a spring is released which generates energy that allows a pin to make contact with a primer causing the grenade to explode and fragment. In the prepper world, the grenade head could be used with a shotgun primer to create a perimeter signaling system or tripwire system.

Lloyd made sure all devices were free of debris and the spring oiled before testing it. He found the fishing line and cotter pins and set them on the workbench. His plan was to set up all thirty of the security devices tonight.

"Dark enough," Lloyd said before yelling for his daughter-in-law. "Nicki, I'm going out alone. I need to get these perimeter security devices set. It will take at least two hours."

"Randall and I will provide cover and they're called tripwires," Nicki said before yelling for Randall.

"Randall, get your ghillie suit on. We need to provide cover for Grandpa. Cali will watch the back," she said.

Ten minutes later Randall and Nicki appeared in ghillie suits.

"Let me guess. Another one of your dad's ideas?" Grandpa asked Randall.

"Absolutely, an additional insurance policy so we're not seen," Randall said with a smile.

"Weapons check," Nicki said abruptly.

Randall, Cali, and Grandpa gave the thumbs-up sign.

Nicki and Randall headed in opposite directions on the property followed by Lloyd who cautiously made his way into the woods near the drive.

"Time to set up the first tripwire," he said silently. He nailed the grenade head to a tree about one to two feet above the ground. He reset the spring and inserted a cotter pin to hold the spring in place. He placed a 12-gauge primer in the modified hole that originally contained the grenade primer. He tied fishing line through the loop on the cotter pin and ran the line to a nearby tree where he tapped another nail into the tree about one to two feet above the ground. He cut the fishing line, pulled it taut, and tied it off on the nail in the tree.

"Process complete. Tripwire one complete," Lloyd said to himself. "Only twenty-nine more left."

Before setting up the next tripwire, he would stop and listen to make sure the area was clear. Except for Nicki and Randall, he knew he should be alone. After all thirty tripwires were set up, he entered the house from the back porch door.

"Are Nicki and Randall here?" Lloyd asked Connie who had also been standing guard duty with Cali from inside the house.

"They were with you. They must still be outside," Connie said.

"Damn it," Lloyd said. "We had a plan, but we never talked about how I would let them know when I was finished."

Several hours later, Randall, and eventually Nicki, came back to the house.

"About time. I've been done for several hours," Lloyd said.

"Seriously?" Randall said while looking at Nicki.

"Our communication skills will get better and better as time goes on. Nothing to worry about. While we're in our ghillie suits, why don't we move the food from the shed and garage into the house?" Nicki asked.

With a worried look, Randall jumped in and said, "It has to be done. The sooner the better. No telling when Frank and his family will be hungry."

"Perfect," said Nicki. "We'll do it later tonight around 2:30 or 3:00 a.m. We need to be cautious," Nicki finished.

Nicki's plan for moving the food was simple. Randall was stronger than Nicki and would be given the task of moving the food from the shed to the house. Not only was he stronger, but he would be faster. Youth and strength had its advantages and with the heavy five-gallon sealed buckets of food, he would need both. Cali knew she needed to help but hadn't been asked.

"I'll help too," Cali volunteered. "I can carry the smaller stuff."

Nicki would set up a protective position outside while Lloyd would man the front door. If either Nicki, Cali, or Randall needed help, he would be available. They had a plan.

33. HUNGRY NEIGHBORS

FRANK COULDN'T STAND BY as he listened to his son constantly whining because they were out of food. He was frustrated that he had seen Oz's Suburban pass his house several times and each time he saw different people being taken to their house. It was as if Oz and Nicki had invited the entire world to their house, yet he and his family were not. As if that was not enough, he hadn't seen Veronica, his wife, in six days, and the constant wonder of what happened to her ate away at him.

He tried several times to walk into town, but stores had already been looted and cleaned out; not to mention the walk took three hours each way. Though Frank thought of himself as strong and confident, in one instance he hid as he watched at what appeared to be a gang of some type break into and steal supplies from a preacher's house. The gang placed the preacher and his wife belly first on the front yard grass and stripped the couple of their clothes, all while laughing as if it was some sort of game. They loaded their van with as much as it would hold, including food, and left the couple for dead or alive as fate would have.

As Frank watched what had just happened, his concern was not for the couple, but how he could become a part of that gang. After all, that's what he had known for most of his life; at least until he was found guilty of second-degree murder and served seventeen years in prison.

Several days later Frank awoke from a nightmare when his thoughts came immediately back to Oz's house. He somehow knew Oz and his family had supplies and he was going to find out one way or another what they had.

As best Frank could tell, it was around 3:00 a.m. and he was wide awake. He stepped out onto his back porch looking toward Oz's house.

"It's time," he thought to himself.

He walked back into the house, got dressed, and cautiously walked to the tree line. His plan was to walk ten feet inside the tree line to make sure he wasn't seen. Even though he was confident the McTateys were sleeping, he wasn't taking any chances. Frank entered the tree line and quickly realized he wasn't as silent as he should be. About every five paces he would step on a branch or twig and knew if someone was outside, he would be heard.

He slowed his pace and continued. About five minutes later he stopped and tried to peer through the trees. It was dark, and with no moonlight to help, he had to take his best guess. Frank knew that Oz's shed was to the south of his house surrounded by forest. He felt confident he could get in the shed, steal whatever was in it, and get back to his house without being heard or caught.

As Frank took a step forward, he heard a loud noise and fell to the ground. He had no idea what had just happened. He remembered seeing a small flash and then heard ringing in his ear. Even though his vision was fine, he was unable to hear.

34. PROTECTING THE FAMILY

NICKI IMMEDIATELY FROZE when she heard the tripwire go off. She motioned for Randall and Cali to take cover. Randall and Cali dropped the food they were carrying and hid behind the engine block on the Suburban just as Nicki had taught them.

Lloyd immediately grabbed the night vision monocular and scanned the area. It didn't take long for him to see an elongated figure on the ground. Whatever, or whoever it was, was clearly not an animal. As he continued to watch the object, he saw it place what appeared to be two hands on the ground and lift itself up. Though he didn't have a night vision scope, Lloyd knew the general direction of the person and fired two, three round bursts at whoever was trespassing on their property. He brought the monocular back to his eye to see the figure hobbling. It appeared as if he had shot them in the left leg. They were going away from their property, albeit at a slow pace.

"That will teach them," Lloyd said to himself. Lloyd walked over to Nicki and Randall and whispered, "Whoever it was is gone. We need to finish getting the food in the house. It's only going to get worse. Randall, your mom and I will continue to keep watch. Nothing, I mean absolutely nothing, will hurt you and Cali."

Shaken by what just happened, Randall and Cali both understood the importance of getting the food inside, and, although scared, they picked up the pace and carried the food into the house.

Frank was in pain and going into shock. He had just been shot twice and had to limp home. His pain became more intense when he had to climb the stairs to his porch before entering his house. Once inside the house, he immediately went to his bedroom and threw himself on his bed. He had no idea how much blood he had lost, and to make matters worse he didn't have first aid supplies or pain medication.

For several hours Frank tried to live with the pain. He did everything he could from not moving, applying ice, and even taking Tylenol, but it didn't work. The pain was unbearable.

"Buzz!" Frank yelled. "Get in here."

Without hesitation, Buzz came running to his dad's side.

"Buzz, I need you to go to Oz's house. Nicki is a nurse. Tell her I need help." Frank thought for a second and realized he was in a very awkward position. Several days ago, he had tried to knock Oz's front door down and even threatened Nicki. Tonight, he trespassed on their property, was caught, and shot. And now, he was asking for help from the woman whose life he terrorized.

"The witch is a nurse. She took an oath. She'll help no matter what," he said to himself.

Without questioning his father, Buzz got dressed and headed down the drive to Oz and Nicki's house.

Camden and Cali had finished moving the food from both
the garage and shed when Lloyd volunteered to take the
security watch for the remained of the night. He couldn't
sleep. He had just shot a person. Though he was confident
it was for the right reasons, it still didn't feel right. Lloyd
peered through the monocular and noticed someone
walking down the drive.

"This night keeps getting better," he said to himself before
waking Nicki. "Nicki, we have someone walking down the
drive," Lloyd said as he gently woke her up.

Lloyd went back to the main window and now saw the
person about 100 feet from the door. He quickly opened the
door and immediately snapped his rifle up to his shoulder.

"Freeze or I'll shoot," Lloyd yelled in his best military drill
instructor voice.

"Sir, please don't shoot. My dad needs help. He's been shot.
He told me to come get Nicki to help."

Confused, Lloyd barked back, "Who are you and where are
you coming from?"

"My name is Buzz and we're your neighbors at the end of
the drive. My dad told me to come get Ms. Nicki. My dad is
hurt and says he needs help."

Nicki was standing behind Lloyd and heard the
conversation. "Buzz, give me a minute," Nicki said.

Nicki needed time to think. As a nurse, she was trained to
save lives, but she was conflicted. This was the man who
tried to break into her house, and had she not shown up,

may have killed her daughter and son. Then he has the gall to trespass on their property, probably to either hurt them or steal their food, got caught, shot, and now is asking for help. This was not about being a nurse. This was about being a parent who protects her family come hell or high water. It went against everything she was trained to do, but she had made up her mind.

She turned to Buzz and said, "Buzz, tell your dad I'm not coming. And Buzz, if anything happens and you're alone, you're scared, someone tries to hurt you, you're welcome at our house. We'll take care of you."

That night, at that moment, Nicki vowed to make sure Buzz always had food and water.

35. LOOKING FOR HELP

TWO DAYS LATER OZ, Naomi, and Cheyanne were camping outside of Griffin, Georgia. Up to this point, the journey had been slow but challenging. Water was plentiful due to the numerous streams and ponds they passed but food was now at a critical point. Oz had brought enough freeze-dried meals and energy bars to last him two weeks but with Naomi and Cheyanne traveling with him, they would need to stock up soon.

Oz also needed to find Naomi and Cheyanne backpacks as well as a bow and arrows for Cheyanne. The sooner the better. They agreed that it would be best to approach a farmhouse and avoid the town. So far, the group avoided any type of confrontation and that's the way they hoped it would remain.

Naomi returned to Oz and Cheyanne after a scouting mission and told them about a farmhouse two miles from their present location. Naomi explained that it was a family of six, and even though they were armed, she felt they would be approachable.

After more discussion, and against Oz's wishes, they agreed it would be Naomi who would approach the family. Once she made contact and knew it was safe, she would signal to Oz and Cheyanne to come out of hiding.

Twenty minutes later the trio hid on the outskirts of the farmhouse and before Naomi left, she whispered in Oz 's ear, "Set up a sniper position. I'm sure everything will be fine, but if it's not, do everything you can to get me out of there. I will not leave Cheyanne alone."

Oz motioned for Cheyanne to take cover as he moved to a position that provided a clear view of the farmhouse, and yet allowed him to be hidden. Naomi slowly turned and headed toward the farm. She exited the tree line and began walking slowly down the driveway with her hands in the air. It didn't take long for a young boy, who looked to be about seven years old, yell in a horrific scream. Moments later, two men exited the house with shotguns aimed at Naomi.

"Don't shoot. I'm not armed!" Naomi shouted.

"Get off of our property now!" one of the young men yelled.

"Can I talk to your father first? Please?" Naomi responded.

"How do you know we have a father?" the young man asked and continued. "Have you been spying on us?"

Now scared, Naomi responded, "No. I have not been spying on you. You look too young to be a father, no offense, so I assumed your father might be here."

Oz watched in disbelief as he saw what appeared to be a man sneaking up on Naomi and, before she could react, placed the barrel of a shotgun to the back of her head.

"Hands up or you'll meet my friend, double ought buckshot," a voice said.

Naomi quickly placed both hands in the air and in a low voice said, "Please don't shot. I'm only looking for food. I don't have much, but I can trade with you."

Without hesitating, the voice said, "Move forward to the house. You move your hands one bit and you're dead."

Naomi did as requested and was soon standing on the front porch of the house. "Tiny, search her," the voice commanded.

A tall, out of shape man approached her and began patting her down. He was bald and Naomi noticed patches of hair as if he was desperately trying to grow a beard. The man placed his hands on Naomi's head and checked her hair before sliding his hands down to her side.

He slowly rolled his hands around to her front chest area when Naomi gave a sharp look and said, "Careful, my friend. There's always pain in things that give you pleasure. These are not for your pleasure."

The man gave a quick snort and then continued to pat her legs intentionally avoiding her inner thighs.

"All good?" Naomi snapped.

The man shook his head up and down. Naomi slowly turned and was now able to see the face that belonged to the voice who held the gun to her back. It was a young woman, most likely in her early twenties. She had long dark hair and green eyes. Her face was weathered, but it appeared as if she was in pretty good physical condition.

"Now, I'll ask you one more time. What are you doing on our property?" the woman demanded before she was interrupted by a man exiting the front porch door.

"Misty, don't treat our guest that way," he said as he admonished her. "My name is Wallace, and as you heard that's my daughter, Misty. That's my son Tiny, and the other man is my son Burt. Now that you know who we are, who are you and how can we help?"

"My name is Naomi and I only want to trade with you. I have a long walk ahead of me and need food. I don't have much to trade, but anything you could do would be appreciated."

"Lady, we don't need nothing. We've been living off the land for five generations."

Naomi questioned the man, "But the power went out. Did you notice that? My friend thinks it will never come back on."

Wallace responded, "Ma'am, we don't have electricity. Never have. Life for us will continue on just as it has my whole life. We live off the land and because we respect it; it produces and provides for all our needs."

"Sir, p-please" Naomi stuttered. "Please, I need food."

Wallace put his hand on Naomi's shoulder, looked her square in the eyes and said, "You mean 'we' need food, don't you?"

Naomi looked confused when she saw Cheyanne and Oz walking down the drive only to be followed by another man with a shotgun to their backs.

"That's my son, Christian," Wallace said with a smile and very methodically continued. "We've, my family to be specific, have been hunting these parts for almost a century. You develop an instinct when something's not right, and we knew something was not right."

As Oz and Cheyanne approached, Naomi felt despair and for the second time in as many days felt hopeless. The thought of seeing her daughter hurt or even killed was the only thing she thought of.

"Don't fret, young lady," Wallace said.

"You and your husband and daughter can spend the night in the barn and we'll feed you. One meal, one night. Then you're gone. Do you understand?" he finished.

Naomi, Cheyanne, and Oz were confused by his words, but shook their head at the same time acknowledging his statement. Christian quickly patted down Cheyanne and Oz and placed their gear on the ground for his father to see.

Without looking at the gear, Wallace said, "You'll get your gear back in the morning. For now, it's time to eat," and motioned for them to enter the house.

Over the next four hours, Wallace shared his family story with the guests and gave them useful information about living off the land during their travels. He gave them quick lessons on plant identification, how to quickly determine what direction they were heading, tips on how to better use the land to camouflage themselves, how to make snare traps, and how to set up perimeter alarms using only what could be found using Mother Nature. It was a good and informative night for Oz. Being exhausted, and with their belly's full, the three meandered to the barn for a good night's sleep.

As Oz woke up the next morning, he was greeted by Wallace who said, "It's time you hit the road. I've packed a few items that might help."

Oz thanked Wallace and with one eye still shut, investigated the bag. There was what appeared to be a package of some type of jerky, dehydrated vegetables, several fresh vegetables, a quart jar that looked like it contained a stew, and a clear pint size mason jar with a clear liquid in it.

"You wouldn't by chance have a couple of backpacks or bow and arrows that I could trade for?" Oz asked Wallace.

Wallace rubbed his chin for a second before saying, "As ironic as this is going to sound, I'll tell you we make our own bows but buy the arrows. I believe we have a longbow I can give you. No need to trade. As I said before, we have everything we need here."

Wallace turned and disappeared into the house. Several minutes later, Oz woke Naomi and Cheyanne up.

Wallace reappeared with a longbow in one hand and a quiver with six arrows in another.

"Who is this for?" Wallace asked.

With sleepy eyes, Cheyanne excitedly said, "For me, sir? At least I think it is."

Oz shook his head up and down and, with great pride, Wallace handed her the bow and arrows.

"The bow is handmade from the earth and will serve you well, young lady. Misty made it," Wallace said before turning to Oz. "At the junction of Highway 92 and Cowan Road, about twenty miles northwest of here is a small outdoors shop called Ed Needles Pawn Shop. Ask for, who else then, Ed. Ed is my cousin. Tell Ed I sent you and you should be able to trade for some of those other things you asked me for."

"How can we ever repay you?" Oz asked Wallace.

"Survive. That's how you repay me; by surviving. And be open-minded that there are still good people in this world," Wallace said as he turned to walk back in the house. With one last piece of advice, Wallace stopped and told the group, "By the way, Ed loves moonshine."

The group dressed, packed, and waved a final farewell to Wallace and his family before hitting the road.

"How are you doing, Naomi," Oz asked as they walked.

"Numb. Still numb. It hasn't hit me yet. I lost my husband, and yesterday someone pointed a loaded shotgun at me," she responded as she brushed her hands through her hair before continuing. "Oz, I can't cry. I can't cry for my husband or even what happened to me. It's like my body shut down. No emotions. I feel nothing."

"It's for the better, Naomi. Who knows what we'll encounter as we move north. I need you focused. We need our bodies to stay alert and ready to act. It's the only way we'll be safe. Once we get to my house, there will be time to rest. Time to properly say goodbye. Time to digest what happened," Oz said as his eyes moved from Naomi to the ground.

"It should take us no more than fourteen hours to walk to Atlanta, but hopefully we can get you and Cheyanne a Bug Out Bag and pick up a few more supplies at Ed's," Oz said. They turned and waved one last goodbye to Wallace and his family before continuing into the cover of the forest.

36. PROTECTING ONE

EVERY DAY, IN THE EARLY MORNING, Nicki would sneak out and put a day's worth of water and food rations on Frank's porch. She wanted to make sure Buzz had food and even provided enough for Frank. She was getting pretty good at knowing Buzz's habits, and around 10:00 a.m. she would hide in the tree line watching to make sure she saw Buzz open the back porch sliding glass door and get the food and water.

Her hope was to get a glance of Buzz and do a quick visual check, to the best of her ability, to make sure he was physically healthy and not injured. It pained Nicki to know that Buzz was the only caregiver Frank had. She couldn't imagine what Buzz was going through, but she would not put her life or that of her family in danger to help a man who would kill given the chance.

Frank looked at his two wounds. They were getting worse and he was now bedridden. The areas surrounding the wounds were green and cloudy in color and swollen. There was a rotting smell emanating from his leg. He had a fever of 101 degrees Fahrenheit and the area near the wound was hot to the touch.

Overall, he was feeling malaise and tired; he just wanted to sleep. As each day went by, he experienced more and more pain and was losing functionality in his left leg. Frank knew that he had made a mistake. He let his ravenousness behavior get the best of him and now it would cost him his life; but he had no regrets. His last words were, "That cold witch. She'll get hers," and then he went to sleep never to wake up again.

Nicki was on guard duty when she saw Buzz walking down the driveway. She wanted to check on him but knew the rule: always go in pairs of two and stay in constant communication.

She grabbed Randall and told him to gear up. Once geared up, Randall went out the back door and cautiously headed into the tree line. Nicki gave him a three-minute head start.

Lloyd took a position at the front door and scanned the property with his binoculars. "Looks clear," Lloyd said.

Nicki went out the front door and began walking down the drive, constantly scanning her environment.

As she approached Buzz, she said, "Hi, Buzz. How are you doing?"

He began to cry and said, "Nicki, my dad's not moving. I can't wake him up."

Through her radio headset she called Lloyd and said "Lloyd, I'm sending Buzz in with you. Have Connie clean him up and make sure he gets fed."

"10-4," she heard over the radio.

"Randall and I are headed over to Frank's house. We need to know his status if you understand what I'm saying." Nicki said.

"10-4," Lloyd responded.

Without having to say a word, she saw Randall stepping over several tripwires headed in the direction of Frank's house. Nicki and Randall walked parallel to one another; separated by thirty feet.

After crossing the field between Frank's and the McTatey property, they approached the porch. Nicki whispered to Randall, "Keep your guard up. You've never cleared a house so make sure you don't point your gun at me. Watch the corners and dark rooms. We'll go slow. Be as quiet as you can."

Nicki and Oz trained yearly at Front Sight in Pahrump, Nevada. They trained every fall with handguns, and in the spring would rotate shotgun and rifle training. Part of the training was house clearing and hostage scenarios. Though it wasn't much experience, it was at least some. Nicki's concern was Randall. He had no formal weapons or tactical training whatsoever. His only training had been the real life experience he gained during the last few weeks when the world went to hell.

Nicki slowly opened the back sliding glass door and entered the house. Randall was right behind her with his handgun pointed down the hallway. Nicki walked slowly around the corner clearing the living room. She gave Randall a thumbs-up sign. Nicki walked in front of Randall and slowly cleared the remaining two bedrooms before finding Frank's room. With her gun trained on Frank, she slowly reached for his wrist, checked his pulse, and confirmed he was dead.

"Randall," Nicki said. "Check the rest of the house for anything we can use. I assume he has no guns. If he did, he would have tried to kill us."

Not finding anything useful, they walked back home. When Nicki saw Buzz, she gave him a big hug and began to cry.

37. THE TRADE

WALKING AT A GOOD PACE, Oz, Naomi, and Cheyanne arrived at the crossroads of Highway 92 and Cowan Road. The trio used a brick wall for cover which also allowed visibility to the store. Oz could see a sign that was barely legible but had the words "Ed Needles Pawn Shop" in faint blue paint. The building itself was rundown, and it appeared that the small porch on the front of the building was leaning to one side. Stacked bricks were placed at the front of the porch and served as stairs up to the main entrance.

The three agreed that Oz would approach the pawn shop while Naomi and Cheyanne stayed behind the brick wall serving as lookouts and backups if Oz ended up in trouble.

With his Bug Out Bag strapped to his back, Oz scanned the area for any movement. Once satisfied that it was safe, he walked across the street and knocked on the pawn shop door. No answer. He went to peer through the window only to find the view had been blocked by windows replaced with wood. As much as he hated to, he knew he had to walk around, behind the building, in hopes of finding Ed. He signaled to Naomi and Cheyanne that he was walking behind the building and to stay where they were.

Oz slowly rounded the corner of the building and saw a small rundown house. At first glance, he thought it was empty, but upon further inspection, he saw signs that someone had recently been there. He quickly scanned his surroundings again and then slowly proceeded to what was possibly the front door. He was now within ten feet of the door when he heard a loud *snap* followed by a searing pain in his left foot. He looked down only to discover he had stepped in a coil spring trap that had tripped and wrapped around his ankle. He held his breath and contained his screams. He was in pain, but the last thing he wanted was to attract unwanted attention. He sat down and with all his strength tried to draw the two heavy jaws apart. He knew he had to get out of the trap and back to the girls as quickly as he could, but was unable to free himself.

As he tried a second time to free himself, he heard a woman's voice say, "Need some help?"

He quickly turned around to see a woman dressed in camouflage clothing holding a double-barreled shotgun in one hand and a small pry bar in the other.

"Please," Oz said to the woman.

"I was just kidding. You're trespassing on my property and you expect me to help you?"

"I'm sorry," Oz said, "We were looking for Ed Needles."

"You'll have to do better than that. You were going to break in and steal my stuff. Maybe you were going to kill me, too. Weren't you?" she said.

"No, ma'am," Oz continued. "I was told by Wallace to ask for Ed. He said Ed might have a few things we need that we could trade for," Oz said.

The woman looked puzzled and asked, "How do you know Wallace?"

"We spent the night in his barn last night. We stumbled upon his house on our journey northward," Oz answered.

"Stay still," the woman said as she took the pry bar and freed Oz from the trap.

Oz rubbed his ankle and though it hurt he didn't feel any broken bones. His combat boots helped to minimize the damage the trap could have truly caused.

"Can you stand?" the woman asked reaching for Oz's hand.

Oz grabbed her hand and stood with the balance of his weight on his right leg.

"Looks like you'll be hobbling around for a while," she laughed.

Oz shot her a searing look and did his best to keep his balance.

"Now, what stuff are you looking for and what do you have to trade? By the way, my name is Ed," she said.

"I should have known," Oz said and continued. "We need a couple of small backpacks, knives, first aid supplies, a couple sets of clothes. And as to what I have to trade, I have silver, a few 9mm bullets, one Glock magazine, and a pint of moonshine."

"The only thing worth value is the moonshine, but I'm sure I can think of other things," Ed said as she pointed to the back entrance.

Oz hobbled into the back entrance of the shop and found it to be disorganized, dirty, and not many supplies to choose from. Most of the supplies appeared to be old, broken, or not practical for what Oz needed. However, one corner of the store had a sign that read 'Emergency Supplies'. Oz headed toward the emergency supplies while Ed stepped away for several minutes and returned with two small backpacks.

"Will these do?" she asked.

"Perfect," said Oz.

As Oz walked around, he picked up several packages of strike-anywhere matches, two basic first aid kits, several t-shirts which he found on a discounted rack, 100 feet of 550 paracord, two emergency blankets, some fishing line, hooks, weights, and bobbers, some hand sanitizer, several boxes of feminine products, four candles, a small bottle of bleach, a jar of Vaseline, and a bag of cotton balls. He placed the items on a counter and took out a Glock magazine with seventeen rounds, a pint of moonshine, and five dollars in pre-1964 silver coins.

Ed grabbed the fully loaded Glock magazine and a pint of moonshine and set it aside. "What else do you have," she said.

"That's it. All I have," Oz said.

"Well, it's not enough," Ed said.

Oz thought for a minute and then said, "Ok, what can I get for the Glock magazine and moonshine?"

Ed reached under the counter and pulled out a four-inch Cold Steel® knife. "Let's make a deal," Ed said. "I'll give you all the supplies on the counter plus this knife in exchange for the Glock magazine and ammunition, the pint of moonshine, and…"

Ed stopped for a minute when Oz saw her eyes slowly scan his body from his head to his toes. Feeling uncomfortable Oz asked, "You mean, sex?"

Ed shook her head up and down. "You get what you want and I get what I want," she exclaimed.

For the first time, Oz looked intently at Ed. She had long blonde hair, hazel eyes, a thin frame, and rather large breasts. As best Oz could tell, she was aged beyond her years but was still attractive. Her hands appeared rough with several calluses which could be easily seen.

"Hard worker," Oz thought to himself.

Oz looked at the gear on the counter and knew some of it could make the difference between life and death. He thought of Nicki and the vows they had taken. He wanted to walk out the door but he was at a crossroads and knew he couldn't do that without affecting Naomi and Cheyanne. This was not about him. As a Christian he knew what he was being asked to do was a sin but he had also sworn to himself to protect the two women in his care. He knew, most likely, he would not be forgiven but had confidence Nicki would tell him to do whatever it took to make it home. He closed his eyes and without verbally saying the words he prayed, "God, please guide me now in my moment of need."

He walked over to the front window, looked out, and saw Naomi's head occasional peak out from the side of the brick wall. Naomi and Cheyanne were now Oz's responsibility and he needed to give them every survival advantage possible.

Oz walked back to Ed and said, "What you're asking me to do breaks the covenants that guide my life. It is true, I am weak, but I will honor my father. I am sorry. No deal."

Ed sighed and then looked down at her breast and then up at Oz before saying, "Your loss but I have to respect a man who truly loves his wife. I hope one day I know what that feels like. Take it all. It won't help me."

Oz opened the front door of the shop, scanned the street in front of him, and walked to where Naomi and Cheyanne were. He handed each of them a backpack and the supplies he had traded for.

He took a moment to reflect and realized that he felt closer to God than he had in years. He had made the right decision.

"So, what took so long?" Naomi asked with an inquisitive look.

"Trading took a little longer than I thought. She was a tough negotiator," Oz said as he smiled.

"Wait a minute. He's a she?" Naomi said.

"Yep. He's a she," Oz replied.

"What exactly did you trade, Oz?" Naomi said with a stern voice.

"Let's just say that she was very creative," Oz said.

"Ok then. No more questions," Naomi quipped.

While the girls prepared the packs, Oz pulled the Cold Steel knife out of his pocket and handed it to Cheyanne.

"Compliments of Ed," he said.

Cheyanne studied the knife and quickly figured out how to open, release the lock, and close the blade.

"Thanks," she said as she put it in her front pocket.

"Onward to Atlanta," Oz said as the group began the day's long hike.

38. ADAPTING TO A NEW WORLD

CALI WAS HAVING TROUBLE ADAPTING to the new world. She missed her friends. She missed her classes and professors. She missed the convenience of the university dining hall. She missed being able to jump in the car and drive anywhere she wanted. She loved her family and knew home was the right place, but it seemed like yesterday she was living in a completely different world.

Now, she was carrying a gun everywhere she went. She had to wear a bulletproof vest and a Personnel Armor System for Ground Troops (PASGT) military helmet. She had to pull guard duty every single day. She wasn't allowed to go outside unless she went with another person. For the first time in her life, she had to eat everything on her plate because food was now more valuable than gold. She thought for a moment and knew she had made the right decision, to come home and not stay at the university. Her family was the most important thing to her, especially when it came to Randall. He was her younger brother and had always been there for her. They were two peas in a pod and always knew they could count on each other.

"Randall," Cali said. "Don't you wish you would have listened to Dad more?"

"What was his Plan B?" Cali asked.

"Did you see the library he created of prepper and survival books downstairs? He has books, magazines, printouts, and posters of everything we need to know. Cali, he has books on plant identification, perimeter security, tactical security, food preservation, gardening, ammunition re-loading, gunsmithing, first aid, natural medications, prepping, radio communications, and survival. It's ironic."

"What's ironic?" Cali said.

"That we go to school to learn new things. To learn what I guess you would call life skills, yet we're going to struggle to do the simplest of things like start a fire, hunt animals, cook food, and the toughest one, learn to live without electricity," Randall lamented.

Cali thought about what her brother just said and asked, "What book do you recommend I start with? I'm completely clueless when it comes to survival and most definitely don't have the right skills. The sooner I get started the better."

"There's an outstanding book called *The Prepper's Handbook* by Zion Prepper. It gives you a great overview of preparedness and really describes the exact situation we're in and what we need to be doing. It's the first book Dad read," Randall said.

"Okay, I'll start with that book," Cali said.

Randall turned to leave the room when Cali said, "Randall, I need you to review the handgun emergency action drills and reload procedures with me. I need to know everything there is to know about my handgun. Mom said it is never to leave my side. I need to be able to defend our family. I need to be able to defend you."

For the next two hours, Randall and Cali reviewed the handgun emergency action drills including, Type I (failure to fire), Type II (stove pipe or failure to eject), Type III (double feed), emergency reloads, and tactical reloads. It was good practice for Randall and Cali.

Unnoticed by the kids, Nicki watched them as they adapted to the new world. She was elated to see them practicing these new and completely unique skills.

"Proud of them. Those exercises could one day save their life," she thought to herself.

39. AMBUSHED

OZ CONVINCED THE LADIES to head north for several hours and then they would turn west. Going west of Atlanta was the best option even though it added an additional day to their trip. The map showed by heading west they would pass several small country cities where they could hopefully restock their food supply.

Oz estimated by taking a more westward direction that it would take about forty-eight hours to walk from Griffin to Adairsville, Georgia. Their route would keep them somewhat safe and invisible as they would be traveling near several large forests that they could use for camping and cover if needed.

After walking for eighteen hours straight, the group needed to rest. They had made good time, but it came at a cost—energy, hunger, and thirst. It was time to set up camp. They chose a spot about 100 yards into the forest. The plan was to eat the rest of the remaining food and hope that within the next day or two they would be able to replenish their supply.

Naomi began to open a Mountain House food pouch when she thought she saw motion. She stopped what she was doing and put her hand on Oz's shoulder while putting her finger to her mouth to signal for silence. She put two fingers to her eyes and pointed indicating that she saw movement in the forest. They both began scanning the immediate area.

Then, the sound of gun fire was heard. The shot rang loud and true. It hit Oz center mass. Oz went to instinctively grab his chest when a second shot rang out. Oz fell to the ground looking up at the night sky. Cheyanne didn't move due to fear while Naomi slowly approached Oz from behind cover. She looked at Oz and then peered up looking for movement or a muzzle flash. She stared into the night but didn't see anything. She slowly crawled the final five feet and grabbed his pant leg. With all her strength she slowly pulled Oz behind a tree. She looked at his chest to check for movement and then placed two fingers on his wrist feeling for a pulse.

"He's alive," she said to herself. She quickly looked for a bullet entrance or exit wound. Nothing. No blood. No wounds. "That's weird," she said.

Then it donned on her. She took off his jacket only to find Oz wearing a Level IV tactical vest. He was unconscious but not dead. Before she could render first aid, she needed to disable the shooter or shooters. Reaching on the ground around her, Naomi found a decent size stick and crawled back to Cheyanne.

"Cheyanne," Naomi whispered. "You need to listen to me and do exactly as I say. Shake your head up and down if you understand."

As if slowly coming out of a coma, Cheyanne shook her head up and down.

"Good," Naomi said and continued. "When I start to crawl to that big tree to your right, I want you to count to thirty and then throw the stick to your left. It will take me about twenty seconds to crawl to the tree and ready my rifle. Are you ready?"

Cheyanne shook her head "yes" when her mother whispered in her ear, "Start counting."

Naomi crawled about twenty feet and then crouched behind a large pecan tree. She slowly raised her body with both knees resting on the ground. She leveled her rifle on her shoulder and waited for Cheyanne to throw the stick.

Naomi heard the stick hurdling through the air, hit several limbs, and eventually land on the ground. She saw the muzzle flash. It was a single muzzle flash.

"One shooter," she said and pulled the trigger on the rifle twice.

Not knowing if she hit the shooter, she waited for one minute before crawling back to Oz. She reached into his fanny pack and took out his night vision monocular and then slowly made her way back to a different tree ten yards away. There was no way she was going to give the shooter the ability to identify her location; she would be constantly moving.

She powered on the monocular and scanned the forest in front of her. As she was scanning, she saw a body lying flat on the forest floor. There was no movement. She continued watching the figure for another thirty seconds before concluding that she had hit and wounded the shooter and, at best, killed them.

She scanned the forest around her looking for any additional movement. There was none. She hung the monocular around her neck, tucked it into her shirt, and crawled back to Cheyanne.

"Cheyanne," Naomi whispered. "We need to be quiet, but I need you to take this rifle and sit by that tree in front of me. If anyone approaches, aim the rifle at them, and pull the trigger. Don't worry if you hit them or not. I'll rush to your side. I need to take care of Oz right now."

"Ok," Cheyanne whispered.

Naomi went back to Oz and removed his jacket and bulletproof vest. She lifted up his shirt and saw two circular bruises one inch apart.

"This man is definitely prepared," she thought. "Had he not had that vest on he would have died."

Before doing anything else, Naomi knew she needed to secure the area of any additional threats. She suspected the shooter was alone but needed to validate her suspicions.

She signaled to Cheyanne to stay where she was as she slowly stood up and peered through the night vision monocular looking for any additional movement in the forest. She saw no movement and began cautiously clearing the immediate area of any threats before arriving at the dead body.

With Oz's handgun in her right hand, she slowly rolled the body over. Naomi was surprised that the shooter was a young man, no older than Cheyanne, dressed in camouflage, and well-armed. He had bled out from a round that had hit him in the femoral artery on his right leg.

"Lucky shot," Naomi whispered before a myriad of thoughts flooded her mind.

She could not understand how such a young man could want to kill or harm anyone. Worse yet, she didn't understand why she was the one who had to end up shooting him.

"Why couldn't it have been Oz," she thought. "Enough. I need to hide the body just in case someone comes looking for him. After that I need to get Oz to a safe location and somehow make a camp for tonight."

Naomi stripped the dead body of any useful gear including a Smith and Wesson M&P® 45 with three extra magazines, a Rock River® LAR-15 with five extra magazines, a compass, flashlight, lighter, and a local map.

Naomi then began piling leaves, branches, and various other natural materials over the body to camouflage it.

"Not the greatest job in the world," she said to herself. "But it will work for now."

Naomi returned to help Oz and realized he was too heavy to carry any distance and that was exactly what she needed to do. She needed to put distance between her group and the dead body but knew Oz would need at least one day's rest. As she continued to devise a plan, she realized the best she could give him would be a couple hours and then they needed to move on. Her worst fear would be that the group that the young man was with would come looking for him and if they found his dead body, well, she could only imagine what would happen next.

Thirty minutes later Oz slowly opened his eyes and began cursing before Naomi could calm him down.

"Oz, be quiet. You'll get us killed." Naomi said while holding her hand over his mouth.

"What happened?" he asked.

"You were shot. I need you to man up and quit being a big baby. You had your vest on." she said with a smirk.

"Damn it, damn it, damn it, it hurts!" he said.

Naomi reached into the first aid kit and pulled out four Tylenol capsules. She gave them to Oz followed by water.

"This is the best we have. Take them. You get two hours rest and then we move on unless you're ready now." Naomi said.

"How long have I been out?" he asked.

"About 30 minutes," Naomi responded.

"In that case, we need to get out of here," Oz said.

Naomi helped Oz up and gestured to Cheyanne to follow. The group headed immediately north at a pace that was comfortable but not too fast for Oz. It didn't take long before they heard noises that appeared to be coming from the area of the dead body. It sounded like a group of pissed off, angry men who didn't care if anyone heard them.

"Oz, we have to pick up the pace right now," Naomi said from behind him.

"I'm going, I'm going," he said while exhaling a deep breath.

40. DESPERATE PEOPLE MAKE DESPERATE GROUPS

NOT EXACTLY SURE WHAT DAY of the week it was, let alone how long it had been since they last left the house, Nicki hugged her son and daughter and said, "I'm going to venture out. I need to get information on what's going on. We can't stay locked up in the house forever and town is our best bet."

"You're not going alone," a voice barked from the other room. It was Lloyd. "I'll go with you."

"No," said Nicki. "We need you to help keep an eye on the house and protect the family," Nicki said.

"I'll go with you, Mom," Randall said.

"Ok," Nicki said reluctantly. Nicki and Randall now had a decision to make. Would they drive the Suburban, which would attract unwanted attention, walk, which would take four to five times longer, or ride bicycles? Nicki quickly thought about it and immediately knew the answer. Bicycling made sense. Bicycles were quiet and would get the two into town in less than an hour.

"Randall, put your vest on. Make sure you have at least four extra magazines with you," Nicki said.

"Done," Randall responded.

"Randall, before we go, I need you to be aware that it's not only men you need to be worried about. Women will be just as dangerous. They will use their body to get what they want. They could even be used to bait you into a trap. Be careful of everyone."

Randall shook his head in acknowledgment.

The weather was good, and as they rode the bikes, the scene was the same as days past. Abandoned cars on every road. The houses they passed looked empty; occasionally they saw someone peek out the windows.

"No way we're stopping; not even if we're asked to help," Nicki said to herself.

As Nicki and Randall approached the outskirts of the town, they could immediately see a small group of people gathered near a local church. Nicki stopped, turned to Randall, and said, "What do you think. It's people gathered at a church. How dangerous could it be?"

"Mom, you realize that you've had to protect your life with a gun, Frank tried to kill us, and now hunger is more rampant than ever? And you're asking me how dangerous can it be?" Randall said suspiciously.

"You're right. Stay to my right about ten feet behind me. Stay where you can keep an eye on the entire group. If I touch my right ear that means I'm getting ready to draw my gun. That's your sign to leave. I'll catch up to you later," Nicki said.

"I'm not, and I repeat, not leaving your side," Randall said and continued. "When you touch your ear, that's my sign to engage if the Stuff hits the fan."

Nicki knew he was not going to change his mind and answered, "Ok, wait two minutes before riding up to the group. Hopefully, they won't catch on that we're together."

Nicki hugged her son, jumped on her bike and rode toward the group. Expecting to see a preacher or minister leading the conversation, Nicki was surprised to see a middle-aged woman taking notes. She had long gray hair and looked emaciated as did the rest of the group. She appeared to be the focal point of the group.

As Nicki walked closer to the lady, she got a quick glance at some of the words written on the note pad, which read: flour, iodine, toothpaste, garden seeds, 45 ACP, wheat, rice, beans, 9mm, shotgun shells, bandages, antibiotics, flashlights, and batteries. The woman looked up and immediately glanced at Nicki.

"Hello stranger," she said.

"Hello," Nicki said. "We're looking for information. Do you know what happened?" Nicki asked.

"That's funny," the lady said. "Everyone around here is starving to death or needs supplies and you're asking what happened. Do you have food or other supplies we could use?" the woman finished.

Quick on her toes, Nicki responded, "We need food, too, but I was hoping you would have information on when the government or state would arrive."

The lady gave Nicki a sharp look and said, "The government is not coming. You're on your own. People are starving and beyond desperate. I recommend that if you have food or supplies, you be a good neighbor and share or at least trade."

The rest of the group began looking at Nicki suspiciously as the woman continued, "You have no signs of malnutrition. Your hair looks like it was recently washed. You have no dirt on you and your clothes are clean. Need I say more?"

Nicki did a quick glance over her right shoulder and saw Randall about twenty feet behind her. She was relieved knowing he hadn't drawn the attention of the rest of the group.

"We don't have food, at most another day's worth, and we take baths and wash our clothes in the creek. It's that simple," Nicki said.

Making direct eye contact with Nicki, the lady said, "Let's hope so for your sake. Now, the true question. Why are you wearing a bulletproof vest? You must have supplies. Why don't you tell us what you have and how much? This will go much better for you if you cooperate. Consider it Socialism where we share everything with everyone."

The group slowly began closing in on Nicki. They blocked any exit she may have thought possible. She needed to signal Randall. She needed her son to leave and head for safety. That was all she cared for. Before she could touch her ear, signaling Randall to head for safety, the sound of gunfire could be heard from behind the group.

Everyone dropped to the ground including Nicki. She slowly raised her head to see Randall with his gun slowly scanning the group of people on the ground.

Using his loudest and most commanding voice he yelled, "If you move you will be shot! Everyone, place your hands above your head and reach as far as you can. Now!"

Nicki stood to her feet and walked to her son's side. A couple of the people in the group lifted their head to see what was going on when they were greeted with Nicki yelling, "Don't be stupid. Listen to him. Keep your heads down!"

Nicki had drawn her Springfield XDM and had it at the low-ready position.

"This was a huge mistake," the lady with the long gray hair shouted, before continuing, "We gave you a chance to help and instead you point your guns at us. You hold us hostage and threaten our lives. We'll remember you. We'll remember your son."

While continually scanning the area, Nicki and Randall made a slow retreat back to their bikes when Randall caught a glimpse of a familiar face.

"That's Stacey," he thought to himself.

He turned to look again when they made eye contact with one another. His heart sank. He immediately felt weak and wanted to reach out to her and help her when his mother pulled him by the shoulder.

"Are you okay?" she asked.

Randall did not respond.

As they rode home, there was only silence. There was no conversation. Only reflection on, yet again, how the world had changed forever.

41. PRIMITIVE SKILLS

AS DAWN BROKE ACROSS THE SKY, Naomi looked down at Oz and Cheyanne. She was tired from pulling guard duty all night. Her thoughts wandered back to Johannes and what had happened. The Navy had prepared her for many things in life but never the loss of her husband and never in those horrific circumstances. She began to feel sorry for herself when she realized that Cheyanne and Oz, to an extent, relied on her to be strong. No matter what she did, no matter what she thought, she had to be strong for both of them. They depended on her.

She returned her gaze to the skyline and saw the beauty all around her. The green trees, the haze coming off the mountains, the rolling valleys, the shifting clouds, and then reality.

"All this beauty surrounded by desperate and evil people," she said to herself.

Startling Naomi, Oz said, "I'm not desperate and definitely not evil."

"Did you read my mind?" she said.

"Nope. You said it aloud," Oz responded.

"Of course," she exclaimed. "If I read the map right, we'll be in Adairsville within the next eight hours. From there, we head to Ringgold and then into Chattanooga. We can keep heading north from there until we hit Nashville, or we can cut east to Cookeville, Tennessee."

Cheyanne looked over to Oz seeing him rubbing his chest and asked, "Does it still hurt? You know, where you were shot."

"Yes, it does. First time and hopefully the last time I'll be shot," Oz uttered.

"Oz, can we camp one more night? We've been going strong for only God knows how long. One day of rest would be good, plus it gives us time to find food," Naomi said.

"I know," he said before Cheyanne interrupted him.

"Oz, why can't we just eat some of the natural vegetation you've talked about," she asked.

Oz took a minute to think before replying, "Naomi, great idea. We'll rest an additional day but make it a learning day. We'll teach Cheyanne the difference between cover and concealment, as well as how to set snares. We'll also spend a little time on wild edibles. In today's world, it's a necessary skill."

The group ate what little food they had after which Oz and Naomi started teaching Cheyanne about tactical survival.

"First, Cheyanne," Naomi said. "I need to teach you an important lesson: the difference between concealment and cover. A lesson you would have thought Oz would have remembered. Concealment is not the place you want to be when bullets start to fly. Concealment does not stop bullets, hence the reason Oz was shot. Wooden doors, car doors, and most house walls, which are made of sheetrock, are examples of concealment. Concealment only keeps you hidden, not protected. Cover, on the other hand, keeps you hidden and protected. Always hide behind things that can stop a bullet. Trees and boulders, in ditches, anything that can prevent bullet penetration. Promise me you'll do that?"

Cheyanne started laughing and said, "I won't pull an Oz. I promise."

"Seriously ladies," Oz exclaimed.

"Now, on to plants," Oz said. "I'm not an expert on the local vegetation but it should be easy enough to identify some good healthy vegetation. The climate and area are somewhat similar to my Kentucky back yard," Oz said.

"But first, let's set some snares," he said.

Oz reached into his backpack and pulled out a ten-foot section of 550 paracord.

"Cheyanne, this is 550 paracord. It's called 550 paracord since it can hold up to 550 pounds before it breaks — a prepper's best friend. When you take the outside cover off, called the sheath," he said as he handed her the sheath, "there are seven additional smaller strands. We're going to use those seven additional strands to set several snare traps. The odds are low we'll catch something, but we need to try. Naomi, is it okay if she comes with me?" Oz asked.

"Fine by me," Naomi said and kissed her daughter goodbye.

"Let me explain what we're doing," Oz said to Cheyanne. "A snare can be used day or night, rain or shine, and in any climate. Look for game trails. To find game trails, look for trampled grass, well-worn paths, animal droppings, tracks, animal shelters, sources of water and food, and broken branches. As I just mentioned, the key is to make sure you place the snare where you see signs of animal life. Snares placed randomly are a waste of time."

Oz chose several locations along the game trail and showed Cheyanne how to make and set a snare.

"Now, let's go get your mom and look for edible plants. Time to forage for food," he told Cheyanne.

With Naomi at their side, Oz said, "First, the basics. The important part of forging is to make sure you know exactly what you're eating. You can do this by visualization, meaning you visually identify physical traits of the plant. Don't limit yourself to visual identification alone. Lots of wild edible plants have look-alikes. Second, you'll need to learn how to differentiate similar plants by smell, feel, texture, etc. It's not a rule, but in many cases, poisonous plants are unpalatable and have a rank smell. That said, taste should only be used if you're sure the plant is not poisonous. Some plants, such as water hemlock, are deadly in very small doses. Third, understand habitats. Simply put, you won't find cattails in the dessert or cactus in the north. Fourth, companion planting is also important. Many plants are commonly found growing by other identifiable plants. Fifth, seasons. You'll need to understand seasons and which plants grow when and where. Sixth, you'll also need to learn which parts of the plant are used for what. For instance, the ripe cooked berries of elderberry are safe to eat, but the bark, stems, and roots are poisonous. And finally, only forage plants that appear to be healthy. Plants can be afflicted by disease, fungi, pests, or pollution. Harvesting healthy plants minimizes the risk of illness and means you're getting more nutritious food."

"Well, I guess I'll put this little green plant down until I know it won't kill me," Cheyanne laughed.

"Yeah, that one they call poison ivy," Oz said with a smirk.

"All right, back on track, ladies," he said. "Some of the common, healthy, greens that we can get this afternoon are dandelions, stinging nettles, lamb's quarter, and acorns. It won't fill our bellies, but it will provide nutrition and hopefully, just hopefully, the snares will catch a little meat."

As the group walked, Oz helped the ladies identify natural edibles. They pulled enough vegetation to feed them for several days. They returned to camp, cleaned the plants, and made a quick vegetable-like stew. Though still hungry, they went to bed with hopes of having meat the following morning.

Early the next morning Cheyanne woke Oz and her mother up. She had excitement in her face. In her right hand hung a rabbit.

"Not bad," Oz said.

"Can you teach me how to clean it?" Cheyanne asked.

"I've only seen it on the internet, but I'm sure we'll figure it out," Oz said with a smile and laugh.

Cheyanne, Naomi, and Oz each got a small piece of cooked rabbit complimented with a nice dandelion salad. Not much, but better than nothing. They would have to continue their hunt for food, but what they ate would allow the group to continue northward on their journey toward Kentucky.

42. KILL OR BE KILLED

THE SOUNDS OF TRIPWIRES going off could be heard from all sides of the house. It sounded as if a stampede had rushed onto the property.

Lloyd scrambled looking through windows on each side of the house. He could see that there were, at a minimum, two people on each of the four sides of the house.

"Nicki!" Lloyd yelled. "We're surrounded. At least two armed people on each side of the house. They haven't approached yet, but it sure in the hell looks like they are going to. Oh yeah, it looks like they have protective vests on to boot."

"Randall, Connie, Cali, grab the AR-15s and rifles. Randall, take the south side of the house. Cali, take the west side. Lloyd, take the east side. Connie, keep the magazines full as we empty them. I'll take the north side!" Nicki barked before turning to Buzz. "Buzz, hide in the closet and do not come out until one of us comes and gets you. No matter what you hear, stay in the closet" Nicki said.

Scared and frightened, Buzz reluctantly opened the closet door and sat down.

Understanding Nicki's orders, each of the family members took their assigned position. "Everyone, vest and helmets on. Radios and headsets on. Radio check in one minute," Nicki ordered.

With the family members geared up and now in communication with one another, they were ready as best they could be.

"If you have a clear shot, fire," Nicki said firmly while continuing. "They won't hesitate to kill you or our family. Now is the time to act. The time to protect our family. Every time one of those bastards goes down, call it out. That will be our queue to move to another position and help where needed."

Before she could say another word, she heard the sound of an AR-15 fire followed by Randall saying, "One down on the south side. One to go."

It was nearly impossible to hear because as soon as Randall fired, all hell broke loose. Bullets began hitting the house, easily penetrating the walls. Randall quickly transitioned to the second guy who was now running full speed toward the house. Randall fired at least twenty rounds before announcing, "Second guy down on the south side." He immediately inserted a fresh magazine.

"Randall, help your sister, now, go!," Nicki shouted into the headset.

"10-4," Randall replied.

"One down on the east side," Lloyd said.

"I've got my two pinned down but can't get a clean shot. They're hiding between the Suburban and the garage. Looks like we'll wait them out," Nicki reported.

The next transmission the family heard over the radio was a scream from Randall, "Cali's been shot! Mom, she's been shot! She's bleeding bad, Mom!"

Nicki listened intently at the sharp piercing screams coming from the bedroom. She could hear Cali in pain and then suddenly, nothing.

"Lloyd, Randall, I need to get to Cali. Randall, take my position. Keep those two pinned down," Nicki said as she fired several blind shots at the two pinned down gunmen before switching with Randall and rushing to Cali's side.

She quickly put her fingers over Cali's carotid artery and felt a pulse. She could see blood seeping from her shirt and quickly isolated the wound. Cali had been shot in the upper left shoulder. Nicki saw the entrance wound and quickly sat Cali up to look for the exit wound.

"Thank God," Nicki said. The bullet had gone through her shoulder.

"The bullet is not lodged in her shoulder. It went straight through. She's losing blood, but she'll be fine," Nicki said over the radio.

"First aid kit. Does anyone know where the first aid kit is?" Nicki said over the radio.

"Downstairs in the room with the ammunition," Lloyd said exhausted.

"Hang on baby," Nicki said as she reengaged herself in the firefight.

As Lloyd was scanning the area for his aggressors, he saw an odd figure off in the distance. He quickly looked through the AR-15 scope but still couldn't make out what the person was doing. He grabbed the binoculars, placed them up to his eyes, and spotted a middle-aged woman talking into a radio. It appeared as if she was talking to someone, but who? Was she a bystander or was she giving the attackers directions? He couldn't be sure. He looked again and saw her point to the left while talking into the radio. Lloyd instantly saw two men running to his right.

"She's giving them directions. She's telling them where to go," Lloyd said to himself.

Lloyd picked up the AR-15 which had been sighted in for 100 yards. He placed the reticle on her upper chest and pulled the trigger. She went down. Lloyd followed up with a second shot, grabbed the binoculars, and saw no movement. As he continued to watch the downed woman, he saw one of the attackers running toward her. The attacker was running full speed in the open appearing not to care whether they were shot at or not. They were going to get to the woman on the ground no matter what. Without emotion, Lloyd quickly transitioned the AR-15, lined the moving target up with the reticle, achieved a sight picture, and pulled the trigger twice. The figure fell to the ground landing on top of the woman.

"I got another one," Lloyd yelled into the radio.

Before the family knew what happened, the sounds of gunfire stopped.

"They're running back into the woods," Randall said.

"Yep, they're carrying away the two I shot," Lloyd replied.

There was no response from Nicki as she headed straight for the basement, grabbed the first aid kit and ran back upstairs to Cali's side.

"I sure hope your dad knew what to put in here," Nicki said to herself.

Nicki opened the first aid kit and pulled out a QuikClot® hemostatic gauze bandage to stop the bleeding. She placed several over the front and back of Cali's shoulder.

"Lloyd, hold these in place. I need to start an IV, but first we need to move her downstairs. Help me," Nicki said.

While Lloyd held the bandages in place, Randall carried his sister downstairs. Once downstairs, Nicki started an IV and told Randall to find clindamycin in their medical supplies.

"We need to make sure her wound doesn't get infected. Hurry," Nicki said.

With Randall getting the medication, and Cali unconscious, Nicki cleaned the wound, replaced the blood-soaked hemostatic gauze with new gauze, and placed an Israeli emergency bandage around her shoulder to hold the gauze in place.

Once Randall returned with the medication, Nicki gave Cali the clindamycin though an IV push.

"We'll watch her and let her sleep," Nicki said.

"She could have died," Randall said as he held his sister's hand.

"But she didn't," Nicki said trying to be strong.

"What happened today creates anger and vengeance in me. I want to kill those men who shot her. Mom, I've never felt such hatred toward anybody like this in my life," Randall said as his tone changed.

"Randall," Nicki said as she began to cry. "What has this world become? Neighbors killing neighbors. My children carrying guns and shooting people. My father-in-law has become the family sniper. And your dad. Where's your dad? We need him!"

Lloyd kept guard as Randall and Nicki watched Cali. Son and mother talked through the night about what had become of the world they previously knew.

43. YOU CAN ONLY LIVE 3 DAYS WITHOUT WATER

HAVING TREKKED FOR FOURTEEN STRAIGHT HOURS, Naomi exclaimed, "If it's not one thing it's another."

"I know. We need water. We'll stop at the next pond or stream we come across," Oz said.

It didn't take long before the group came across a small wet weather stream. He turned to the ladies and said, "I made sure we kept the water bottles because of their many uses; one of which is it disinfect water. Our two primary concerns with water are cryptosporidium and giardia."

Naomi, Cheyanne, and Oz approached the small stream. Oz took a plastic water bottle and filled it completely. He then took a clean sock which he had in his Bug Out Bag and filtered the water of solids by allowing the water to flow through the sock into another water bottle.

"Ok, we've removed debris from the water. The big stuff," Oz said. "We have to now disinfect it. There are a couple of ways. The first and easiest way is to boil it. It's not an option for us because we need to save the remaining fuel for our camp stove. The second thing we could do is place the water bottle over the coals of a fire but not directly on the fire and let it boil for one to two minutes. We don't have

277

time to start a fire so we're going to use a method using a tincture of iodine. We'll add five drops per quart to clear water and ten drops per quart to cloudy water. We'll let the bottle sit for thirty minutes before drinking. It will task funny, but again, it's safe to drink."

Cheyanne made a face but was so thirsty she was willing to drink directly from the pond at this stage if she had to.

"Oz, how did you learn this stuff," Naomi asked.

"Lots of books followed by lots of practice and many mistakes," Oz said.

With drinking water now replenished, the group foraged for plants, set a few snares, and made camp for the night.

Cheyanne woke the next morning and saw Oz sleeping. She looked around and didn't see her mother.

"She must be on guard duty," she thought.

Before they started their daily trek, she thought it would be a good idea to take a quick sponge bath at the pond. She couldn't remember how long it had been since she last took a shower. She grabbed a t-shirt from her Bug Out Bag and headed to the pond. The morning was beautiful, and as she stopped to listen all she heard was silence.

"That's the loudest noise I've ever heard," she said to herself.

She looked around, didn't see anyone, or anything for that matter, and slowly took her shirt off. She placed the t-shirt in the water and cleaned her face, arms, and chest, and then put on a clean shirt.

She took her pants off and began to clean the rest of her body when she heard an unfamiliar voice say, "Very nice. Don't stop."

"Wish I had money to give her. You know, like at the strip clubs," said another voice.

Cheyanne quickly looked up and saw two men. Both men were dirty and didn't take their eyes off her. One of the men appeared to be in his fifties or sixties, had rotten teeth, a ripped shirt, ripped pants, and duck taped shoes. The other man had a scar going across his cheek and what appeared to be a broken nose. He had rotten teeth and dirty hair; Cheyanne could smell him from ten feet away.

"Can I help you?" she said.

"Oh, yeah. You're going to help us. Help us both," the man with the ripped shirt said.

Cheyanne quickly pulled her pants up and began running. She didn't get more than five feet before she was tackled, flipped onto her back, and her pants pulled down.

Cheyanne tried to scream at the top of her lungs but before she could say a thing a hand was placed over her mouth. The man with the scar began to take off his pants when the other man shouted, "Hey, it's my turn. You went first last time."

"I went first last time because I found the woman," the man with the scar said. The two men continued arguing with one another for another thirty seconds. This gave Cheyanne enough time to pull out the four-inch Cold Steel knife.

With the two men still arguing, she ran the blade of her knife across the hand of the man who had his hand on her mouth. He instantly released his grip and yelled with a voracious scream that could be heard for miles.

Cheyanne quickly rotated the knife forty-five degrees and drove it deep into the stomach of the man with the scar. He fell on his side and clutched his stomach. Cheyanne began screaming and running which instantly woke Oz up.

Oz quickly scanned the campsite and didn't see Naomi or Cheyanne. He grabbed his Glock and ran in the direction of Cheyanne's voice.

As the pond came into view, he could see the situation was well under control. He saw Cheyanne shielded by Naomi who had the two men at gunpoint.

Oz ran up to Naomi and Cheyanne and asked, "What the hell happened?"

"My daughter left camp alone. She didn't wake up or tell either one of us. They were going to rape her and probably kill her. This will not happen again!" Naomi said looking squarely at Cheyanne.

Cheyanne only looked down realizing she had made a huge mistake.

"What do we do with these assholes?" Oz asked.

"We castrate them," Naomi said without hesitation. "Cheyanne let me have your knife."

Naomi took Cheyanne's knife, turned to Oz and said, "Take Cheyanne back to camp. I have it under control."

"Are you sure?" Oz said.

"Yes, I couldn't be more sure of anything," she finished. As a precaution, Oz took out some paracord and tied both men's hands behind them and bound their feet.

"There," he said. "A little extra insurance."

Oz took Cheyanne back to camp and remained ever vigilant just in case Naomi needed help. Before he could think another thought he heard the screams of one of the men followed by the screams of the second. Several minutes later he saw Naomi and asked, "Are you okay?"

"Oz," she said. "Who have I become? In the last days, I've been raped, my daughter was almost raped twice, I've killed, and now, I just cut the balls off two pedophiles. Oh yeah, I cut their ropes. If they survive, they get to live."

"You're adapting Naomi. You're adapting. I just need to remember to never get on your bad side," Oz said as he began packing up camp.

44. BACK AGAIN

"I WAS READING THROUGH your dad's SHTF Manual and I'll be damned if he didn't mention LP/OP. We had those in Vietnam. They were the first line of defense for us," Lloyd said talking to his grandson.

"After what happened last night, I think it's time to find a good location and establish one."

Randall was still focused on his sister and only gave a slight nod.

"I'll take care of it," his grandfather said.

Against the family rules, Lloyd went outside by himself. He looked the property over assessing the terrain and elevation. At first glance, there really was no ideal location for an LP/OP. As he continued walking the property, he noticed a location that would work. It was in the tree line in between Frank's house and the McTatey's. It would provide natural cover, allow for a 360-degree view of the property, and was well within a rifle's distance to the house. The only problem was that it didn't allow for much reaction time.

"Better than nothing," Lloyd said to himself.

Before he could continue to the next task at hand, he heard Nicki say in a snippety voice, "Father-in-law, you never leave the house alone. This is your last warning. Do you understand?"

"Understood," Lloyd said as he stared at the ground.

"Randall," Nicki said over the radio. "Please come stand guard duty for your grandpa. He seems to think he's invincible. Put your vest on under your ghillie suit and wear the PASGT helmet. I want you armed with your Springfield and AR-15."

"10-4," said Randall who appeared from the door several minutes later.

As Nicki looked at her son, she no longer saw the young man of weeks ago. She saw a man wearing a bulletproof vest, PASGT helmet, ghillie suit, and carrying two firearms. A man who would defend his family to the death. That was her son and she was proud of him.

As Randall stood guard duty, his grandpa worked to create an LP/OP. It would provide an early warning to the family. With the tripwire securing the outer perimeter and the LP/OP securing the inner perimeter, the family had a simple but basic security system. It would give them the warning they needed.

Lloyd used branches and downed trees to create the framework of the LP/OP. It needed to blend in with the environment and not easily seen.

Randall scanned the entire perimeter of the house looking for anyone or any movement. The last thing he wanted was someone watching his grandpa constructing the LP/OP.

After working on the LP/OP for eight hours, Lloyd had reached a point in the construction where it wasn't complete but could be used. The last task of the night was to run telephone cable from the LP/OP to the house and connect the EE-8A phones. Oz bought the phones years ago and knew there was no real practical purpose or reason to have them. But today, without electricity, they were the perfect communications tool.

With the EE-8A phones connected in the LP/OP and in the house, Lloyd went inside for the night.

"Nicki, the weather looks like it will be clear tonight. The LP/OP isn't complete but can be used. I've set the phones up and they're ready to be used. I would recommend either you or me man it tonight. We just repelled a serious attack. They may want vengeance," Lloyd said.

"You're right. I'll man it tonight," Nicki said. "Just make sure the phones work and someone answers if I call."

"They do work, and I'll be the one to answer," Lloyd proudly said.

Several hours after the sunset, Nicki positioned herself in the LP/OP. It was a nice night temperature-wise, but with the bulletproof vest on she felt hotter than it was.

"It's not lingerie, at least not the kind I like," Nicki laughed as she sat in an old lawn chair. Nicki settled in for the night, remaining vigilant, and constantly scanning for movement.

Time went by slowly for Nicki and she was excited to see the sun rising. As she was enjoying the view, she was suddenly caught off guard and jumped when she heard one of the tripwires go off. She immediately grabbed her binoculars and scanned the area. To her relief, she caught a glimpse of a deer running away. She put the binoculars down and just as quickly brought them back to her face. She thought she saw something else moving. Within seconds she saw the movement of several bodies. She grabbed the EE-8A, wound the crank, and a sleepy Lloyd answered.

"Get everyone up. Get everyone ready. They're back. They're avoiding the tripwires. Assume worse case. They want vengeance. Make sure to hide Buzz," Nicki said quietly so as to not alert anyone nearby.

She picked up the binoculars and scanned the remaining areas of the property. She counted at least fifteen people. Most of them armed with guns but several with crowbars and baseball bats. She slowly turned and looked behind her and saw five individuals; two armed with guns.

She picked up the phone, wound the crank, and quickly said, "Twenty in total," then hung up.

She turned to the closet aggressors, flipped the AR-15 safety off, sighted in one of the men carrying a rifle and fired twice. The four remaining men scattered in every direction. The only one she cared about was the other man with the rifle. She saw him run behind a tree and waited for him to appear. She didn't see his body, but he had made the mistake of leaving his foot out in the open. She aimed and pulled the trigger. The man was in immediate pain and made the mistake of moving out from behind the tree. Nicki placed three shots in various parts of his body before he dropped.

Nicki was unable to hear how her family in the house was doing as the sound from her AR-15 had temporarily deafened her. Though not able to hear, she quickly turned around searching to find the other three men — or any target for that matter.

What she saw horrified her. She saw a person with a baseball bat beating down her front door while another person was preparing a Molotov cocktail.

"No one's going to burn down my house," she said as she placed the man in her gun sights. Before she could fire, she saw the man fall and instantly catch on fire as the Molotov cocktail exploded in his hand. Someone from the house must have shot him. Muzzle flashes erupted from all over the property. She quickly realized that there was a good chance that her house would be overrun.

Randall took the west side of the house and was outflanked. He got very few shots off. He was pinned down. Lloyd would belly crawl from room to room, fire, and then move. He wanted to give the illusion that the house was well armed.

Several minutes later he heard the smoke alarm going off. Lloyd ran to the kitchen and saw a fire that would engulf the house within minutes if it wasn't extinguished. Before he had time to act, Connie ran in with a fire extinguisher and handed it to Lloyd. Lloyd pulled the pin and aimed the extinguisher at the base of the spreading fired. He pressed the handles together and swept the extinguisher across the fire. Thirty seconds later, the fire was out and the extinguisher empty.

"I love my son," he said before running to help Randall.

Oz always purchased the bigger 40-pound fire extinguishers because he knew, if used correctly they would put out most fires.

The attackers had finally identified Nicki's location and began concentrating fire on her position. She had no choice but to duck and take cover. Her only hope was that Randall and Lloyd could hold them off, but in her heart she knew she would probably not survive the day.

45. JUST IN TIME

NAOMI, CHEYANNE, AND OZ walked from Lebanon to Oz's house throughout the night and into the early morning. It was an uneventful but long walk; all accomplished without stopping. They were excited to get to the house and rest.

As Oz, Naomi, and Cheyanne approached Oz's house, they could hear gunfire coming from the direction of his house.

Oz immediately began running toward his house when Naomi grabbed his shoulder and said, "Stop. You know you can't run into a gunfight. We need a plan."

Oz pushed her hand away and continued walking toward the house.

"I'm telling you to stop. You saved my life now let me save yours," Naomi begged.

Oz reluctantly stopped and looked at her before saying, "Ok. What's the plan?"

"This is your part of the country and your house. You tell us what the plan is," Naomi said frustrated.

"First, we hide Cheyanne," Oz said.

"Cheyanne you follow me and when I say stay, you stay right where I tell you until your mother or I come to get you. Do you understand?" Oz said frantically.

Cheyanne shook her head up and down.

"Keep your bow ready to shoot, protect yourself at all times, but one more time, do not move from where I tell you to stay. Naomi, my house is down that drive. I'll approach it from the west and you approach it from the east. It will be easy to identify my family members. They should all be wearing the Italian military Vegetato battle dress units (BDU). The uniforms were similar to U.S. BDUs, but a different pattern. If you come across someone not wearing the uniform and think it might be one of my family members, ask them their last name. If you don't hear the words McTatey, Foster or Balgemann, then they're the enemy. We need to move, now," Oz finished.

Oz and Cheyanne immediately turned into the forest and disappeared as Naomi walked the tree line for approximately 100 yards before turning toward Oz's house.

Oz motioned for Cheyanne to sit and stay hidden behind a large fallen tree. Once he saw she was safe, he briskly walked toward his house. As he walked through the forest and closer to his house, he noticed fishing line tied off from one tree and ending at one of his grenade heads on another tree. The fishline could only be seen when the sun's rays reflected off of the string.

"Hot damn," he thought to himself. "Someone set up my tripwires."

Now more cautious so as not to set off a tripwire, he could see at least a dozen people either firing at his house or getting ready to torch it. Oz took up a position of concealment and readied the Rock River LAR-15.

Naomi quickly ran through the forest knowing she needed to get into position. Her military training told her that the quicker the firefight ends, the better. Before she could take another step, she heard a horrendous sound. The sound came from right where she was standing. Temporarily immobilized, she quickly checked her body to make sure she wasn't injured. She was fine but could not hear a damn thing. She quickly saw that fishing line had been tied to a tree and then to a grenade head.

"A tripwire," she said to herself and continued toward Oz's house.

Oz took out two people getting ready to throw Molotov cocktails at the house and then concentrated his fire on the west side. He had caught them off guard. Using cover as much as he could, he moved his position to a southern point and eliminated three more threats; they didn't see it coming.

Before Oz could move to another position something collided with his head. The last words he heard was, "You're going to pay for what you did. Pay with your life!" Then his eyes closed.

Randall saw his mom pinned down in the LP/OP. He counted three or four people running toward her location.

"Grandpa," Randall said. "People are running toward Mom. Looks like they got her pinned down. She's in trouble."

"I see them!" Lloyd yelled over the radio.

"Grandpa, I have to help her," Randall said with a quivering voice.

"No. I'll go, Randall. You switch positions with me. Cover me. If you get hurt, I'll never forgive myself. No time to argue."

Lloyd placed a fresh magazine in his handgun and rifle and headed toward the front door.

"Right behind you, Grandpa. As soon as you open the door, I'm going to fire a volley in every direction. When you run, don't stop until you get to the LP/OP," Randall said.

Lloyd opened the door and began running for the LP/OP. Randall followed him onto the porch, knelt on one knee and quickly scanned the area firing three rounds in every direction. The bolt on his AR-15 locked back. He quickly ejected the magazine, inserted a full magazine and sent the bolt home. He continued with his three-round burst.

Lloyd could see the LP/OP, and Nicki was indeed pinned down. He was going to do everything in his power to save his daughter-in-law. Lloyd was about to engage a man running toward him with what looked like a sledgehammer when he felt a sharp sting in the back of his leg. He fell and without thinking quickly got up and shot at the man.

Lloyd hit the man in the shoulder and chest, and he fell to the ground. With a slow limp, Lloyd continued to head to the LP/OP. A second and third bullet hit him. Lloyd felt warm blood spurting from his neck and placed his hand over the wound hoping to stop the bleeding. He then said a silent prayer. His prayer was for the safety of his wife and family and, oddly enough, the hope that he would see Fred, his pet Shar Pei, who died many years earlier.

"I'll meet you all on the rainbow bridge," he said as his breathing became shallower and shallower and he collapsed to the ground.

As Naomi broached the tree line, she saw a group of three people converging toward something, but she was unsure of what they were approaching. She saw what appeared to be gunfire coming from the ground but didn't see anyone only the end of an AR-15 firing straight up.

"Must be a foxhole or something similar. Probably Oz's family," Naomi thought.

She dropped to the ground and placed the reticle of the Ruger PC Carbine center mass on one of the men and fired two rounds. The body fell limp. She quickly transitioned to a second person and pulled the trigger twice more.

"Like shooting fish in a barrel," she said to herself.

Naomi saw a crazed woman turn in her direction. Naomi knew she was looking for her and the direction of her gunfire. Before the woman could determine where Naomi was hidden, she fell to the ground with her chest completely blown away. Naomi looked and saw where the shot came from. It came from an older man wearing full combat gear and a military uniform that Oz described. Naomi watched as the man fell to the ground. She knew it had to be one of Oz's family members and said a quick prayer in hopes he would get up, but he did not.

Out of her left side eye, Naomi caught a glance of a man running wildly at her.

"Does this ever end?" she said out loud.

As soon as the man jumped into the tree line toward her, he was met by a volley of armed fire. The last thing in life he saw was Naomi.

Cheyanne had heard the gunfire. It was coming from everywhere. She was scared. She understood what Oz had told her but felt the need to move. She stood up and moved from tree to tree taking cover and getting closer and closer to Oz's house. Bullets were flying everywhere. Cheyanne crouched and prayed that the gunfire would stop but it didn't. She stood and continued moving when she saw Oz down on the ground. A man appeared over him with a baseball bat. The man with the bat was saying something to Oz as he brought the bat above his head. Cheyanne quickly drew an arrow from her quiver and nocked the arrow. She aimed the sights and let the arrow fly. The arrow hit the man high on the right shoulder. He dropped the bat and began screaming. Cheyanne nocked another arrow and slowly began walking toward Oz and the man. She seemed unaware of the battle that was raging around her. Her sole focus was on Oz.

The man looked at Cheyanne and started yelling, "You witch! You shot me!"

He picked up the bat with his left hand and started walking toward her.

"Don't do it. Please, stop," Cheyanne said as tears streamed from her eyes. "Please, stop."

The man was now within ten feet of her when she released the arrow, striking him in the stomach. She nocked another arrow and placed a third shot perfectly centered in the middle of his neck striking the carotid artery. Blood began spurting everywhere as the man grabbed for his throat. He fell to the ground in a pool of blood and stopped moving.

Cheyanne ran to Oz. She put her fingers on his wrist and felt nothing. She tried again but this time pushing harder on his wrist. Nothing. She tried one last time and felt relieved when she felt an ever so slight pulse. She would stay by Oz's side until help arrived. She grabbed his AR-15 and was ready to kill anyone who came near him.

46. REUNION

AFTER WHAT SEEMED LIKE AN ETERNITY, the gunfire had ceased. The bodies of men and women were strewn throughout Oz's property. Randall immediately picked up the phone and cranked the handle.

"Answer. Answer. Mom, answer the phone!" Randall said frantically. There was no answer.

"Grandma, go from room to room and report what you see. Are there still people out there or did they bug out? I need to know if they're regrouping," he said.

"Ok. I'll call over the radio," his grandma said. Randall peered out the window but did not see any movement from the LP/OP. He wanted to leave the house but knew he couldn't. It was too risky, and he would protect Cali and his Grandma come hell or high water.

Randall turned and continued looking through the window waiting to see his mom walk in the door any moment when he saw his grandpa on the ground motionless. Panic set in. For the first time in his life, his thoughts turned to terror and he froze. The thought of not seeing his mother or grandfather again weighed heavy on his mind.

Naomi remained in her position and waited fifteen more minutes to ensure everything was clear before beginning to walk toward the LP/OP. She needed to make sure that whoever was in there was okay.

Her training had taught her not to walk directly up to a foxhole or LP/OP, as she would more than likely end up dead. Instead, she crawled within ten feet of the LP/OP and yelled, "My name is Naomi and I'm with Oz. If you are a family member of Oz you need to come out with your hands up, identify yourself right now, and tell me what his last name is. If you don't come out or you get his last name wrong, I will shoot you." There was no response. She repeated her instructions and saw two hands appear out of the LP/OP.

"Don't shoot. My name is Nicki and our last name is McTatey," Nicki said.

Naomi immediately lowered her rifle and walked up to Nicki extending her hand. "I'm Naomi and I'm with your husband," she said.

"Where's my husband?" Nicki said.

"We split up to help defend the house. I'm sure he'll be around soon. Can you contact your family in the house? The last thing I want to do is walk across your property, be seen as a stranger, and get shot," Naomi said.

Nicki went back into the LP/OP and dialed the house. Randall answered and heard his mom say, "Don't shoot. I'm coming out with a friend. Cover us."

"Mom," Randall said with a panicked voice. "Grandpa is on the ground near the LP/OP. I can't see him moving. Get to him quickly. Grandma said the remaining attackers bugged out. I think the fighting stopped. Please help Grandpa, Mom."

Naomi helped Nicki out of the LP/OP and handed her the AR-15. They both cautiously walked out of the tree line immediately seeing Lloyd on the ground not moving.

As Cheyanne protected Oz, she saw her mom and another woman walking out of the tree line to the house. Cheyanne left Oz's side and while behind cover, waived her arms hoping to get the attention of her mother.

Nicki quickly brought her AR-15 to her should and yelled, "Keep your hands in the air where we can see them and slowly walk toward us!"

Naomi put her hand on the barrel of the AR-15, lowered it, and said, "That's my daughter."

"Sorry about that," Nicki said.

"Don't be sorry. In this new world we need to always be ready," Naomi responded.

"Mom, Oz is unconscious. He needs help," Cheyanne said as her voice trembled.

"You take care of him and I'll check on Oz," Naomi said.

Naomi ran toward Cheyanne who pointed into the forest. She ran as fast as she could until she found Oz. He lay on his back. Naomi noticed his chest slowly moving up and down and was instantly relieved. She ran back to Nicki who was aggressively working on Lloyd. Both men needed to be taken into the house where the medical supplies were.

Nicki told Naomi to go inside the house and get Randall. She would need help moving Oz and Lloyd into the basement.

As Nicki frantically worked on Lloyd, she saw Randall and Naomi carrying Oz into the house. She knew in her heart he would be okay and turned her attention to Lloyd.

In her head she said the words, "Oz, I knew you would make it home."

Several hours later, Oz slowly opened his eyes and though groggy, was excited to see Nicki staring at him.

"How's the love of my life?" Nicki said with a smile.

"Major headache, but I'll be fine," he said and reached up to hug her.

"Come in you two," Nicki said with a smile.

Randall and Cali came running in.

"We missed you, Dad," both kids said.

"Buzz, do you remember Oz? You haven't seen him in a long time, but he and I are going to be taking care of you from now on," Nicki said.

Oz looked completely perplexed by Nicki's statement when Buzz looked up at him and said "Yeah. He used to help my daddy mow the lawn."

"It's great to see you again, Buzz," Oz said as he realized that by Nicki's look and comment they were now responsible for him.

"Cali, what happened to your shoulder?" Oz said.

"As they say, it's a long story, Dad," she responded.

"Hello Chief Petty Officer," Oz said shifting his attention to Naomi and Cheyanne.

"Morning, sir," Naomi said.

"We did it, we all survived?" Oz exclaimed excitedly.

As far as Oz knew, everyone he loved had survived that terrible day.

Nicki held Oz's hand and began crying.

"What's wrong?" he said.

"Your dad was shot three times," Nicki began. "Only one of the three shots lodged in his body. The other two went through him which is a good thing. I had to cut away some tissue and muscle to get to the one lodged in him, but I eventually pulled it out. I cleaned all the wounds and stitched them up. His neck wound is the most concerning. He won't be able to move for weeks for fear of not healing properly. The bullet nicked his jugular vein and he lost a lot of blood. I did everything I could, including something that in the real world you would never do."

Oz looked perplexed but waited for his wife to continue.

"I gave him a direct human-to-human blood transfusion. I know he is AB-Positive and can receive any blood type. Thank God. Grandma and Naomi volunteered to donate. Now we sit and pray that he'll survive."

"I'm proud of you and you should know that you did the right thing. It will work! Going forward, we'll all being doing things differently. The old ways are gone. If we're going to survive, we're going to have to use ingenuity as you did." Oz said as he grabbed her hand.

Later that night, Nicki approached Oz crying and said, "Oz, I can't get BJ off my mind. Did he have a Bug Out Bag?"

"He has a Bug Out Bag. It has everything he needs to make it to Brian and Elizabeth's. BJ knew that if he couldn't drive to Kentucky he was to go to their house. I have an agreement with Brian that if BJ doesn't show up to their house within five days of an SHTF, and he and Elizabeth are safe, Brian will find a way to get to SIU and find BJ," Oz said.

"I can't just stand by and wait for him. Not knowing if he is safe is painful," Nicki said in a muffled voice.

Oz thought for a moment and then hugged Nicki. "I'll set up the shortwave radio tomorrow and we'll try and contact Brian and Elizabeth. They know the emergency communication protocol we set up. If they're okay there's a good chance BJ is with them," Oz said.

Nicki kissed him on the lips and turned to check on the rest of the family.

47. THE NEW BEGINNING

EARLY THE NEXT DAY, Oz, Nicki, and Naomi were discussing the challenges each had faced in the past weeks when Naomi said, "Oz, this is a new beginning. You know we'll have to prepare even more now. Survival is no longer guaranteed."

"I agree with her, Oz," Nicki said while looking at Naomi with a smile. "In the short time since the EMP I've seen rape, murder, hunger, desperation, and the will of people to do anything to survive."

"I, too, have experienced the same," Naomi said and then began crying. Oz knew Naomi and Cheyanne had a difficult road ahead of them but knew that he and Nicki would be steadfast in their support for both of them.

"Well, then," Oz said. "We have three main priorities. One, re-secure the house and property. Make it better and more secure than before. Two, find BJ and get him home. We have no idea if he left Illinois or is on his way. Three, get Naomi and Cheyanne home. California is a long way away, but I promised I would do everything in my power to get them home."

Before Oz could continue, Naomi interrupted and said, "Cheyanne and I have been talking. When we lost Johannes, we lost our family. Yes, we have a house in

California, but we lost our home when he died. We have nowhere to go. This is our home if you'll have us."

With that, Naomi began crying and hugged Cheyanne.

Nicki immediately walked up to Naomi and Cheyanne, embraced them and said, "You're welcome in our house. You're family now, and besides," Nicki continued through tears of her own, "it will take both of us to keep Oz under control."

Out of nowhere, a faint, barely audible but familiar voice said, "Randall, it's time to get your dad's SHTF- Elevated Threat Manual out. We will never be caught off guard again. Let's get to work."

It was Lloyd. The group rejoiced but realized that he, and they as well, had a long way to go.

Oz, Naomi, Nicki, Connie, and Randall worked hard for the next several days re-establishing the LP/OP, securing the house and property, and setting up the shortwave radio. Cali was making a slow recovery and, with the help of Nicki, would begin physical therapy soon. Lloyd would take many weeks, perhaps months to recover. Nicki's primary concern was an infection, but as a nurse, she had confidence in her abilities and with the medications they had stored, knew that Lloyd would have a high probability of recovery.

Using the shortwave radio Oz was able to contact Brian and Elizabeth. Their situation was dire. Within 10 miles of their house was a federal prison. After the power was completely lost, the area experienced something it had never seen before — a mass prison escape. Brian had learned that in a complete power outage the prison doors would automatically open. This was a safety precaution that prevented prisoners from being exposed to events such as fires.

Brian further explained that even when outside their jail cells, prisoners would only have access to their quadrant and most definitely no access to the outside world. As with most things, the prisoners discovered a vulnerability in the system and were able to escape en masse. To make matters worse, BJ had not arrived at their house. Brian knew he had agreed to find BJ, but given their circumstances he needed to protect his family. The responsibility of finding BJ now fell on Oz.

In the next couple of days, Oz and the family had some very important decisions to make, tasks to complete, and realizations to understand. Would they bug out or would they remain at the house? Would they be attacked again by the same or different group and, if so, would the family be ready? If they stayed, would they find like-minded people and be able to form coalitions, or could they find other Mutual Assistance Groups (MAG)? Would they be able to grow and store enough food for the upcoming year? Would they be able to find others with whom they could trade and barter with? When and how would Oz find BJ?

Though there were many more questions than answers, Oz knew that he had to take action. This is exactly what he told his family time and time again, and because they had prepared, they were safe — at least for now. Oz's focus shifted to worry for BJ, Brian, and Elizabeth. Not knowing if they were safe weighed heavily on him. He would do everything he could to make sure that they were. Though

he had just arrived in Kentucky, he was ready to travel to
Illinois and risk his life yet again for the safety of his family.

REFERENCES

Enforcement, U. S. (n.d.). Fentanyl, What Is It? Retrieved December 16, 2018, from https://www.dea.gov/factsheets/fentanyl

Esmé E Deprez, L. H. (2018, May 22). Deadly Chinese Fentanyl Is Creating a New Era of Drug Kingpins. Retrieved December 15, 2018, from https://www.bloomberg.com/news/features/2018-05-22/deadly-chinese-fentanyl-is-creating-a-new-era-of-drug-kingpins

Lee Cantrell, P., Jeffrey R. Suchard, M., Alan Wu, P., & al, e. (2012, October 8). Stability of Active Ingredients in Long-Expired Prescription Medications. *American Medical Association*. Retrieved December 02, 2018, from https://jamanetwork.com/journals/jamainternalmedicine/fullarticle/1377417

Merriam-Webster. (2018, November 18). *Merriam-Webster*. Retrieved from Merriam-Webster: https://www.merriam-webster.com/dictionary/normalcy

Prevention, C. f. (2018, May 7). *Remembering the 1918 Influenza Pandemic*. Retrieved from Centers for Disease Control and Prevention: https://www.cdc.gov/features/1918-flu-pandemic/index.html

Made in the USA
Monee, IL
30 May 2021